Nightwhispers
Volume 1
Premiere Edition

Four erotic romances.
Heat you'll have to feel for yourself.
And passion that will leap off the pages.

Tempting
Myla Jackson

Sanctuary
Delilah Devlin

Dark Heat
Leigh Wyndfield

Awakening
Vivi Anna

WHISPERS
Goose Creek, South Carolina
<u>www.whisperhome.com</u>

Published by: Whispers, 107 Clearview Circle, Goose Creek, SC 29445

Trademarks Acknowledgement The authors and publishers acknowledge the trademarked status and trademark owners of the following trademarks mentioned in these works of fiction:

Hummer–Nov 10, 1992 Owner: AM GENERAL MOTORS CORPORATION DELAWARE P.O. Box 7025, South Bend INDIANA 466347024

Enter the Matrix – June 12, 2002 Owner: Time Warner Entertainment Company, L.P. Warner Communications Inc., a Delaware corporation and American Television and Communications Corporation, a Delaware corporation PARTNERSHIP DELAWARE 75 Rockefeller Plaza New York NEW YORK 10019

Starbucks–Starbucks U.S. Brands, LLC LIAB Co.

Exxon–Exxon Corporation

Lone Ranger–Golden Books Publishing, Inc.

Tempting by Myla Jackson

Sisters and elite members of the Paranormal Investigative Agency (PIA) use themselves as bait to discover who's kidnapping young women. When one of the sisters disappears, the other turns to a vampire, a breed she's sworn to kill, for help.

Sanctuary by Delilah Devlin

In the post-Apocalyptic future, a woman rancher runs a last refuge for human survivors of a nuclear winter in West Texas. When the security of the sanctuary is breached, she must place her trust in one of the creatures freed by perpetual darkness.

Dark Heat by Leigh Wyndfield

When healer Caelan angers her King, she's thrown into prison where she bargains her body to a warrior. Their special powers unite, turning lust into something unforeseen. Soon they are forced to choose between freedom and their growing love.

Awakening by Vivi Anna

Branlyn has been having sensual, hot dreams about a stranger with blond hair and pale eyes. He awakens not just her body but also her memories of her childhood home and the horrible tragedy she witnessed there. After fifteen years of running, it is time to go back to face her past. When she returns, she finds not only her dream man waiting for her in flesh and blood, but a dark seductive power that wants to possess her body.

What Reviewers Are Saying

From Just Erotic Romance: "...Delilah Devlin's "Sanctuary is one heck of an action-packed, futuristic paranormal ride..."

From Ecataromance: "...Sanctuary will leave you breathless!..."

"Hot Gossip by Tawny Stokes is a keeper...!"~Joyfully Reviewed

"The sex was very hot and magical... [Dark Heat] a story any romance lover will be sure to enjoy."~Just Erotic Romance Reviews

"Action packed and fast paced, Tempting quickly captured my attention and held onto it with a firm grip."~Just Erotic Romance Reviews

Tempting

Myla Jackson

Myla Jackson

Chapter One

Reggie Gallagher ducked behind the last in a row of dumpsters and braced her hands on her knees, dragging in huge gulps of air. Sweat ran down the side of her face, and the black ribbed-knit tank top clung to her breasts. The coastal humidity and heat acted like a steam bath even when she was standing still. For the moment, all she could hear was the ragged gasps of her breath wheezing in and out of her straining lungs. And despite the retched stench of the waste beside her, she welcomed the respite from the chase.

Where was Madison? She'd been right behind Reggie until now.

The quiet of the alley was broken when pounding footsteps entered and raced toward her.

Risking a stealthy glance around the hard metal corner of the dumpster, Reggie confirmed the runner, and she reached out to snag her and pull her in beside her.

"Can't...stop." Madison bent low, her shoulders heaving with the effort to fill her oxygen-starved lungs.

"Breathe," Reggie ordered and tapped the miniature headset positioned inside her ear like a hearing aide. "Where the hell are Jordan and Mike?"

"It's...as...if...they disappeared." Madison sucked in air and gushed, "Ah, shit! I can't breathe. I don't know if those guys saw me turn down here, but they can't be far behind."

"Then let's go." Reggie shot another glance around the corner of the dumpster. The alley was empty. She waited another second and then grabbed her sister's hand, pulling her along behind her.

"There!" The shout of one of their pursuers echoed off the brick of the multi-story structures rising up from their concrete foundations. The buildings spread over entire blocks, channeling Reggie and Madison through the worst part of Houston, leaving few places to hide or take cover. How had the mission gone south so fast? Where was their backup?

"They'll catch us at this rate," Madison shouted, between gasps. "Gotta split up."

"No!" But before Reggie could tighten her grip, her younger sister pulled free and swung left, sprinting west away from the downtown area.

Reggie glanced back at the group of six men closing in behind her. If she played her hand right, they'd follow her and leave Madison alone. The fastest runner on the team at the Paranormal Investigative Agency, she could outrun every man, except perhaps the boss. Tanner was made of iron and muscles. No one could outrun, out gun, or outsmart him.

But if she wanted to live, Reggie had better make it her goal to beat all of his records and then some. She just hoped the hell Madison got away.

Summoning every last ounce of energy, she punched out, running straight for two blocks to ensure the bad boys behind her wouldn't branch off and pursue her sister. Just as she was about to veer east, a shot rang out and something hard and fast slammed against her left shoulder, spinning her around so quickly she crashed into the brick corner of an office building.

Surprise numbed the pain for the first five seconds until her heart resumed function, kicking her blood through her body and out the small hole the size of a quarter on one side of her shoulder. A glance backward confirmed the exit point was a lot bigger. Her stomach lurched, and the pale glow of the streetlamps dimmed. No. She couldn't pass out. *Not now. Have to run. Have to get farther away from Madison.*

As fog crept in around her peripheral vision, Reggie rounded the corner she'd been aiming for and set off at a swift jog, her pace slowing more each time her heels hit the pavement.

No. This couldn't happen. She would not be another one of the victims she risked her life to protect. No way would the gang members or bloodsuckers take her down like they'd done her father.

Heartless bastards! All of them.

Although Tanner said there were good vamps out there, Reggie had it firmly in her mind that the only good vampire was a dead vampire. She repeated the words like a cadence, motivating her legs to keep pumping and her feet to continue moving away from her attackers.

"The only good vampire is a—" With only half a block between her and the six men, she reached the end of the street and swung a hard right, running into a solid wall of steel. Her forehead made contact and then her chest, knocking what little air was left from her lungs. The force of the collision made her bounce backward, her head snapping up. With no air to sustain breathing and her vision blurred, the ground sucked her downward. As her knees buckled, her mouth completed her sentence, "—dead vampire."

"I like to think of it as the living dead." A deep voice with one of those guttural, and incredibly sexy, foreign accents filled her senses, and strong arms reached out to catch her before she hit the pavement.

Her brain cloudy from blood and oxygen loss, Reggie was thankful for the strength of the man in front of her. But she had to get away. Those men would catch up and do who knew what to her. How the hell had the ambush they'd set up for the gang turned into a trap for her and Madison? Where was the rest of her team?

The gang had been waiting for them as if they knew she and Madison were the bait and they'd be alone. How had they known? The entire situation stunk. Could there be a snitch on the inside at PIA? Would Reggie and Madison end up missing like the thirteen young women to date?

Bull shit.

She and Madison weren't victims. They were the good guys sworn to catch the filthy scum taking advantage of lone women.

Reggie struggled against the vice grip holding her chest-to-chest with the stranger. When she tried to right herself, her head swam, and her knees refused to engage enough to hold her upright.

"Let me go," she said with more bravado than conviction that she could stand on her own once released.

He chuckled, his chest vibrating against hers. "If I do, you'll fall."

Footsteps rang out on the streets behind her, and her body stiffened. "Let me go!" No matter how strong this guy was, he couldn't go against six men and hope to win. For that matter, Reggie didn't know if he wasn't one of them. Had she run right into the enemy?

The men rounded the corner and skidded to a stop, their leader at the front—Cesar Dominguez, a man Reggie knew from the mug shots on file at the agency and the snake-dragon tattoo on his right arm. He carried a nine-millimeter pistol and had it pointed at the man holding her.

That settled one question in Reggie's numb mind. Her rescuer wasn't one of the gang she'd set out to capture. She would have sighed her relief, but she still didn't know who the hell he was.

"Let me have her, and I won't shoot you," Cesar said, stepping forward.

Her captor paused, not like a hesitation, but as if to make sure his answer was understood. "No." A single word, no negotiation, and no compromise.

Reggie could like a guy like this if she wasn't so uncertain of his alliance. Anyone as incredibly gorgeous and sexy, with an accent that could melt metal, had to be a bad guy. What had he said to her? He liked to consider it living dead? What the hell had he meant by that?

Thoughts swirled around inside her head like melting whipped cream in a stirred latte. Why couldn't she focus?

Could it be the gallon of blood she'd lost running down the street? Reggie trained her blurry gaze on Cesar and clung to sexy man's chest to keep from slipping to the ground.

"If you don't turn her loose, then you die." He pointed the weapon at the dark man's chest.

Before Cesar could squeeze the trigger, tall-dark-and-sexy dropped his hold on Reggie, smacked the gun from Cesar's hand so hard it flew high overhead and crashed through a window. And he was back so fast he caught Reggie before her knees gave out.

"What the fuck?" Cesar shook his empty hand, his eyes wide.

"My friend, Nic, is a show off," another voice said from behind them.

So her captor's name was Nic. Reggie leaned her head back to peer around the man holding her up, which proved to be a big mistake as the world spun several times before it settled in place.

An even taller man, towering well above six feet, stood behind her guy, wearing a black muscle shirt and black jeans. Where her captor was as dark as a moonless night, this new man was a vision of light. White hair fell to his shoulders, and his pale blue eyes shown in the limited glow from the nearby streetlamps. He was beautiful and built like a Norse god, with muscles bulging beneath the scrap of a shirt.

Even if she hadn't lost a gallon of blood, Reggie might have swooned over these guys. "Where do they come up with guys like you and your buddy here?" Was that her voice, the one that sounded like a drunken sailor? Her head lolled, and her vision blurred.

No. She wouldn't pass out. Good PIA's didn't crap out on the job. No, sir. "I'm a good agent," she muttered and struggled to keep her head upright.

"I'm sure you are," he said soothingly. "But could you shut up for a moment?"

"No way to treat a lady," she pouted and leaned her head against the soft jersey of the black T-shirt he wore, liking the feel of all that muscle beneath her cheek. She could fall asleep cradled as she was in his arms if her shoulder wasn't aching so badly.

"Do you boys need more convincing?" Nic called out.

Reggie's head jerked up, and she glared across at Cesar and his gang of thugs. "Yeah, what he said." If she weren't so dizzy from blood loss and knocking into this man named Nic, she'd get her ass in gear and fight.

"Please." Nic frowned at her. "I can handle this."

"Just trying to help."

"I don't need your help," Nic said.

"Too bad." She pushed away from him and faced Cesar. "You'd better slither back into the gutter you crawled out of, or you'll be the one to die, punk."

"Could you have been a little more inflammatory?" Nic asked, shaking his head.

The twinkle in his eye was too cute, and if her shoulder wasn't hurting so badly, she might be tempted to ask for his number when they were done kicking Cesar's ass. "I aim to inflame."

"Seems you hit your mark. Let's hope he doesn't hit his." The twinkle left Nic's eyes as Cesar slid a knife out of his pocket and clicked it open.

Reggie's heart leaped at the glint of steel flashing in the glare of a streetlight, instantly regretting her taunting words. With a knife that big and ugly, someone was bound to get hurt. She hoped to hell it wasn't Nic. It would be a shame to scar any part of his handsome face.

With a wave of his knife, Cesar motioned his minions forward, and they circled Reggie, Nic and the Norse god.

Blondie laughed out loud, his mirth booming off the high rises. "Do they really think they can frighten us?"

"You're not doing much to persuade them otherwise,

my friend." Nic's lips twisted.

"Then let me demonstrate, since you seem to have your hands full." He flexed his muscles and stalked the man nearest him.

"Thank you," Nic said, his voice dripping sarcasm.

Apparently these guys knew each other well. Reggie watched in utter amazement as the Norse god proved he was god-worthy and lifted the man off his feet with one hand and tossed him twenty feet. And he didn't even grunt or break a sweat.

Swaying slightly on her feet, Reggie wished Nic was holding her steady. He'd seemed so solid and strong. As if he could read her mind, his arm snaked around her middle, and she gladly leaned into him. She never leaned on people. Why did she want to now? Maybe she was already unconscious and this was all a really weird dream.

Cesar lunged at Nic, slicing the wicked knife through the air. Nic dodged neatly, shielding Reggie from the deadly blade. "If you're through over there, I could use a hand here," he called out over his shoulder.

"Just cleaning up the little ones. You can handle him for a minute, can't you?"

Reggie couldn't believe these guys. She and Madison had high-tailed it out of Dodge when they realized their backup had flown the coup and left them holding the trap by themselves, six to two. Not good odds when the six were mean looking, tattoo-bearing thugs. But Nic and his Norse-god friend hadn't even batted an eyelash.

Nic shifted her to his left arm. Cesar took advantage of Nic's distraction and shot forward, plunging his knife into Nic's gut.

"Ha!" Cesar said. "Not as great as you thought you were, are you?"

Nic glanced down at his belly as blood stained his shirt. Then he looked at her as if annoyed. "Pardon me for a moment."

He stood her on her own and then turned to Cesar.

"You've irritated me long enough, human."

Reggie's knees buckled, and she dropped to the pavement, the jolt sending pain slicing through her injured arm. Though the pain made her see squiggly bright lights in the darkness of the night, she tried to prop herself in a sitting position with her good arm.

Nic lifted Cesar off the ground and flung him ten yards to the south as if he weighed little more than a sack of sugar. How did he do that?

Some things about Nic and his Norse friend weren't adding up. What had he called Cesar? Human? And they were both incredibly strong. She stared at the cut in his side as he dusted his hands off. It wasn't bleeding anymore.

A cold chill shivered across Reggie's skin. Something wasn't clicking, but her head was too fuzzy to make sense of it.

Damn! Reggie slumped back to the hard black surface of the street. At least Nic and the Norse god were handling Cesar. She didn't have the strength nor could she see straight enough to do anything but lay back and watch the show.

And it was a terrific kick-butt event, with Nic tossing thugs like firewood. She'd have to remember to thank them for the entertainment when she felt more herself. And maybe get the man's number. He was a man a girl could sink her teeth into and so vigorous, he'd probably be great in bed. What a babe.

Chapter Two

"Why didn't you leave her where you found her?" Torsten Lang pushed his long blond hair back from his forehead and circled the woman on the dining table. "Or are you collecting strays again?"

Safe in his penthouse apartment, twenty-six stories into the Houston skyline, Nicolae Kovak needn't fear discovery or interference from Cesar's disbanded gang of punks. The only danger now was the woman he'd been foolish enough to bring into the secrecy of his lair. But he couldn't leave her on the street, not alone and as weak as she'd been.

"They would have come back for her." Nic stared down at the woman's deep red hair and skin a pearly shade of alabaster dusted with ginger-colored freckles. Her breathing was shallow, her breasts barely rising and falling to the rhythm.

"Did she pass out on her own or did you have some influence?" Torsten asked.

"I put her in a trance," Nic responded. Although, she'd already been in a mild state of shock from blood loss and running into him.

Torsten leaned close to sniff at her neck. "Ummm. She smells tempting."

His friend's gesture sent a rush of blood to Nic's face, and his fists tightened. "Back off."

Straightening, Torsten leveled piercing blue eyes on Nic. "Unless you plan on keeping her, you need get her out of here before she wakes."

"You're back so soon?" Melisande's lilting voice preceded her into the room. When she stepped into the dining area, she ground to a halt, her gaze fixed on the woman lying across the table. "What is she doing here?"

"Bleeding, at the moment," Torsten said, his gaze never leaving Nic. "Shall we serve her up for dinner? She's in the right place."

"Don't be crude, Tor." A faint dip in her delicate brow signaled Melisande's displeasure with Torsten's remark. She strode to the table and perused the woman as if examining a new bedspread for the queen-size bed in her room. "She's pretty in a manly way."

Nic's frown deepened. The woman's curves had burned an indelible impression on his hands. "There's not a manly bone on this woman's body." As soon as the words left his mouth, he realized Melisande was fishing for the answer to his involvement with a strange woman.

The twinkle in Melisande's eye could not be mistaken. Her lips stretched into a grin. "What is it about this woman you felt it necessary to risk all of us by bringing her here?" She lifted a strand of fiery red hair, the coppery highlights reflecting the light from the overhead chandelier.

Nic had asked himself that question all the way back to the penthouse suite, carrying the woman in his arms, refusing to allow Torsten to share the burden for even a step. "Some of Andrei's Dragóns would have taken her. I couldn't leave her to their machinations."

"So you brought her here? Couldn't you have taken her to a hospital or dropped her at one of those 24-hour trauma centers?" Melisande shook her head. "This is too messy, especially for you, Nicolae."

"Melisande is right. We'll have trouble when she wakes," Torsten added.

"I couldn't leave her." Why was he defending his actions? He was in charge here. "The deed is done."

"Which brings us to the next question." Melisande stared down at the redhead. "What shall we do with her now?"

"Looks to me like we have at least three choices." Torsten held a finger in the air. "The first is to dump her back on the street."

"Not an option." Nicolae stepped toward the woman

as if preparing to defend her. Her trance was so deep, when he lifted her wrist, he could barely feel the pulse.

"Which leads to your next option, you can turn her into one of us." Torsten tapped a hand to his chest.

The idea appealed to Nic, but he felt the woman would want to make that choice herself. In all his four hundred and twenty-eight years as a vampire, he refused to force the choice to turn on an unconscious person. "No, I will not turn her."

"You can heal her and set her free when she is ready. As you did for me." Melisande's voice carried through the air.

Melisande had been with him for the past five years, not as his lover, but as his friend and his backup source of the blood he needed to survive. He'd healed an injury inflicted by her abusive father. She was one of the strays Torsten alluded to.

She placed a hand on his arm and looked up at him with her dark brown eyes. "If you choose to keep her here until she wakes, be careful. She could blow your cover."

"If you don't have the stomach for it, I'll sacrifice my services and heal her." Torsten clapped his hands together. "She's pretty if you like red hair and pale skin. Me? I prefer a sun-drenched wench of darker skin tones. But I never turn down a pretty woman, especially one with hair the color of polished copper."

Nic's teeth clenched. "I'll take care of her and heal her. After that, I'll be the one to decide what to do with her."

"You don't know how she'll react when she finds out you aren't human. She might be frightened. Or worse still, she might not like vampires." Melisande's gaze roved over the woman's face as if recalling her own initial fear.

Nic snorted. He already had an idea about her feelings about vampires. Did he think he could change her mind? "I know the risks for us," he said, his voice coarse, impatient. Time was wasting, and her wounds needed tending.

But would she want him to touch her? What was it she'd said when she'd run into him? The only good vampire was a dead vampire? A smile tilted his lips upward. Was she afraid of vampires? He couldn't imagine this woman being afraid of anything. Hadn't she proven her strength and determination when she'd stood up against the Dragóns? Even after she'd been wounded.

The woman deserved to walk away whole, even if it was a vampire helping her to do so. He didn't have to turn her, but she might think that was his intent when she came to.

"Are you sure you want to do this?" Melisande asked.

Nic sighed. "Yes."

He gathered the red-haired woman into his arms, her blood smearing across his sleeve. Had he not fed an hour earlier, the hunger would have been washing over him in waves. The scent of blood drew him like no other, but he'd had over four hundred years to learn to control his blood lust. He hoped the lessons learned would carry him through the other urges not so easily controlled.

He carried her to his room and turned to close the door.

"Need my assistance?" Torsten asked, his gaze focused on Nic not the woman.

"I do not wish to be disturbed."

"What if she tries to kill you?" Melisande asked.

"I'll take my chances." With a slight kick, the door swung shut, blocking out Torsten and Melisande's worried faces.

When he laid her on the bed, she was like a rag doll, completely limp and unresponsive. Her wounds were not mortal, but she'd lost enough blood to weaken her. The trance did the rest. But as soon as he started the healing process, she'd awaken.

Maybe she'd be frightened. More likely she'd be shocked and angry, thinking he was taking advantage of her. Perhaps that was the reason he'd brought her here in the first place.

This woman and her foolish bravado intrigued him as no other in many years.

Nic glanced at the clock. Dawn was only an hour away. If he planned to do this, he'd need to do it quickly.

Without another thought to the consequences, he pulled a knife from the sheath in his boots and slipped it beneath the hem of her shirt, the blade slicing through threads until he peeled back the tank top exposing the wound and a shell-pink, lace bra.

For a woman all in black, the pink bra was a pleasant surprise. In order to heal her, he had to strip her clothing away to expose all entry and exit wounds.

He flipped the front clasp and her breasts spilled out of the lace and into his hands. Okay, so he probably hadn't needed to remove the bra, but he couldn't resist, and the straps might prove to be in the way across her back.

His cock flicked against the confines of his trousers, and Nic ground his teeth together to stave off his rising desire. Although the surge of lust was inevitable, he had no business coming on to this semi-conscious woman.

When he rolled her to her side, she moaned, a low, weak sound in the large room. Careful not to cause her further pain, he eased the remnants of her shirt over her shoulder and down her arms. The back of her shoulder was a mess of blood and torn flesh from the bullet's damaging exit. At least he needn't worry about removing the slug.

Once he had her top half stripped, he removed his own boots and his bloodstained T-shirt. Then he climbed in the bed beside her and went to work.

Healing an open wound was a delicate line for him to walk, with the taste of blood on his tongue and the silkiness of female flesh beneath his fingers. He'd die a thousand deaths before he finished the job. Resisting her would be a monumental task.

Melisande had been the only other person he'd

healed. Doctors were available for this kind of thing. For centuries, he'd lived a quiet existence, blending into the shadows of the places he lived. If he healed every wound, he'd leave himself vulnerable, and others would come to realize the truth of his existence. If they learned of his true nature, they'd hunt him down and kill him. Fear of vampires lead many to destroy them without considering they were still people beneath the undead exterior.

Nic had contemplated that death on occasion, but he wasn't ready to give up on life such as it was. He had Torsten to keep him company and the occasional woman to warm his bed. Melisande provided sustenance when available donors were limited. What more could he want?

The woman beside him lay as still as death, her peaches and cream skin cool to his touch. He skimmed his fingers over a breast and up to the base of her throat where her pulse beat the strongest. With a deep breath, he leaned into her his lips pulling back as his teeth extended.

How easy it would be to sink into her jugular and suck the life-giving blood from her body. To make her immortal to stand beside him for eternity.

He skimmed the long incisors across her neck, pressing lightly, without breaking the skin.

A surge of desire rolled over him like waves crashing against the shore. Struggling against instinct, he proceeded down the base of her throat and across her collarbone to the injured shoulder. He sniffed at the blood still oozing from the wound, like a thick, rich wine to be sipped.

He tasted the nectar, savoring the flavor or her, his body responding to her naked breasts beneath his chin, within easy reach of his mouth. Each pearly mound jutting upward, begging him to take them into his mouth.

She stirred beneath him, her back arching upward, a breast pressing against his chin.

Turning his face just a little, he captured the nipple between his teeth, letting go immediately. He realized his mistake at once. If he didn't get back to the task at hand, he'd be lost in his own uncontrollable lust.

He turned her onto her stomach, putting those luscious breasts beneath her and out of reach of his roving lips and baser instincts. Then with long sure strokes, he laved the wound on her back until the shattered flesh grew together, the scar shrinking until it disappeared.

She stirred in his grasp, groaning and pushing against the bed.

The taste of her blood an aphrodisiac to his senses, Nic closed his eyes as the red-haired goddess rolled to her back.

He inhaled and let out a long breath, schooling himself to a calm he didn't feel. Yet, he fought a losing battle against his body. He had to complete the work and get her out of his bed before he did something they would both regret. He opened his eyes and stared only at the entrance wound, refusing to note the peachy tips of her breasts, now pebbled into tight beads.

With an economy of effort, he sealed the entrance wound and leaned back to inspect his work. The injury wouldn't leave a scar to mar the perfection of her skin.

If he were a gentleman, he'd get off the bed and walk away. He even made a move to do just that.

She shifted beneath him, her hands rising up his torso to clasp around his neck, pulling him closer until his chest rested against her full, ripe breasts.

Nic froze, his arms braced on either side of her shoulders, his mouth hovering over hers.

Her breath blew softly against his lips, the tangy scent of mint filling his senses.

Move away, he willed his body. But the body wasn't going anywhere. Nestled against the soft curves, he couldn't tear himself away.

Her leg curved around the back of his calf, and she pressed her crotch to his thigh. "Love me," she whispered, her eyes closed, her body caught in a lusty dream. She probably didn't know who she was or what she was doing, only that she needed to be loved.

Nic wondered who she was dreaming of. Did she have a boyfriend or a husband lurking in her thoughts and somewhere in Houston? With a quick glance down at her hand, he heaved a sigh. No ring. Good. Then who was she thinking of in her lust-filled trance?

He knew the intensity of lust, having experienced it when he was turned so long ago by the venomous vampire he thought he cared for. Had he known the consequences of making love to her and letting his passion take over, he might have chosen differently. But Katarina hadn't given him the choice. She'd fooled him into drinking her blood, turning him into a vampire just like her. When she'd taken what she wanted, she left without a trace. No goodbyes, no false declarations of love.

Swearing never to trick an innocent, Nic knew he couldn't make love to this woman. He had to be very careful. Caught up in lust, he might forget himself and turn her against her will.

In the meantime, he rolled to his back trying to ignore her attack on his body. For attack was what it was since he fought to resist with every fiber of his being. The draw was too strong, and when her hand drifted over his abdomen, Nic couldn't resist her any longer. He'd only let her touch him, he wouldn't make love like she begged him to. She wasn't in her right mind, still caught in the grip of the trance.

"Please." She nibbled at his ear, sinking her teeth in a little harder than a nip, enough to make him jerk against her. Her hand slipped beneath the waistband of his pants to fondle his cock.

Nic groaned, his nerve endings titillated, testosterone flaming downward, filling him to tight, rock-hard proportions. Resistance might as well be torture. As a vampire, he was even more prone to the call of desire than the average man and much more likely to move on it. Before he could stop himself, his hips thrust against hers in an uncontrolled spasm. Mind over lust, he reminded himself, backing away.

When he shifted, her other hand slipped beneath his hip and pulled him against her, his cock pressing into her belly.

The moist pressure of her mouth moved from his earlobe to his lips, leaving a trail of fiery kisses along his jaw line.

With her hand still in his pants and her tongue delving between his teeth in the exact rhythm of sex, she had him. Nic realized this was going to be harder than he imagined. Feeling his defenses crumbling, he tried to pull her hand away from his cock.

She bit into his bottom lip and held, her hand remaining just where she wanted it, stroking, massaging and stirring his fires to flame.

"You'll regret this in the morning," he whispered against her ear. His lips were so close, and her skin had warmed, the peaches and cream texture teasing him until he had to touch his tongue to her neck to judge for himself if she tasted as good as she looked.

He found her to be a heady combination of sweet and salty, like a tangy Margarita, cool to the lips yet warming the pallet as the tequila works its magic. He could drink her all up if he let himself. And maybe he would.

Chapter Three

Reggie writhed against the sheets, her body burning with need now that the pain was gone. With eyelids too heavy to lift, she gave in to the desire crumbling her inhibitions to dust.

It was only a flight of the imagination, a wild and sensuous escape from reality, and she didn't want to wake up until she'd had her fill. In her fantasy she reached out, her hands finding a warm, solid body to skim across. He was the tall, dark and sexy man she'd run headfirst into in an alley. Had that been in her dream? Her mind tried to make sense of him. He must have been part of her fantasy. No human could launch another person into the air as if he weighed less than a cat.

Settling back, she entwined her hands around his neck and pulled him over her, desperate for a kiss to start. And that would only be the beginning.

He resisted slightly, and she reached up to press her mouth to his. She wanted him to make love to her. Did she say it out loud? Had she begged him? Not caring one way or the other, she looped a leg over him to prevent his escape. If he wouldn't come to her, she'd surely go to him.

It was a dream after all, and she could do anything she damn well pleased.

"Make love to me me, Dream Boy." Her hands slid down his torso and into the confines of his trousers.

He was hot and hard and larger than any man she'd ever slept with. Ah, the power of dreams. She could have him any size she wanted. But she wanted him inside her. Now.

"Too many clothes," she said against his mouth. She pushed him to his back and straddled his thighs, her eyes still refusing to open even though her body was wide awake and flaming.

Not caring, she felt his beauty with her fingers,

running her hands across his chest, sparsely sprinkled with coarse hairs. Her fingers traced a path of curls down his torso to his belly button and lower until the curls disappeared into the waistband of his trousers.

"This will never do," she grumbled, sliding further down his legs. Making quick work of the button, she grasped the zipper and gently slid it downward. Unencumbered by briefs or boxers, his cock sprang free and into her waiting hands.

She grasped him and held on, willing her eyes to open to see his magnificence. How could this be a dream when it felt so real? And her usual fantasies included the visual. What was wrong with her eyes to cheat her out of the full effect?

The cock she held twitched, pulsing warmly, filling her palms.

Her hands slid upward to the velvety tip and back down to the base, where his balls nestled in a tangle of hair. Her dream guy moaned and captured her hands. "Much as I'd love to continue this, you should wake up," he said, his voice deep and as tempting as his body.

"No," she whined. "I don't want to wake up." Where she'd wanted to open her eyes, now she squeezed them shut, afraid if she opened them, her dream would be over, and she'd crash to earth into her cold empty bed.

The man between her thighs sat up, taking her with him until she balanced in his lap, her breasts tickled by the hairs on his chest. Sitting up, laying down...it didn't matter. She liked the feel of his skin against hers with the light musky scent of his maleness assaulting her senses.

A kiss feathered across her lips and then words puffed against her ear. "Open your eyes, pretty lady."

Despite her new determination to keep her eyes closed and make the dream last all night long, her eyelids lifted, and she stared into the face of her rescuer from the alley. She definitely was dreaming.

"Am I awake or asleep?" she asked, her voice a

whisper, tentative against the silence of the room.

He smiled, the twinkle in his eyes making him even more than devastatingly handsome. "You're awake."

She could fall into those mesmerizing eyes, and she swayed toward him, the incremental movement enough to establish their nudity was not a dream. His hands splayed across the skin of her lower back, holding her steady, the texture of his fingers pressing into her flesh, reassuring at the same time as it was unsettling.

As if she was still struggling out of the fog of sleep, she glanced down at her breasts. The rosy nipples were taut and pointed where they nestled in the dark curls sprinkled across his upper body.

"I must be dreaming," she argued, feeling a frown pull her forehead downward. She glanced back up at him, tipping her head to the side. "I seem to have lost my shirt."

He nodded toward the floor. "I had to cut it off you."

"I don't understand." As she shook her head, her hair brushed across her shoulders, the feel of it on her skin sending tingling nerve flashes downward where her jean-clad bottom rested against his thighs. His cock rose out of the unzipped flaps of his trousers, huge and strong, ready and resting in her palms.

"Wow!" At first she just stared and then realizing she still held a stranger's penis, she jerked her hands back. "What the hell's going on?" She struggled to free her knees of the tangled sheets.

His fingers curled around her waist. "Slow down before you get hurt."

Slapping at his hands, she rolled to the side and stood, searching for something to cover herself. She grabbed for a pillow and held it in front of her like a shield. "Who are you, and where am I?"

"I'm Nicolae Kovak." The sexy lilt of his words sounded Russian or Romanian. "I brought you to my apartment because you were wounded and in need of my assistance."

Balancing the pillow against her breasts, she felt along her shoulder for the bullet wound and found nothing. A quick glance over her shoulder confirmed there was no wound there as well, no sign of an entrance or exit wound. Her foot nudged the ruined black tank top on the floor. It was coated in dried blood. Her blood.

"How?" She stared across the bed at him, watching him wearily as he stood and carefully zipped his cock into his pants, the resulting tent almost comical if the entire situation wasn't downright insane. What a shame to cover such magnificence. She inhaled a deep breath and let it out slowly. "I'll ask again. What the hell's going on?"

"First, tell me what you were doing out in that alley with the Dragóns chasing after you."

She crossed her arms over the pillow and held it tight. "Why should I tell you?"

"It might help me to better explain my actions."

"So you can lie better?"

"I would not lie to you, pretty lady." He frowned. "Have you a name? I can't continue to call you pretty lady although the truth is evident." His gaze scraped over the tops of her shoulders and the pillow she held in her arms. "It's only right to know the name of the woman who just shared my bed."

"I didn't share your bed." Anger fueled her words. "You kidnapped me and drugged me or something."

"I did what I had to do to protect you." He shrugged as if his crimes meant nothing. "Your name?"

She thought to refuse answering him, but what did it matter if he knew her name or not? "Regina Gallagher."

"Regina." Her name rolled off his tongue like a caress, and tingles slithered across her skin despite the shock of the uncompromising position she'd found herself in.

"Most people call me Reggie." Why was she telling him this? Had she lost her senses? She couldn't even blame it on her thoughts still being fuzzy. Her head was clear, and her mind raced through possible scenarios for escape.

"Why would they call you Reggie when Regina is such a lovely name?"

"Whatever." She eyed the door, determined to get out of there, yet too curious to leave. "I answered your question. Why don't you answer mine?"

"Fair enough." He crossed his arms over his chest.

"Why did you really bring me here?"

"I told you already." He walked around the end of the bed to stand in front of her, effectively blocking her escape route. "You were injured and needed attention."

She hadn't mistaken the slight pause before the word 'attention'. "Impossible. If I had been injured, there would be signs of a wound still. Nobody heals that fast." As she said the words, she glanced again at her ruined top.

"Ah, but you see the blood, do you not?" He'd caught her glancing down.

"It doesn't make sense."

"When you came into this room, you had a bullet wound in your left shoulder." His gaze captured hers and held.

"Just how long ago was that?"

He glanced down at his watch. "One hour."

"But if I was wounded, where is the wound? This whole situation doesn't make sense."

"We can talk when you're properly dressed." He sighed and turned toward the closet, reaching in for a plain white pinpoint oxford cloth shirt. When he turned back to hand it to her, he said, "I have the ability to heal some wounds."

"Like magic or something?" Reggie snorted. "The only people I know who can heal a wound that fast are—" All the blood rushed out of her head, and she remembered her last thought before she'd passed out earlier. "Oh damn! You're a vampire."

Chapter Four

Nicolae thought she might pass out when her cheeks turned a pasty gray. Just as quickly as they'd gone pale, they burst into a raging red.

"No fucking way!" she said.

He grimaced. "Do you always use such colorful language?"

"If you find my language offensive, tough."

"Actually…" He studied her closely. "It makes me consider the possibilities."

"It's not even a remote possibility because first chance I get, I'm going to stake your sorry vampire ass!" Her gaze darted around the room as if she were looking for the wooden stake to carry through on her promise.

"If you plan to kill me, you'll have to drive a stake into my heart not my buttocks." His lips twitched as he fought to contain the smile threatening to break loose. He shook the shirt in front of her face. "Please, put this on. I find your breasts very lovely and distracting."

She slapped his hand away and almost dropped the pillow in the process, one side dropping low enough to expose her peachy nipple.

Nic's cock nudged against his pants, reminding him he'd left his body in an unsatisfied condition, and he'd pay for that in pain until his arousal subsided. If she kept dropping the pillow, that would be a while. "Put the shirt on," he said, his voice more harsh than he'd intended.

"I don't want your damn shirt, your healing, or anything else from you. Just let me out of here." She tried to step around him.

His hands reached out and clamped onto her bare shoulders, the warmth of her skin sending heat waves rippling through him, keeping his erection in the constant state of granite. He let go and stepped back but not out of her way. "I can't let you leave. It's not safe."

"Why?" She stared up into his eyes, hers widening and her mouth dropping open. "You didn't."

"Didn't what?

She rushed to the mirror hanging over the mahogany dresser. Stretching her neck to the side, she pushed her long red hair back to expose the white column of her throat. "If you can heal wounds, how do I know you didn't bite me and turn me into one of your stinking kind?"

"I didn't turn you, and we don't stink unless we choose to."

"Bull!"

"You didn't seem to mind my scent before you were fully awake."

"I'm talking about what you've done to me. If you made me a vampire, I'll kill you." She turned and shot him a look of pure venom. "And when I do, I'll make it slow and painful.

"Step outside when the sun comes up, you'll know the truth then." He nodded toward the window. The heavy drapes, pulled to the side, allowed a stunning view of the city below. The clouds hung low over the city, reflecting the glow of streetlights, making it that much brighter in the darkest hours of early morning.

"I will," she said, again eyeing the door. "If you'll just let me by…"

"You can't leave until morning."

"Why the hell not?"

"Cesar's Dragóns are still roaming the streets as well as other less agreeable people."

"People like you?"

"I'm not here to harm humans." He sighed. "I came to help."

"Help?" Reggie snorted. "Help yourself to a woman alone in the night? If that's the case, I'm here to stop you and every other blood-sucker I can lay a stake into."

"Big words for just one woman. How do you propose to take out the entire population of vampires?"

"One vamp at a time, buddy. One vamp at a time." She reached behind her and jerked a drawer from the dresser. With one hand holding the pillow, the other swung the drawer against a doorframe, splintering it into pieces, one of which was sharp and long enough to pierce his heart. "Starting with you."

Nicolae shook his head. "How can I convince you that I'm one of the good guys?"

"Seems the only way you'll convince me is by letting me stake you through the heart." She advanced on him, the stick pointed at his chest.

"Need help in there?" Torsten's amused voice called out.

"No. Everything is under control," Nic said, never taking his gaze away from Reggie's. He could always put her back in a trance, but this was much more interesting. He hadn't felt this alive facing the possibility of death at the hand and stake of a beautiful woman in a long time. Perhaps never.

The sound of the door opening was followed by a long low whistle. "She's even lovelier without the shirt. I can see why you wanted to keep her to yourself."

"Not now, Torsten," Nic said, hiding a smile. "She's not all too fond of vampires." He agreed with Torsten that Reggie was lovely with or without the shirt.

"Interesting," Torsten said. "Some of us aren't as bad as others. We don't all go around raping, killing, and draining our victims."

Reggie growled and leaped at Nicolae. "Move, vampire!"

Nicolae reached out and captured her wrist, knocking it against his thigh until she dropped the stake. Then he spun her around, thrust her arm up the middle of her back, and pressed it between her shoulder blades. "Now see what you've done, Tor? You made her angry."

She dropped the pillow and elbowed him in the side. "Let me go."

Nic doubled over but didn't release his hold on her arm, ratcheting it higher up her back. "I don't want to hurt you," he said between gritted teeth.

"Then let me go!" Her foot kicked backward, landing a glancing blow to his shin.

"Not until daylight. The streets aren't safe at this hour." He clamped an arm around her middle, pinning her free arm to her side, and pulled her tight against his chest. "Stop wiggling."

"No." She struggled, her breasts rubbing against the top of his arm, causing him more consternation than the blow to his shin.

"How can I talk sense into you when you won't be still?" he said, grunting as she jabbed another elbow into his ribs.

"You're a vampire. I don't listen to vampires. I kill them."

"Not today, you don't."

"Are you sure you don't need help?" Torsten asked. "She seems to be getting the better of you."

Just what he needed—a persistent pest to distract him when he had his hands full. "Get out!" Nic roared.

The door slammed, none too gently, leaving Nic and Reggie alone again.

Reggie planted her feet on the ground and lurched forward in an attempt to throw him off balance and over her shoulder.

But Nic was ready. He lifted her high into the air and marched her to the bed, tossing her to the sheets face first.

Reggie twisted onto her back at the same time Nicolae threw himself across her body, trapping her flailing arms and legs beneath him.

She fought like a hellcat for several more minutes, and then sagged against him, as if all the wind left her sails.

"I have to go back out," she said, her voice sounding strained and frantic. "Please, let go of me."

He pulled her arms up over her head and held them

pinned to the bed, as much affected by her quiet plea as her spirited resistance. But he couldn't let her go. Not yet. "No."

"You don't understand. I have to go back out."

"Why?"

She inhaled and blew the breath out before answering. "It's my job."

"Your job?"

"Yes. We were the bait to lure the person responsible for the disappearances of the thirteen women you might have heard about in the papers. Vampires do read, don't they?"

"Not all of us are animals," he said. Although the animal in him wanted more than words from this woman. "What did you mean bait?"

"Bait to draw out the kidnappers."

Anger as fiery as a red-hot poker seared through his veins. "Bait? What fool would send a women out as bait?"

"Hey, it was my idea, okay?"

"Then you are a fool." He frowned down at her. "What are you—some kind of cop?"

"We're with the Paranormal Investigative Agency. We search out and destroy bad vampires like you," she practically spat the last word in his face.

"That explains a little. But you were alone when we found you. Where are the other members of your team?"

"That's why I have to get back out there. My partner is out there alone."

"I'll send Torsten out to see if he can find him. What does he look like?"

"He's a she. And why would I tell you what she looks like? So Blondie there can capture her, too? No thanks."

"Whatever you choose to believe, you're staying put. You're safer here."

"I'm no safer here than out there with Cesar's thugs." Reggie bucked beneath him, renewing her fighting against his superior weight and strength.

Her pelvis pressed against his engorged cock, and he had to bite down hard not to moan. "You have my promise we will not harm you."

"As if a vampire's promise is worth anything? Ha!"

Her struggle was beginning to wear at him. If she didn't settle down, he might be tempted to shut her up in other ways. "When I give my word, I stand behind it."

"Just let me go," she said, her breathing coming in gasps, each breath making her breasts rise toward him.

Fighting anger and frustration, he wondered how much he could he stand and not touch. If he were to let her loose before morning, she'd be right back out in the same amount of danger she'd been before. "I won't let you go." Truth was he didn't want to let her go. He wanted to fill his hands with her and bury himself deep inside her warm moist center.

"I won't tell anyone where you are. You can blindfold me and lead me out if you have to, but I need to find Madison. She's all I have left."

"You won't be able to help her now, and I won't allow you to go until daylight." The sweet swells of her body were making him crazy. If he didn't get away from her, he'd do something he'd regret. Nicolae grabbed for the shirt she'd slapped aside and tied a sleeve around her wrists.

"Don't you dare," she said, her lips thinning into a straight peachy pink line, her body struggling beneath him.

"I'll do what I have to." He tossed the shirt around one of the posts on the headboard and pulled the fabric until her hands were snug against the wood. He tested its strength before he rolled away from that luscious figure.

His body already missed the warmth of her beneath him, but he had work to do. "I'll be back when the sun comes up." One last look at her half naked body, and he left the room.

* * *

As soon as Nic left the room, Reggie twisted and struggled until she'd flipped over and worked her way to her knees.

With her fingertips, she worked at the fabric trying to untangle the knot he'd tied so expertly. Her twisting to her knees had only complicated the matter and pulled it tighter. The more she tried, the more she realized the knot wasn't getting any loser.

She should have put the damned shirt on when he told her to instead of giving him the perfect method of restraint.

"Want me to untie it for you?"

The sound of a gentle feminine voice behind her made her yelp.

"I'm sorry. I didn't mean to startle you." A pretty pale young woman with hair the color of milk chocolate eased through the doorway and into the room, shooting a look back over her shoulder. "I shouldn't be in here, but I wanted to talk to you."

"Is that right? Only talk? Or are you one of them?" Reggie jerked her head toward the door.

The girl's mouth curved into a soft smile. "No. I'm not a vampire, if that's what you mean."

Anger fired through her veins. Maybe she was one of missing women. "Are you a prisoner, too? What's your name?" Maybe she matched a name on her list of missing women. Or worse, there were more unreported women missing.

Her musical laugh floated through the room as she crossed the room to Reggie. "My name is Melisande and, no, I'm not a prisoner. I live here."

"I don't understand. You're not a prisoner, you're not a vamp, and yet you choose to live here?"

"Yes." She reached out and tugged at the shirt, pulling the sleeves through the knots. Her glance strayed to Reggie's naked breasts several times during the process, her cheeks growing redder by the minute.

When Reggie's hands were finally freed, Melisande stepped back, twisting the shirt in her hands.

"Eh-hem." Reggie rubbed her wrists, wondering about this woman who seemed so young and naïve. "Could I have the shirt, please?"

Melisande glanced up her eyes wide, the flush in her cheeks deepening. When her gaze landed on Reggie's full breasts, she turned away, shoving the shirt at her without looking. "Please. I didn't mean to…I'm sorry. Oh, hell…" her voice trailed off, and she turned her back to her.

"Are you embarrassed by my nakedness?" Reggie chuckled. "You're a strange bird. A woman who lives with vampires is embarrassed by a little nudity, when she has two of the most gorgeous men I've ever seen under the same roof." She shrugged her arms into the voluminous sleeves and buttoned the middle three buttons. The shirt hung to her knees. Since it was the only garment offered, she'd make do. Her tank top was toast.

"I know you must think I'm silly. I see the guys running around with next to nothing on, sometimes even naked, but there aren't many women around."

"With those two, that's hard to believe." The thought of Tor and Nic traipsing around the apartment with nothing on made her blood shoot to her head and low in her belly at the same time. Whew! She'd seen a good portion of Nic exposed, and he would be hard to forget.

"They never bring them back to the apartment. They don't want anyone to know where they live. It's been that way since Nic brought me to live with them."

"Nic bringing you here, was it your choice or his?" Reggie tied the shirttails around her waist with a firm yank. Did she need to sneak Melisande out of here as well as getting her own butt out? If she had to drag Melisande around Houston, it would slow her from finding Madison, but she didn't feel right leaving her here.

"Mine, of course," she said with conviction. "I really didn't have anywhere else to go, and I've never felt safer."

But Reggie stared at her for a long moment. "Aren't you afraid they'll try to make you into one of them?"

"Oh, no." She shook her head, her straight brown hair swirling around her shoulders. "Nic was turned against his will around four-hundred years ago by a woman he thought he loved. Such a sad story." Melisande sighed.

Nic was in love with another woman? The thought didn't sit well with Reggie, and her fingers curled into a tight ball. She hadn't considered Nic might be taken. "Is she still around?"

"Oh, no. She left as soon as she turned him. Broke his heart." The girl shrugged. "That's why Nic swore he'd never turn a soul who didn't want it. Tor feels the same. They won't turn me unless I want them to."

So the woman wasn't around, and Nic had morals. Reggie found that hard to believe, especially after he'd tied her to the bed. "You're not considering letting them turn you, are you?"

"Maybe someday. I want to have a regular life first."

"Regular? Honey, you live with vampires. There's nothin' regular about that in my books." She glanced toward the open curtains. The battleship gray of pre-dawn crept across the Houston skyline.

"I know. But I hope to have a career and maybe a husband and children someday." She turned toward Reggie. "I'm going to college, you know."

Reggie raked a hand through her tangled hair and then planted both fists on her hips. "Then what the hell are you doing with them?"

"I love them," she said as if it were the most natural thing in the world. "They're my family."

"Don't you have a real family?"

Her head dipped low. "No."

Reggie had to lean close to catch her answer. "What happened to them?"

"My mother died when I was a baby, and my father...wasn't much of a father to me." She looked up, her gaze finally meeting Reggie's. "Nic saved me and brought me here."

"My mother also died with I was a baby." She and Melisande had something in common, but losing their mothers was as far as it went. Her father had raised her and Madison in a loving, supportive environment. That's why his death had hit her so hard, and why she didn't trust vampires. Especially ones with dark, sexy eyes and a body to drool for.

"It's hard growing up without a mother," Melisande said.

"Not if you have a father who gives a damn and a sister you'd give your life for."

"What's that like?" Melisande asked. "Having a father who cares? Mine didn't. He only wanted me for one reason." Her voice dropped to a whisper, and her gaze shifted to her feet.

She didn't name that reason, but Reggie had seen enough in her life as a cop before she joined the PIA that she could guess by what she didn't say. Melisande's father was a sexually abusive son-of-a-bitch. For a brief moment, she could respect Nic for taking this woman-child away from that kind of life.

She reached out and grasped the woman's hands. "Melisande, come with me. I can find you a place to stay and get you set up with scholarships and everything. You don't have to stay here."

"Leave?" Melisande stared up at her as if she'd shaken a screw loose. "Why? I'm happy for the first time in my life. I can come and go as I please, and Nic is paying for my education. I have everything I could want."

"But you're living with vampires." Had they brainwashed her? Was she in some kind of trance?

Didn't she get it?

However, Nic had been very persuasive, sexy, and unlike any other man she'd ever met. The touch of his skin against hers hadn't been like she'd thought it would be. He didn't feel at all dead. His body had been warm and pulsing with life, just like one of the living.

Could she be wrong about vampires? Was there such a thing as a good vampire, or was it all a part of his act? Mentally shaking herself, she stared across at Melisande. "Don't you understand? The two guys in the other room are vampires, creatures of the night. Honey, they're bloodsucking monsters!"

"No. *You* don't understand. They might be vampires, but they're more human than my father. He was the monster." She yanked her hands from Reggie's. "The sun's up. You can leave now."

Chapter Five

The door closed behind Reggie with a resounding slam. She hadn't bothered to say goodbye, thank you, or kiss my ass as she left.

And Nic hadn't tried to stop her. He couldn't hold her captive forever. Having promised to let her go at sunup, he wouldn't go back on his word. Even when his insides screamed he was a fool to let her go.

Why should he care?

"I still think you took a big risk letting her leave on her own." Torsten leaned against the bar separating the kitchen from the living area. "She could lead the authorities back here."

"She won't," Nic said, wondering if he was right. Although he'd healed her wound, she hadn't wanted him to. She didn't like vampires, and she was bound and determined to kill every last one of them. What made him think she wouldn't come back with a bunch of her buddies at the PIA and finish him off?

Nothing.

He was living on wishful thinking, and that kind of thinking got a vampire dusted.

"She's pretty, isn't she?" Melisande entered the living area from Nic's bedroom. "I can see why Nic's enchanted by her. Although she didn't seem to share the sentiment."

"I'm not enchanted." He shot a fierce frown toward Melisande.

She smiled.

"I pulled her out of a tight situation, that's all," he continued as if he needed to explain himself. Like he *ever* explained his actions.

"Then why did you come out of there with a hard-on the size of Copenhagen?" Melisande's gaze flicked to Nic's pants, still slightly bulging from his tumble with Reggie.

Nic's frown transferred to his friend. "I'm not immune

to a sexy woman. That doesn't mean I have feelings for her. She's a vampire-hating stranger, for the love of God. She tried to kill me."

"Stimulating, wasn't it?" Torsten grinned. "I don't think I've seen you this intrigued with a woman. Ever."

"Enough," Nic said, his voice firm. All he wanted was to put her out of his mind. "We have bigger problems to worry about than a PIA agent." Even if she had hair the color of fire and skin so soft...Nic forced himself back on track. "Seems our man Andrei is up to his old tricks."

"Are you sure Andrei's behind the gang attack last night?" Torsten asked.

"I saw a tattoo on Cesar's arm." Nic's chest tightened when he thought of the shots they'd fired at Reggie and how they'd hunted her down. "It was Andrei's mark of the dragon."

"How bad is that?" Melisande asked.

"We have no idea how many gang members he might have recruited. They've already captured thirteen young women."

"Damn." Torsten shoved a hand through his long blond hair.

"We may not have much time." Nic stared at the curtains covering the windows, the daylight edging in around the sides making him squint.

Frustration welled up inside him. He needed every hour of the day and night to find Andrei. He was as slippery as they came and too evil for too long to change.

"Not much we can do until nightfall." Torsten yawned. "I'm for some rest."

"What about me?" Melisande asked. "I can go out during the daylight."

"No!" Both Nic and Torsten shouted in unison.

"You two treat me like a baby. I'm twenty-three and old enough to make up my own mind."

"Yeah, and you fit the profile for Andrei's buyers." Nic touched a hand to her cheek. "Young, pretty, and alone. We know you can make your own decisions, but we can't help you during the daytime. Andrei's been known to get his human minions to work the dayshift for him."

"Still…" Melisande frowned. "I feel so useless. While Reggie's out fighting the bad guys, you two keep me cocooned from everything in here. I'm getting bored, and I want to go back to my classes."

"You will, ma petite, soon enough." Nic pressed a kiss to her forehead like he would a child. At twenty-three, she wasn't much more than a child. "Let us take care of Andrei first. No woman is safe out there right now."

"You let Reggie go," she pointed out.

"She's trained in law enforcement and self-defense," Nic said. "Taking care of herself is second nature."

Melisande's brows rose. "Then why didn't you let her leave when she wanted to instead of waiting until daylight?"

Gotcha.

Nic clamped his lips closed. He wasn't going down that path. He hadn't wanted her to leave, but he'd promised her by daylight.

"I think our Nic has met his match in Reggie. Wouldn't you say?" Torsten laid an arm across Nic's shoulders, a smirky grin quirking his lips upward. "In the meantime, let's get some rest for the night ahead. We have a lot of work to do in order to find and rein in Andrei."

* * *

Heads popped up over the tops of walled cubicles as Reggie stormed through the offices of the Paranormal Investigations Agency. When she reached Blake Tanner's office, she marched in without knocking, slinging the door open so fast it crashed against the wall. "Where's Madison?"

She'd been by their apartment before she came to the station. No amount of calling raised her on her cell phone. Reggie's last hope was that she'd made it back to the station in the time it had taken for her to get from

Nicolae's penthouse to the station.

Tanner rose from the chair behind his desk, a phone pressed to his ear and scowl on his face. "I understand, sir. We have our best people on the case and hope to have it wrapped up by tonight." He nodded as if the man on the other end of the line could see him. "Yes, sir. I understand how important the safety of the city is to you. Yes sir, I'll keep you informed. Thank you, sir." The line clicked loud enough that Tanner jerked the phone away from his ear with a wince. Then he set it back in its receiver and turned his full attention to Reggie. "Have a seat."

"I don't need a freakin' seat. I want to know where the hell my sister is."

Tanner looked her square in the eye, one of his better traits. He didn't waste words or hold back on the truth. "She never came in after the mission went south. I have ten people out combing the streets for some sign of her and so far, I've gotten no reports."

He walked around the desk and reached out to pat her back, the movement awkward but well intentioned. The man was typical Type-A and didn't know an emotion until it slapped him in the face. But not a man or woman on his team had any doubt he'd give his life for every one of them. "I'm sorry, Reggie."

"Well, sorry ain't cuttin' it." Brushing away a tear, she glared at him through watery eyes. She would not break down in front of this man or any other, for that matter. "She's my sister," she whispered, biting hard on her lip to keep it from trembling.

"I know, and we'll find her." He turned away, his motions jerky. The man probably wasn't used to tears on a team consisting predominantly of men. If she and Madison hadn't gotten in his face and more or less worn him down, they would never have been allowed on the team. "We recovered Macias and Jones where they'd set up audio surveillance."

Reggie gulped back her tears, her breath caught in her

throat. "Dead?"

"Didn't even have a chance. Necks broken and both drained. Looked like the works of vampires. Up until you walked in the door, we thought you and Madison were going on our list of missing women."

He didn't complete the thought. Instead of both of them going on the missing women list, Madison would be the only one unless she miraculously appeared in the next few hours. Where the hell was she?

"I have people out looking for you both. I'll let them know at least *you're* back." He sighed and sat behind his desk, rifling through the stack of files until he unearthed one. He glanced across at her. "I take it you're not going to get any rest after being up all night?"

"You got that right. I can't rest until I know where Madison is."

"Good, then you can follow up on a lead we just got. An A. Skirko owns a warehouse on the waterfront. Word on the street has it that he might be involved somehow with the disappearances. I want you to take Humberto and check it out. And this time, don't lose your partner." His words weren't said with malice, but he meant it nonetheless. The rule in this business was to fly with a wingman and never let him out of your sight.

Reggie understood, but her reckless sister didn't always play by the rules, and sometimes that came back to bite her. Hopefully, this time the bite wasn't from a vampire.

"By the way, where were you? Why didn't you report in?" Tanner pinned her with a stare. "You had us all worried."

Now was the time to tell her boss she'd been detained by a vampire and held until dawn. If she were a good agent, she'd do it without hesitation. An image of Nicolae Kovak sprang to mind. The image where he wasn't wearing a shirt and neither was she. Her body tensed all over again. "When I lost Madison, I hunkered down in a safe place until daylight."

His attention was back on the stack of documents in front of him. "Smart move. Next time, try to get a call in to me."

* * *

"Yes, sir." She spun on her heal and headed to her desk. Once seated, she gathered her thoughts. Where was Madison? The only leads she had were the Dragons and the folder Tanner had given her.

The Dragóns were a diverse group of gang members, primarily from the poor neighborhoods. Kids who'd been left to run the streets by parents who were either too spaced out on drugs or just didn't give a damn. Those kids grew into criminals, running in packs like rabid dogs, ripe for any illegal way to make a buck. Nothing was off limits to them. Stealing, killing, and kidnapping women would be right up their alley. But was there a bigger fish to fry at the core of their work?

Reggie poured over the file of A. Skirko, foreign-born businessman with substantial financial holdings in the Houston area, including shipping ties and warehouses along the waterfront. She jotted down the addresses of the places that might be used to hold over a dozen, make that fourteen women, counting Madison. Reggie refused to believe any one of them was dead, and her sister was only waiting for her to find her and save her sorry ass.

And she'd kick it from here to tomorrow, after she was safe and sound back home.

"Bert?" she yelled, as she rose from her desk.

"Yo, Reggie, good to see you back in one piece. Like the shirt." He nodded at the cleavage no amount of tying could cover.

He was a notorious, yet harmless womanizer, but all-in-all not too bad. Reggie had worked with him on occasion when Madison was out sick. "Keep it in your pants, Casanova. We have work to do."

In one of the agency's nondescript gray sedans, they

traveled east along the congested highways crisscrossing the metropolitan spread that was Houston toward the inland waterways and ports. When they turned onto the road where one of the warehouses was located, Reggie caught glimpses of the water between the rows of buildings.

Clouds churned in the sky, blotting out the sun and turning the water to a perpetual dark gray.

Reggie parked the car three buildings shy of their target, pulling around back out of sight. When she got out, she was hit with the full force of the coastal humidity the air conditioner had effectively cut up to this point. "Remind me why I live in Houston?" she grumbled.

Her family had been in Houston as far back as her great-great grandfather. They'd settled in this area, coming all the way from Ireland to start over in the new world. Why couldn't they have found a cooler, drier place to start a new life?

With her sister's life hanging in the balance, she had to hurry. Reggie broke into a jog, covering the distance between the buildings with Bert barely keeping up.

All the warehouses looked pretty much the same, and she feared she'd lose count or get the wrong one. Then she recognized the symbol painted in bold black across the back door of one of them. She'd seen it in the file and on Cesar's arm in the form of a tattoo. It was a circle made of the coil of a snake's body with the head and tail of a dragon. "I'll take door number one."

"Sure this is it?"

"Absolutely." She grabbed the doorknob on the off chance it would open, only to be disappointed. The door was locked.

"How do you suggest we get in?"

"There has to be a way." She scanned the walls of the steel and metal sided building. Without so much as a window close enough to the ground to crawl into, the place was a veritable fortress.

A truck rumbled along the street out front, slowing to a stop.

Reggie ran toward it, calling back over her shoulder, "Come on."

Tucked in the shadow cast by the morning sun, Reggie and Bert skimmed along the sheet metal siding to the front where a delivery truck stood. The driver honked three times and waited.

When the giant doors rolled open, a man stepped out to speak to the driver.

"Be ready. We're going in," Reggie said, never taking her gaze from the truck.

"What? Are you crazy?" Bert whispered. "We don't know how many people are inside."

"A chance we'll have to take." Especially if her sister was inside. "I tell you what, you stay out here and keep you eyes peeled for trouble."

"I can't let you go in by yourself."

"Better just one person than two. That way, if I get in trouble, you can go for help. If I'm not back in twenty minutes, call Tanner."

"I don't like it."

"Tough. I'm going." The truck's engine rumbled, and it rolled past the building, and then backed in. Reggie crept up to the passenger side and crouched low, walking inside with the truck until she passed the doorway at which time, she ducked behind a stand of crates on pallets.

Her heart hammered against her ribcage as her eyes adjusted to the darker interior of the warehouse. As soon as the truck cleared the entrance, the giant doors closed.

Good. She was inside, and the alarm hadn't gone up. Male voices echoed in the cavernous interior. Reggie peeked around the corner of the crate.

Eight men stood around the newly arrived delivery truck, all looking like one or the other of Cesar's thugs — tattooed, earring-wearing muscular guys in black. Great. Her nightmare from last night. Only this time there would be no vampire to rescue her. He was safely tucked in his apartment until sunset. Definitely a limitation in her book. Not that she wanted him to save her.

While the men focused on the truck, Reggie moved away from the door and farther back into the warehouse half the size of a football field. Stacks of wooden crates rose to ten feet high, creating a maze for Reggie to work her way through one row at a time. Until she came to a solid block of containers thirty feet wide and thirty feet long. Reggie edged her way around the periphery until she found an entry into the stack.

Voices carried to her, sounding closer than before, and she could hear footsteps moving her direction.

Before she could think, she ducked into the wall of crates, finding a neat row of more wooden boxes. Only these weren't stacked. Fourteen of the coffin-sized containers lined the walls, each with the tops off and white blankets covering the contents.

"Are they ready for shipment?" a male voice asked. "The boss doesn't want any more screw ups."

"They're ready." Reggie recognized Cesar's voice from last night. Damn she was right in the middle of something.

She ducked behind one of the crates in the shadows of the far corner and held her breath. If they caught her, it would be up to Bert to get word back to the PIA. By then, it might be too late.

The footsteps halted in her little room and paused in front of one of the boxes.

"When do you want us to seal the containers?" Cesar asked.

"Not until the last minute. Each box is ventilated, but we don't want to risk keeping them confined for too long. Our customers want them fresh not suffocated."

What were they talking about? Reggie tried to read between the lines. Were they discussing fresh foods or the missing women? Anger boiled inside her. How could these animals play with lives the way they did? But she knew how psychopaths worked. They had no remorse.

"Are they drugged?"

Cesar said. "Sort of. The boss put them in some kind of trance. They're asleep until he wakes them." "Must be nice to be a vamp. Wish I could use that trick on my old lady." Cesar laughed.

The other man remained silent.

"Well, anyway, the boss oughta be happy with this shipment," Cesar continued, all humor wiped from his voice.

"He'd have been happier if you'd gotten the other sister last night."

Reggie smothered a gasp. Although she'd guessed they'd been talking about the women, hearing reference to her sister almost made her blow her cover. As angry as she was, she could take two men, but the other six, and who knew how many more there might be, could take her out, and where would that leave her sister and the other thirteen young ladies being held hostage?

"That wasn't our fault. She had help," Cesar said.

"Another reason the boss was pissed."

"Hey, that guy nearly broke my arm!"

"He let you live."

"Barely," Cesar muttered. "What did the boss say?"

"Nothing. Come on. We have work to do before the boss gets here tonight."

The men left the room, their footsteps carrying them away from the crate room and Reggie.

For the first time in the past few minutes, she breathed. When she thought the coast was clear, she jumped to her feet and pulled the white blankets aside one at a time. Beneath each was a woman laid out in what looked like makeshift coffin-like structures lined with rich colored fabrics. Velvet, satin, taffeta — no expense spared to outfit and present the merchandise. Reggie's stomach rebelled, and she fought the urge to throw up. All were young and beautiful and in a deep sleep.

When she reached the last one that stood closest to the entrance, her hand shook as she yanked the blanket aside.

There, nestled in white satin sheeting was her sister with the flaming auburn hair. She wore a black lace skirt and an old-fashioned black corset, cinched tightly to emphasize her already generous bust line.

"Madison," Reggie whispered into her ear. She couldn't breathe until she felt the beat of her sister's pulse. Then she patted Madison's cheek. "Wake up, Madison. Wake up." She increased the sharpness of her slap until realization sank in. No matter how hard she tried, she wasn't waking her sister. Whatever "the boss" had done had all these women in a deep trance.

Reggie stood staring around the room. How could she get Madison and all the rest of the women out? They were like dead weight. Even if she could carry her sister, she couldn't get past all the men out front. And if she did, what would happen to the rest of the women? If these people knew they'd been discovered, they'd leave and take all the evidence with them.

Much as she hated doing it, she had to leave Madison and go get help. Lots of help.

Making a quick pass around the room, she put the blankets back the way she'd found them. Then dropping a kiss on her sister's cheeks, she whispered, "I'll be back."

Chapter Six

The sense that Reggie was in trouble forced Nic to do something he hadn't done in a long time— venture out during the daytime.

If the clouds weren't covering the sun's deadly rays, he wouldn't even attempt going out until dark. As was typical of Houston, clouds came in from the Gulf, sometimes lingering all day and night. The weatherman had predicted cloudy skies until close to midnight.

"I'm not feeling good about this," Torsten said, shoving an arm into the long, lightweight overcoat with the high collar.

Nic pulled gloves onto his hand and adjusted the collar of his black trench coat upward to protect the back of his neck. "Being a vampire can be a pain."

"But we live forever," Torsten countered.

"If we aren't staked in the heart by well-intentioned citizens, fried in the daylight, or otherwise dusted."

Torsten stopped halfway into his coat and stared at Nic. "Tell me again why the hell we're going out?"

"We have to stop Andrei."

"Uh huh. Andrei. Right." The expressive lift of Torsten's eyebrows conveyed a lot more than the sarcasm in his words. "I'm thinking its one redhead that's got you all excited."

"I'm going out for one thing and one thing only—to bring Andrei down."

"And if you get a little taste of red, you'll be all that much happier?"

"Quit teasing him, Tor." Melisande emerged from Nic's room, carrying two broad-brimmed hats like the gangsters wore in the early nineteen hundreds. "Wear these."

"You don't think we'll stand out with those?"

"No more than you'll stand out with the black trench

51

coats on a hot and humid day in Houston. Just tell them you're going to a Matrix convention if anyone asks."

"By the way, where are we going?" Torsten stood at the door, settling the hat at a jaunty angle on his long white hair.

"PIA headquarters." Nic stepped past the slack-jawed Norseman and strode down the hall. A small smile quirked his lips upward.

The drive to PIA headquarters was nothing less than hair-raising. Daytime traffic in Houston was worse than anything Paris at night had ever been.

"Tell me again why we're going to PIA headquarters? Do you have a death wish or what?" Torsten gripped the armrest of the HUMMV hard enough to leave permanent grooves in the leather.

"That's who Reggie works for, and I think they may prove of assistance in our quest to find and eliminate Andrei and his band of Dragóns." He swerved around a car and zipped off the exit ramp leading to the collection of high-rise office buildings of downtown Houston.

"This idea doesn't make sense, Nic. You know how the PIA works—kill the monster now and ask questions later."

"They won't harm us."

"Are you sure?"

No, he wasn't. But by showing up in the daytime, he might get past the front desk without them really knowing what they were. "Just remember to remove the coat, hat, and gloves before we get to the front desk."

"Great." Torsten leaned his head back, his sunglasses pointing to the ceiling. "I'm riding with a lunatic to a destination no sane vampire would walk into without a submachine gun and extra ammo belts."

"I'm telling you, they'll be glad to see us." He hoped.

"Sure. Whatever." Torsten rode in silence for the rest of the short drive into the parking garage of the office building housing the PIA headquarters.

After parking in the darkest corner next to the elevator, Nic climbed out and removed his hat, gloves, and jacket.

Torsten did the same, squinting at the light peeking in from beneath the parking decks. "You sure the sun's not coming out today?"

"The weatherman said cloudy until midnight."

"Since when has the weatherman gotten it right?"

"Let's hope he's right today. I don't plan on frying. Not with the possibility that Andrei's behind the missing fourteen women."

Feeling completely exposed and a little nervous about walking during the daylight, Nic kept to the darkest path leading to the elevator and breathed a sign when he climbed in and scanned the sign indicating what could be found on each floor of the fourteen-story building. P.I.A. Headquarters was located on the second floor. He punched the button and grinned at Torsten.

The tall blond Norseman shook his head. "You owe me big time for this."

* * *

Getting out of the building took a little more time than getting in. The truck wasn't going anywhere until midnight, and the big doors remained closed. Reggie worked her way around the building, hugging the shadows for ten minutes until she came across a door leading out—the door that had been locked from the outside at the back of the building. She scanned the door handle for any signs of security alarms. There were no warning signs that an alarm would go off if she opened it.

She had to take the chance. The only other opening was at the front, and a man was stationed there. On the count of three, Reggie took a deep breath, opened the door, stepped out, and closed it behind her. She didn't hear any sirens or buzzing sounds to indicate an alarm had gone off. But she wasn't taking any chances. The quicker she got out of sight the better off the women inside would be.

She sprinted toward the edge of the side of the building where Bert was supposed to be waiting. He stood with his back to her, checking around the corner and down at his watch.

"Psst!"

Bert jumped and spun toward her, his eyes wide until he recognized her. Then he was running toward her, and they beat a hasty retreat to their car parked three long buildings away.

Once they were on the road and away from the warehouse district, Reggie's heartbeat returned to semi-normal.

"What the hell happened in there?" Bert demanded.

"I found them."

"The women?"

"Fourteen of them."

"Damn."

"Yeah." And it was killing her that she'd left them there. "We have to get back to headquarters for help. This is a bigger operation than the two of us can handle."

"No kidding." He leaned back and turned his head toward her. "You all right?"

"No." But she had to hold it together until this was all over. "Madison is in there."

"Damn."

Spinning sideways into the parking garage, Reggie parked the car in a no-parking zone next to the elevator and leaped out before the engine had time to completely shut down. She punched the elevator button, and when it didn't open immediately, she turned to the stairwell, climbing the three flights from the garage to the second floor.

When she burst through the door into the offices occupied by the PIA, heads turned. With the lives of fourteen women hanging in the balance, Reggie didn't waste time on pleasantries. She jogged through the rows of cubicles straight to Tanner's office.

She didn't wait for permission to enter. She pushed through the door. "Tanner, I found them."

Tanner wasn't alone. Sitting with their backs to her were two men in long black trench coats, one with sooty black hair down to his shoulders, and the other with hair longer than hers and so blond it could be considered white.

She swallowed her heart and felt it land like a rock in the pit of her stomach. "What the hell are you doing here?"

Nicolae Kovak and Torsten Lang stood as one and turned toward her. Torsten's face was split in a long grin, whereas Nic's face was set in a serious frown. Even the frown looked sexy on the man.

What was wrong with her? Good-looking men never had the impact on her like this one. Why couldn't he be human?

"Reggie, it's so good to see a friendly face." Torsten hugged her like a long-lost friend, not the stranger she'd met during the wee hours of that dark morning when she'd needed saving from a pack of rabid gang members. When Torsten stepped backward, Reggie could see her boss's angry expression.

"Care to explain?" he asked.

"Not really," she said.

"We were just telling Agent Tanner about the incident this morning," Torsten said.

"Thanks," Reggie said. Nic still hadn't said a word, and it made her all jittery inside. She found herself anxious to hear his low baritone voice with the foreign accent.

"Next time you debrief me on an operation, don't leave out the important details," Tanner said.

Worry for her sister pushed through her thoughts of Nic. How could she think of him at a time like this? "How did they get in?"

"Walked in during broad daylight," Tanner responded.

"The cloud cover helps," Torsten offered.

"They want to help recover the women and bring in the guy responsible for their disappearances."

Reggie put aside her uneasiness and turned to Tanner. "I found them."

"The women?" Tanner's frown lifted. "Where?"

"In the A.S.E. Warehouse near the waterfront."

"Why didn't you bother to call in? We could have sent someone over in a matter of minutes."

"I didn't trust the lines. Another part of last night I didn't mention was that I think someone knew about our set up and sabotaged it before we even started."

Tanner's jaw tightened. "We've lost two good men already and possibly Madison. Think it's an inside job?"

"I didn't want to take the chance," Reggie said.

"It's just as well you didn't send anyone down there immediately," Nicolae finally spoke up, his voice turning Reggie's knees to mush.

"Why is that?" Tanner crossed his arms over his chest as if daring Nic to say anything he wanted to listen to.

Nic's lips thinned. "If you retrieve these women now, you will not deal with the main problem."

"Andrei Skirko," Torsten filled in. "A.S. of A.S. Enterprises."

"What exactly did you learn at the warehouse?" Tanner shot the question at Reggie.

"They plan to move the women tonight at midnight. They have the truck in place, and their boss is due to be there for the event." She looked from Torsten to Nic. "I take it the boss is this guy, Andrei?"

"Yes. He's a four-hundred-twenty-two-year-old vampire we've been following off and on over the centuries cleaning up after him." Nic stepped closer, his presence raising her body temperature with each step.

Reggie held her ground, refusing to let him know she responded in any way to his presence, even though her heart was hammering in her chest and perspiration popped out on her upper lip. "Why should we trust you?"

"We have the same interests at heart," he said, his voice soft and directed only at her.

"I seriously doubt that," she said, her voice a little less convinced than her body. What was wrong with her? She shouldn't be even mildly attracted to Nicolae Kovak. He was a vampire; she was human. It was just wrong.

"Be that as it may." He winked and then turned to face her boss.

A good thing, too, because her skin was tingling all over, and her mind wasn't focusing on anything past his lips.

Nic swept his arm out. "We of the vampire world are very much like you."

Tanner snorted.

Nic nodded but didn't comment on the derogatory sound. "There are good vampires," he nodded toward Torsten, "and very bad vampires. When a bad vampire is out of control, Torsten and I are sent in to...fix things."

"So you're some kind of vampire cops?" her boss asked.

"More like special forces. We come in, assess, identify, and eliminate the problem. We work on our own or with local police forces and even the federal government. Check with the CIA. They'll vouch for us."

"Thanks, I will." Tanner punched a button on his phone. "Maury, call the CIA and ask if they've ever worked with a Nicolae Kovak and Torsten Lang. Get on that ASAP."

"Thus our reason for being here." Nic continued when Tanner switched off the intercom. "Which I was getting to before Agent Gallagher arrived." He shot a glance back at Reggie.

The glance lit a fire in her, and she stepped forward. "I don't really care why you're here. We need reinforcements to go into that warehouse and retrieve those women."

"And if you do, you might save these women, but

Andrei will be free to do it all again." Nic stared hard at Reggie. "If not in Houston, in some other city where women are equally vulnerable to him."

"What is he doing with them?" Tanner asked.

Torsten stepped forward. "He's selling them in foreign countries as sheep to other vampires."

"Sheep?" Reggie asked.

The muscle in Nic's jaw twitched. "It's a crude term for someone who feeds the needs of a vampire, whether it's blood or lust."

"In other words, they're trafficking women, forcing them to be sex slaves and blood donors for the highest bidder?"

"American women bring a higher price." Nic's tone was hard.

Reggie spun on her heels. "I'm getting Madison out of there, and I'm gonna bust some serious heads while I'm at it."

Nicolae laid a hand on her arm, dragging her to a halt before she reached the door. "You can't. Andrei will get away. Hopefully, they don't know you found them, and they'll continue with their planned shipment. We have to be there when it happens and when Andrei shows up to direct operations."

"I hate to say he's right, but the vamp has a point, Reggie." Tanner glared at Nicolae. "You can let go of her arm now."

Nicolae held on for a second longer and then released her, leaving his warm imprint on her skin.

"But I can't just leave Madison there." Reggie stepped up to Tanner's desk, trying hard to ignore the other two men in the room.

"We'll get her out of there, but we need to get Andrei as well." The PIA lead tapped a pen against the hard metal of his desk. "How?"

Reggie stared at him. "I can't believe you're going along with vampires while my sister is lying in some warehouse waiting to be shipped out to the highest bidder. Did you consider these guys might be lying?"

"I told you I haven't lied to you," Nic said, his voice as warm as melted chocolate.

Fighting to control her temper, she faced Nic. "I don't know that, and I've never trusted the word of a vampire. It's one of your kind who killed my father."

A muscle worked in Nic's jaw. "I see."

"What do you see?" She stared at him, refusing to back down or be sucked in by his handsome looks. "All I see is the enemy in friendly territory."

The phone on Tanner's desk buzzed, and he punched a button. "Tanner."

"Sir, CIA says the two names you gave me check out. They also said these guys are the pros, and to let them be fully involved in whatever operation you're conducting."

"Thanks." He stabbed the button and stared across the room at Reggie. "I know how you feel about Madison. I feel the same way. She's one of my people."

"No, you *don't* know how I feel," Reggie said. "She's *my* sister not yours."

"Granted," he nodded. "However, we need to take out Andrei so he can't do this to other women."

"Precisely," Nic agreed.

"I don't trust you even if the CIA swore on a stack of Bibles. You're vampires!" Or was it herself she couldn't trust around Nicolae? He'd saved her from Cesar and hidden her until daylight to keep her from getting hurt. What had he done so far to prove himself untrustworthy?

He was a vampire. A vampire Tanner was willing to believe in. Should she? For her sister?

"Agent Gallagher," Tanner said in a warning tone. "If I have to, I'll pull you off this case."

Her heart stopped cold in her chest and then it leapt into motion, beating twice as fast as normal. "You can't do that. Not while my sister is in that animal's hands."

"Then you have to have confidence in me and believe

they will get Madison and the other ladies out alive." Her boss stood with his hands propped on his hips.

She stared from Tanner to Nic and back to Tanner. If she wanted to be there when it all went down, she had to shut up and go along with their tactics. Pushing her shoulders back, she gave Nicolae a cold stare. "What's the plan?"

Chapter Seven

"How in hell you got Tanner to agree to this, I'll never know." Reggie wasn't letting go of her anger any time soon. Nic suspected that if she did, she might fall apart. The worry for her sister had to be colossal.

"I really think he wants you to keep an eye on me or vice versa." Nicolae leaned against the counter of her kitchenette, studying her as she paced from her refrigerator to the stove and back.

"You're the vampire. It's not as if I can easily dispose of you if you tried to do something. Hell, you can out muscle me by at least ten to one." She slammed a jug of orange juice on the counter and turned. "What do you want with the PIA? Can't you fight your own kind without our help?"

"Yes, but there's just the two of us, and Andrei's got a few more on his side at the moment."

"Uh-huh. Yeah. And I'm supposed to feel good about leaving my sister in that hell hole?" Her eyes filling with tears, she turned her back to him and yanked a skillet from beneath the cabinet, giving him a terrific view of black denim molded to her firm, rounded bottom.

He had to count to ten before he could think straight and then count ten more before he could form a coherent sentence. "It only makes sense to wait until midnight to catch Andrei. Tanner has people watching the warehouse throughout the day and evening in case any trucks come or go."

"I should be there. I'm just glad he handpicked the team." With a flick of her wrist, she turned the knob on the stove and the burner beneath the smooth surface glowed red. "I still hate to think there's a leak in our department." Placing the skillet on the burner, she sprayed it with cooking spray.

Nicolae liked the casual ease with which she moved

around the kitchen as if she were as at home here as out on the streets busting badass monsters. "You're a strange woman, Regina."

She turned, a frown creasing the smooth skin of her forehead. "Me? I'm human, *you're* the vampire, and you're calling *me* strange?"

"Last night I saw a tough young woman stand up to a crowd of really nasty men." He nodded at the stove and the pan. "Tonight I see a completely different side of you working in a kitchen as if you know your way around."

A smirk lifted the corner of her mouth. "A girl has to eat to keep up her strength. I'm not passing out on the job. My sister needs me."

"These days, women who work in jobs like yours don't always have the time to cook."

"Don't get the wrong impression. I'm not very domestic. Ask me to clean a bathroom, and I'll throw the toilet brush at you. This—" she waved her hand at the stove, "I call self-preservation. My sister was—" her voice broke, and she turned away, the moisture back in her eyes. "My sister and I live together, and she's a really lousy cook."

She touched her finger to the middle of the pan and jerked it away. "Ouch!" Her finger went into her mouth, and she looked across the room at Nicolae as if waiting for him to say something. "Why are you really here?" she blurted out around her finger.

He wanted to answer her, but he couldn't think past her lips. Just that little movement of putting her finger in her mouth had him salivating and wishing he was the finger. The way she'd touched him last night still lingered in his body's memory, crying out to finish what they'd started when she was still in the grip of his trance. Only this time, he wanted very much for her to be fully awake and participating with her eyes wide open.

The longer he stared, the wider her eyes grew, her gaze darting to his mouth.

He knew he shouldn't, but he couldn't resist stepping closer until he stood toe-to-toe with her in the middle of the kitchen. "As I told you before, I'm here to bring Andrei down."

"No." Her finger slipped from her lips, and she stood looking up into his eyes, hers wary. But she didn't back away. "Why are you here in my apartment?"

"I wanted to make sure you were safe. It's dark outside."

"I've been around in the dark by myself before. I don't need you to protect me."

Her defiance pleased him. He liked a woman who wasn't afraid to stand up for herself and speak her mind. Especially if she had flaming red hair, smooth, creamy shoulders and… "Did you realize your skin is the color of cream sprinkled with cinnamon?"

Her breath caught on a little gasp. "My freckles are none of your concern, and you're changing the subject."

"Yes, I am." His hands came up to clasp her elbows. "I came here because I find you intriguing, and I want to know you better."

"Me?" she squeaked and backed into the stove.

Taking it as a good sign that she hadn't tried to knee him or hit him with the skillet, he closed the distance. His hands slid up her bare arms to her neck, his thumbs skimming her jaw. "You're a beautiful woman, Regina Gallagher."

"And you're treading on dangerous ground, vampire," she said on a whisper, her lips full and open, ready for —

The harsh scent of something burning broke through his concentration. Gripping her waist, he spun her away from the stove and the smoking skillet with the blackened cooking spray.

Regina grabbed the pan and held it under the faucet, the spray hissing until the pan cooled. She stood with her back to him longer than necessary as if avoiding the unavoidable.

* * *

What was wrong with her? He was a vampire, for godsakes! A gorgeous vampire, wearing a black trench coat, looking for all the world like he'd stepped out of a Matrix movie ready to sweep her into his arms and carry her off to have hot and dirty sex. Sweat beaded on her upper lip and between her breasts. "Don't," she said, surprised at how ragged her voice sounded to her own ears.

"Why, when we both feel it? Regina, it's inevitable." Stepping up behind her, he removed the pan from her grasp and laid it in the sink. Then with slow, deliberate movements, he turned her in his arms and stared down into eyes, his own a piercing pale blue.

"I need to eat," she said, her hands fluttering against his chest. She needed to eat? What was wrong with her? This vampire who looked good enough to eat was about to kiss her and all she could say was 'I need to eat'? *Think, Reggie*!

"I need you." He bent to take her lips, his mouth covering hers, his tongue licking at her bottom lip.

Her lips parted on a gasp. Think?

Think what?

Think about how good he felt against her, how warm his lips were pressed to hers. How gently he touched her, smoothing his hands down her back to curl around her hips and bring her even closer.

Nicolae dove in and plundered, thrusting his tongue through her teeth to duel with hers.

Thought wasn't an option. Feeling, tasting, and touching were instinctive and natural, and she thrust back with both her tongue and her hips. The hard evidence of his arousal pressed into her belly, making her want more.

Reggie's hands crept up his chest and circled behind his neck, tangling in his hair and tugging him closer. At the same time, her lips moved against his, voicing a thought as random as this encounter. "This is wrong."

"Maybe so, but I can't help myself." His kisses moved from her mouth to her throat.

Had he tried to resist the draw between them as much as she had?

Hard, sharp teeth skimmed over the sensitive skin of her neck, and she didn't fight him. He could sink his vampire fangs deep into her jugular and drain her dry, and she'd welcome it gladly.

"You must have me in another one of your trances," she whispered, her head thrown back to give him better access.

"No, my Regina, I want you on your terms." He grasped the hem of her tank top and dragged it up her waist and over her head, tossing it to the kitchen table.

She could have resisted. Instead she pressed her body against his, shoving his coat from his shoulders.

When he let go of her long enough to straighten his arms, his black trench coat fell to the floor, the buttons clicking against the ceramic tile.

Skin. She wanted to be skin-to-skin with him, and it couldn't be soon enough. Taking charge, she ripped his black T-shirt up and over his head, slinging it to the floor. Then her hands moved over the rivet at the waistband of his jeans and yanked it loose, sliding the zipper down with more desperation than care.

"Easy," he said, his hands grasping hers. Then he slid his jeans down, kicking off his shoes until he stood naked and proud, his penis hard and pointed in her direction.

Reggie's breath caught in her chest. Last time she'd seen him, she'd been in the shock of waking up from a trance. Now that she had time to study him from head to toe and all those gorgeous parts in between, she was speechless.

His sultry look turned confused. "What?" He glanced down at himself and back to her.

"Are all vampires as well equipped?" she asked,

excitement feeding through her veins like fire on dry tinder.

"Not that I go around looking at other vampire's cocks, but I'd venture to say it's one of the perks." His eyes narrowed into the dark and sexy look of the hunter. "My turn."

She stood like a deer mesmerized by oncoming headlights, frozen to the kitchen floor, her bottom leaning against the kitchen sink. When she should be remembering what happened to her father at the hands of a vampire, all she could think about was what this vampire's hands were going to do to her.

As she stood in her bra and jeans, Reggie's body sweltered in her own skin.

Nic moved closer, his body calling out to the inner wanton in her.

Feeling highly overdressed, Reggie was ready to shake free of all encumbrances standing in the way of her and him.

He slid his engorged cock against her belly. Instead of telling him to get lost and running like a frightened child, she pressed closer, unable to quell the surge of unbridled lust washing over her like a tidal wave pulling her under and dragging her out to sea.

His hands tugged her jeans over her hips and downward until he knelt at her feet to lift her legs one at time, releasing her of the stiff fabric.

"I'm going to hate myself later," she moaned, her legs spreading wider as his hands rose up the insides of her thighs.

"Maybe so, but I'm going to love you now." His fingers slipped into her folds until he found her moist center. First one then two fingers slid in, abrading her vaginal wall with the rough texture of his hands.

Reggie squirmed, her legs spreading wider, giving him more access to her. She clamped her teeth on her tongue to keep from begging him to take her.

Dragging his moistened finger between her folds, he swirled her juices around and around the little nub of her clit, teasing but not touching the swollen tip.

When he flicked his finger against that special place, she rose on her tiptoes, her hands clutching at his hair, pulling him closer.

He grabbed her by the hips, hiked her bottom up onto the counter and replaced his finger with his tongue, lapping at her hypersensitive clit in much more aggressive and sensuous strokes.

Reggie welcomed the cold countertop against her hot ass as she spiraled toward that ultimate peak. Spurred by that magical tongue laving her clit, her body erupted into a cataclysm of sensations. Her orgasm was so exquisitely intense, she didn't realize she'd shouted out loud until she heard Nic chuckle, his breath warm against her thighs.

"Stop laughing. You did that to me."

"But you yell with such gusto." He kissed the inside of her thigh and looked up at her with those wickedly blue eyes gleaming.

"Shut up and fuck me." She tugged at his hair until he stood and wrapped her legs around his waist, his penis positioned at the opening to her pussy, the velvety head poised to plunge into her slippery depths.

He hesitated.

"Oh for the love of Mike, do I have to do everything?" She grabbed his hips and slammed him home, her cunt absorbing all of him inside, the walls stretching to accommodate his size.

As he moved in and out of her, she leaned back, her head resting against the cabinets. "Why," she inhaled sharply as her body clenched around him, reveling in his strength. "Why did you stop a moment ago?"

He pumped in and out of her, his eyelids drooping over those ice-blue eyes, his lips pulled back over his teeth, exposing the long incisors. "I was going to scold you," he said, his voice breathless and strained.

"Scold me?" she asked, as he pressed deeper. How much better could this get and she not fall apart?

"For saying fuck." His body rammed hard on the word, and he held steady, the muscles in his arms and legs tense. "But I decided I like it when it's you." He pulled back slowly, hissing as he did, and then he rocked into her again, holding her hips against his.

His cock pulsed inside her, the sensation pushing her over the edge yet again. She cried out, grasping his shoulders, holding on as she rode the wave until they both coasted in to the shore and collapsed against each other.

When she could breathe again, she pushed back without breaking their intimate connection and stared down at where they were still joined, his cock still hard and deep within her.

"Definitely a perk," she said. And then the world came back to her like a train wreck. Her body stiffened, and she pushed against him. "Damn."

"What?" He slipped free of her warm, moist center, the cool air in the apartment a shocking blast to his heated shaft. His hands retained their hold on her thighs.

"I shouldn't have done that." Her voice was soft and sad, and her eyes filled with tears. "I shouldn't have made love to the enemy."

Chapter Eight

She slapped his hands away and pushed him aside, running from the room, her tight, white ass sexy even as she disappeared around the door into her bedroom.

He followed her across the living room and stood in front of her closed door. "Regina, I am not the enemy. Why do you refuse to believe me?"

"Are you a vampire?" she called out through the wooden panels.

"Yes but not by choice."

"Then you're the enemy!" she shouted. "I can't believe I just did what I did. My sister will never forgive me, and my father, God rest his soul, is probably rollin' in his freakin' grave. What was I thinking? Where are my black running shoes?"

Nicolae smiled as he listened to her run-on ranting.

She might regret now, but she'd be back again. He'd bet a trip into the sunshine on it. The amount of passion they'd shared couldn't be a fleeting blip on her radar. It came from deep within her. Otherwise she would not have reacted with such vigor and intensity with a being she professed to despise.

However, if he didn't settle the issue of Andrei Skirko and free Reggie's sister and the other women purloined from the streets of Houston, there wouldn't be a next time. Of that he was certain. Regina's sister meant a lot to her. If something were to happen to her while they had been making love, Regina would never forgive herself or him.

While she busied herself in her room, Nicolae returned to the kitchen. After he dressed, he cleaned the burned skillet and cracked two eggs into it.

When Reggie emerged, showered and dressed in black, he held out a plate to her. "Sit and eat." He didn't ask, he ordered. Knowing she'd refuse, he was prepared to take up the gauntlet.

"I'm not—"

He held up a hand. "When was the last time you ate?"

Pressing her lips together, she looked as though she might not answer. "Yesterday at noon."

His brows rose. "And you're arguing with me? Sit. And. Eat." He plopped the plate on the table and pulled the chair out for her.

"I'm not hungry." She said, but her gaze followed the plate to the table. "Okay, so maybe a little." She sat and picked up a forkful of scrambled eggs.

"Hard sex tends to work up an appetite."

She glared at him over the fork. "Don't expect a repeat performance." She shoved the fork in her mouth and chewed, continuing to frown.

"I don't expect anything," he said, leaning against the refrigerator, his arms crossed over his chest. It was true. He didn't expect anything, but he knew she'd come around with enough of the right persuasion. If only they had more time.

A quick glance at his watch, and he straightened. "When you're ready, we need to go."

Her fork clattered to the plate, and she stood so fast her chair teetered on two legs and crashed to the floor. "I'm ready."

* * *

No matter how much experience she'd had with late-night stakeouts, Reggie couldn't control her galloping heart rate. Hovering in the shadows across the street from the A.S.E. warehouse, she tapped her finger to the headset, hoping it was in good working order as she awaited the signal to move in.

A hand on her arm made her jump. "Don't do that," she whispered.

"I think he's been dying to touch you for the past thirty minutes." Torsten chuckled. "Not that I blame him. You do look pretty amazing in black."

"Leave it alone, Torsten," Nicolae warned.

"You're too obvious, Nic," Torsten continued. "Can't you see she doesn't want anything to do with you? Isn't that right, Reggie?"

"Right," she answered. If she said it often enough, perhaps she'd feel it. At that moment, though, she was scared. Scared for her sister and scared for herself.

How had she gotten in so deep with Nic in less than twenty-four hours? And he a vampire, no less.

No matter how much she damned her own actions, she couldn't stop thinking about the way he'd held her and touched her. Just thinking about him made her go all warm and wet between the legs.

What she didn't understand was why he hadn't tried to bite her even when she gave him ample opportunity. Twice now he could have sunk his vampire teeth into her. Yet he hadn't.

Melisande had said a woman had turned Nic. She hadn't given him the choice, forcing him into a life of immortality. A life some would find appealing.

Reggie got the impression Nicolae found living forever was lonely. Another chink in the wall she'd attempted to erect around her heart where Nic was concerned. In her attempt to hate him, she didn't want to know the heartless bastard might not be heartless after all.

Her thoughts drifted again to her kitchen and the image engraved in her mind of Nic standing there naked and beautiful, his cock hard and huge for her. Her breath caught in her throat, and her body caught fire all over again.

Nicolae leaned close. "Thinking about me?"

"No." She instantly regretted how weak her answer sounded. Mentally, she shook herself. Was she going soft? How could she keep her edge against the vampires, werewolves, and other creepy creatures roaming the streets of Houston if she couldn't keep her thoughts out of Nicolae's pants?

A long black limousine drove up to the doors, which

immediately opened as if the people inside had been watching and waiting for it to arrive. Once the vehicle slid inside, the rest of the PIA team moved into place. This was it. The black limo had to be the one carrying Andrei.

"I'm moving in," Blake Tanner said into the radio. He had insisted on being the lead with the C4 explosives they planned to use to breach the doors.

A shadow slipped across the face of the building and stopped directly in front of the large doors, now closed to the outside. After ten seconds, he moved back the direction he'd come.

Over the radio, she heard, "Five, four—"

Reggie ducked behind the protection of the building and leaned against the solid muscles of Nicolae Kovak. As much as she tried to tell herself not to get used to having him around to depend on, she couldn't help the sense of security lent to a tough situation.

He shifted his thigh against hers, and that surge of heat he'd inspired earlier warmed her belly and dampened her panties.

Damn. How was she going to explain him to her sister?

If Reggie had been vampire hater, Madison was twice as bad. She'd been the one to find her father and hold him as he gasped his dying breath. Her hatred ran deep and unbending.

"—two, one." A loud explosion echoed off the sides of the buildings, shattering the relative silence of the waterfront.

"Move in!" The call went out over the radio.

Reggie and Nicolae raced across the street and into the gaping hole filled with smoke that used to be the large sliding doors.

Shouts rang out, and bullets zinged over their heads.

As planned, Reggie dove to the left behind the stacks of crates. She rolled to her feet and ran toward the back of the building where her sister and the thirteen other women were kept. Nicolae and Torsten followed her through the maze as the other agents worked through the resistance, creating a needed diversion.

At the first sign of trouble, Andrei would head for the women. Not only did they make for good resale, they would also be useful in negotiating himself out of the current circumstances.

Reggie, Nic, and Torsten had to get there first.

As they neared the crate-sided room, Nic reached out and snagged her arm, indicating he should go first.

Since their enemy was another vampire, Reggie didn't argue. Somewhere between last night on the street with Cesar and now, she'd allowed herself to trust Nicolae. Trust enough to save her sister. If Andrei was as bad as they said he was, she wouldn't stand much of a chance. As she followed Nicolae, she bent to retrieve the wooden stake wedged like a knife in her boot sheath.

"I hope you don't plan to use that on my friend," Torsten whispered as they moved around to the open end of the room.

"Not unless he's been lying to me all along," she said and hoped the hell she hadn't misplaced her trust. Madison was the only family she had left in this world. She couldn't bear to lose her. Nor could she stand the thought of going on alone.

When they rounded the corner of the giant stack of crates, Nicolae stopped, and Reggie all but crashed into him.

When she steadied herself against his back, she felt his muscles go rigid.

Reggie's heart skipped several beats and crashed to a halt when she moved around Nicolae to see their nemesis. A man, as dark and dangerous looking as Nic, stood in the doorway of the makeshift room. Draped across his arms was the unconscious body of her sister, Madison.

"Andrei," Nic said, his tone more of an accusation than a greeting.

"Ah, Nicolae, what brings you to this part of the world? I thought you were enjoying the night life in Paris." Like Nicolae, Andrei's voice was heavily laced with a foreign accent.

"You know I go were the scum lands."

"Tsk, tsk. Always doing the council's dirty work, are you? Saving the unworthy innocents. Who was there to save us from a fate worse than death, huh, Nic? Brother?" His voice rose, echoing off the wooden walls and disappearing toward the high ceiling.

Brother? Reggie staggered backward, cold hard dread settling in the pit of her belly. She stared at the man she'd allowed herself to trust. Had he lied to her? Was this nothing more than an elaborate trap?

"We didn't have a choice when we were turned," Nicolae was saying. "That doesn't make it right to do the same to others."

"You think that's why I brought these lovely ladies here?" Andrei's eyebrow rose.

"Not really." He crossed his arms over his chest. "I see you as one with a complete lack of control."

"Control." Andrei snorted. "You preach of control, and what does it buy you? Nothing. Whereas, I can have everything and everyone money can buy. Do you know how much these women will bring on the sheep market?" he asked.

Reggie's fear melted as a blast of white-hot anger burst forth. "You bastard! These women are people not cattle." She lunged toward him, brandishing her stake.

Nicolae's arm shot out, clenching around her elbow, hauling her back behind him. "Stay out of this."

"Is this man your brother?" she demanded.

"He used to be," Nicolae said, his tone filled with sadness.

"My brother disenfranchised himself from me over our many years of shared immortality. He fancies himself as a crusader for the less fortunate." Andrei lifted Madison higher. "I've taken the life of this less fortunate. What are you going to do? Kill me? You don't have the balls to do it."

Reggie gasped, her chest squeezing so tightly she couldn't breathe. Nic's narrowed into slits. "I'll kill you just like any other rogue I'm sent out to retire."

"Where's the family loyalty, brother?" Andrei sneered.

"My brother died centuries ago." Nic's jaw tightened, and he stepped forward. "Put the woman down."

"No." The smile on Andrei's face was an evil taunt.

"Let go of my sister." Reggie strained against the hand holding her back, no longer willing wait for the two vampires to duke it out.

"And such a tasty treat she was. Unfortunately, I didn't save anything for the sale. Ah well, what's one loss? I still have thirteen left."

"Let her go, Andrei." Nicolae's voice was low and deadly.

"Always out to save the innocent," Andrei said, his face drawing into a scowl. "Such a shame you're too late to save this one." He straightened his arms, and Madison dropped.

Her body hit the concrete with a soft whomp, and she rolled to her back.

Reggie jerked out of Nic's grasp and dove for her sister.

The scene erupted in a flurry of movement as Torsten and Nicolae leaped for Andrei.

The evil brother dashed into the room full of inert bodies.

As the men crashed and thumped against the wooden crates, Reggie knelt next to her sister and felt for a pulse. Her hand moved from her sister's cool cheek to her neck.

A sob rose in her own throat as she searched for any indication there was still some life left in her. Then the faintest nudge tapped against her desperate fingertips and then another. She was still alive but barely.

"Reggie?" Madison whispered.

As Reggie leaned forward to hear her sister's words, the loud crashes from inside the crate room faded into the background.

"I'm dying," she said, her lips a ghastly shade of blue, her cheeks pale and gray.

"No, Madison. You can't. You're all I have."

Her sister's chest jerked as she tried to laugh, her lips twisting into a humorless smile. "I'm dying just like our dad."

Anger surged in Reggie's veins. "I won't let this happen. He won't get away with it." Grabbing the stake she'd dropped on the floor, she left her sister's side and walked into the room.

Torsten flew through the air, hit the box next to her, and slid to the floor. Nicolae and Andrei were locked in a fierce battle to control the splintered board in Andrei's hand.

Without stopping to think or even reason through her actions, Reggie strode forward and swung the stake as hard as she possibly could.

Seeing the stake coming at him, Andrei pulled Nicolae around and in front of him.

At the last second, when Reggie though for sure she'd killed the wrong vampire, Nic backed up and the sharpened weapon plunged into Andrei's heart.

"That's for my sister!" She shouted. Then she ran back to Madison and collapsed across her, sobbing. She couldn't die. Not Madison. Not her beloved sister.

* * *

All the pressure on Nicolae's arms slackened as Andrei staggered backward and sagged against the corner of a wooden box containing one of the women he'd kidnapped.

Hundreds of years peeled away, leaving Nic facing the dying face of his younger brother. Andrei had always been out for a good time, womanizing and drinking into the dark hours of the morning. "I'm sorry we couldn't see eye to eye," Nic said softly.

"As am I," Andrei gripped his chest and exploded into a cloud of dust that smelled of death and old bones.

Nicolae doubled over, the ache in his heart equaling the pain in his gut.

Torsten's strong arm circled his shoulder. "I'm sorry about your brother, Nic, but you're needed."

Reggie.

Forcing his grief to the back of his mind, he looked around to find Reggie sprawled across the near-lifeless body of her sister.

Reggie looked up at him, eyes red-rimmed, tears trailing down her cheeks. "Help her."

"Andrei drained her," Torsten said. "She's dying,"

"Don't let her die. You can't!" Reggie moaned, wrapping her arms around her sister as if by sheer force she could keep her alive.

"I won't turn her unless she wants it," Nic said, his heart breaking along with Reggie.

"You're a vampire. You can heal her like you healed me."

He shook his head. "Andrei took her too far."

"Then take her the rest of the way. I'd rather she lived as a vampire than not at all," Reggie stared down at her sister, her tears soaking the dying girl's cheeks. "Please."

"No, Reggie. I won't be a vampire." Madison's eyes opened slowly, like it took more effort than she had left in her. "Let me die."

"No!" She leaped to her feet and ran to Torsten. "If he won't do it, you can. How do you do it? Tell me!"

"I'm sorry, Reggie. I'm with Nic. I won't go against his wishes."

Reggie turned to Nic, the fear and sadness of losing the only sibling and family left to her emanating from her green eyes. She came to him and wrapped her arms

77

around his waist, burying her face against his chest. "Please, I beg you."

He wanted to do as she asked more than he could stand, but Madison didn't want to be turned. "You'll have to take it up with your sister. I won't turn her against her will."

Reggie stared at him, tears welling in her eyes. "Then turn me," she said, quietly. "Turn me so I can save my sister."

"No, Reggie, don't do it." Madison lifted an arm toward her sister and, it fell back to the ground.

"I won't stand by and let you die."

"I'd rather die than be one of them." Madison's voice was fading, and her eyes closed as if keeping them open was too much effort.

Reggie dropped to the ground beside her sister and gathered a limp, cold hand in both of hers. "They aren't all the same, Maddie. There are good ones and bad ones. Nic and Torsten saved you and all the other women. Don't you see? You could be one of the good ones." A sob escaped, racking her body.

Nic knelt beside her and cradled her in his arms, his heart breaking for her. "Do you really believe what you said?" he asked. "Do you believe I'm not the enemy? Do you trust me?"

"Yes," she cried against his shirt. "Please don't let my sister die. I love her so much."

The relief of hearing her say she trusted him and that she didn't think of him as the enemy was like a heavy curtain being lifted to let the sunshine in. Taking a deep breath, he let it out slowly. "All right, I'll turn her."

The racking sobs stopped and she stared up at him through watery eyes. "You will?"

"Nic, remember how you felt when you were turned and didn't want it," Torsten warned.

But Nic could only see the tentative smile on Reggie's face. If he didn't help her sister, that smile would disappear. He'd risk Madison's anger for Reggie's love any day. "Give me that stake."

Reggie leaped to her feet and retrieved the stake from where it had fallen after she'd dusted Andrei.

"Sounds like they have the rest of Andrei's gang under control." Torsten laid a hand on Nic's shoulder. "Are you sure you want to do this?"

"I've never been more sure." Reggie was the first woman to capture his admiration in centuries. He didn't want her to lose her sister when he had the power to save her. "I want a chance at love."

"And you hope to buy that love with her sister's life?"

"If need be." Nic frowned, not liking the way Torsten made it sound. "Madison will learn to deal with being a vampire, just as you and I have."

Reggie pressed the stake into his palm and said, "I'll help her come to terms."

He took the stake with one hand and captured her hand with the other. "We'll help her, together."

Reggie smiled and turned to Madison. "What do I need to do?"

"Just believe." Nic braced himself and then stabbed the stake into his wrist. Blood gushed from the fresh wound, spilling out onto the ground.

Dropping to his knees beside Madison, he lifted her with his uninjured arm and pressed his wrist to her mouth. "Drink, Madison."

"No." Too weak to fight, she turned her head to the side.

Reggie knelt beside Nic and held her sister's head straight. "Do it, Madison," she said, her voice choked with tears. "I love you, and I won't let you die."

Trapped by the two sets of hands holding her, Madison had no choice but to drink the blood of a vampire, and Nic hoped the hell he was doing the right thing.

"How much does it take?" Reggie asked, her voice

only a whisper.

"Just a drop is all that's needed." That's all it took to turn him more than four hundred years earlier.

When Madison's throat moved, and she swallowed, Nic laid her head on the concrete, and he moved back.

"What happens now?" Reggie asked.

"You sister joins the ranks of the living dead. By morning, she will no longer walk in daylight and live to tell. Her thirst for blood will have to be fed to sustain her life, such as it is. And if she isn't staked, beheaded or otherwise dusted, she can live forever."

Reggie stood next to Nic and wrapped her arms around his middle. "I understand your reasons for not wanting to turn her. Thank you for saving her anyway."

Nic pushed a strand of her red hair behind her ear. "I don't know that I have. I hope she won't awaken to hate you and me both."

"I'll take that chance," Reggie said looking up into his face.

"Just like you took a chance on me?" He rested his hands on her hips, his pulse leaping in his veins. "Any regrets?"

She smiled. "Only one and I plan to remedy it soon."

Nic frowned, a picture of her staking Andrei flashed through his mind. "Does it involve staking anyone in the immediate vicinity?"

She laughed and the sound was like music. "No stakes." She stood on her tiptoes and pressed a kiss to his lips. "My one regret is that I don't know much about you. I want to know everything."

He pulled her against him. "How long do you have?"

"A life time," she said, resting her cheek against his chest.

He slid his hands beneath her shirt and up the middle of her back, liking the silky smoothness of her skin. "I don't know," he stared toward the ceiling. "It might take longer for me to tell you everything. Are you willing to stick around for awhile?"

Her fingers found their way inside his shirt. "As long as it takes, baby. As long as it takes."

Sanctuary

Delilah Devlin

Chapter One

Kate McKinnon pulled up the collar of her old leather duster to ward off the chill wind that bit the back of her neck. One glance at the darkening sky reminded her of the passage of time. Daylight was a-wastin'. Soon, she'd have to head back to the safety of the ranch house.

She cinched her "stampede" string tighter under her chin to prevent her hat from flying away and nudged her horse forward to follow the fence line, looking for any breaks that might indicate trouble.

She wasn't worried that cattle might have slipped through a hole in the fence. Most of the herd she'd run roughshod over was gone. More worrisome was what might have come inside. The dense cloud cover above hadn't allowed even a glimpse of sunlight to peek through all day.

Perfect conditions for the monsters to come out and play.

Any one of her men could have been assigned this duty, but Kate liked being on her own. Every once in a while, she needed to ride the fence to harken back to a time when the worst thing she might find was a cow mired in the mud or a calf circled by buzzards. On the open range with only herself to argue with, she found some peace. Not that she could ever really escape her problems.

The radio squawked where she'd clipped it to the bridle of her horse. "The southwest corner's clear, boss," said Sam Culpepper, her ranch foreman. "I'm headin' back to the ranch."

She unclipped the mike and held it to her mouth. "I'll turn back at Wasp Creek. Almost there now."

"Hope you found somethin' for Cass's stew pot. I didn't see sign of deer or rabbit."

Kate grimaced and pressed the talk switch. "Well, I found a bird."

"Turkey?" he asked, a hopeful note in his voice.

She glanced at the black-feathered carcass hanging upside down from a string tied to her saddle horn. "You got that half right."

"Shit."

That was when she spied slackened barbwire and knew they had a problem. "Sam, we have a break."

"I'm right behind you. Wait for me," he rasped.

"Wait? Yeah, right," Kate replied, knowing any delay in catching the varmint was unacceptable. The creature could wipe out the rest of their meager herd as well as endanger the lives of those living at the ranch. What pissed her off most was Sam wouldn't have issued that order to any other ranch hand. At times like these, she regretted ever asking him into her bed.

"Goddammit, Kate, I'm on your ass! Wait!"

Kate grinned and spurred her horse into a canter. When the troubles began, Sam had appointed himself her guardian. Since "caution" didn't appear anywhere in her vocabulary, she'd made it her mission in life to make his job as onerous as possible.

Not that she was foolhardy. She followed the fence and kept her gaze alert to any movement in the brush around her, and her horse didn't appear nervous in the slightest—Kate had learned to trust Lucy Lu's instincts.

The break, when she found it, was small and low—the creature had crawled in on all fours. Prints leading into the brush indicated one animal, but she wasn't ready to celebrate just yet.

The thunder of hooves, more than she'd expected, came from north along the fence line. She drew her rifle from its scabbard and turned it sideways to double check her load. Mentally, she counted off her earlier shots—three rounds were all she had left.

Sam pulled to halt beside her, his expression promising retribution. Danny's horse ground to a halt behind him, his two pit bulls close on his buckskin's hooves. The dogs whined, and their tails wagged frenetically. They'd already picked up the scent, but they'd wait until Danny gave the order to track.

"Don't you have a lick o'sense?" Sam ground out.

Kate smirked. "You only live once. Sometimes."

Sam shook his head, his gaze narrowing. "We'll talk about this later." Then he took the lead, following paw prints in the dry dirt until they entered an arroyo.

He nodded to Danny, and the ranch hand swept out his arm, index finger extended, giving the command to the dogs to follow the creature into the ravine.

Sam slipped off his horse and grabbed his rifle. "You stay put. Watch the horses. Danny, follow me."

Kate tamped down her impatience at Sam's overprotective streak and dismounted. So she was stuck watching horses again. She settled her rifle barrel on her shoulder, kicked the dirt, and listened to the radio as the men talked between themselves while they tracked the animal.

The wind shifted. A subtle turn that blew west then east, like a lazy wag. Lucy Lu whinnied, and Kate felt the prickles that always preceded the feeling she needed to get the hell out of Dodge. It raised the fine hairs on the back of her neck.

The radio squawked. "Kate, he's doubled back! Get the fuck out of there!"

"Get out, my ass," she whispered. She had three horses to protect and her daddy's old rifle in her arms.

Resisting the urge to check her chamber one more time, she waited while the horses whinnied nervously and pulled at the reins tied to a scrubby live oak, causing it to creak and obliterating any possibility she might actually hear the beast's approach.

Instead, she took her cues from the horses' actions—the direction their ears pricked, which way they instinctively pulled against their reins. She faced the mouth of the arroyo.

When it burst, snarling, from beneath the cover of brush, she was ready. She slammed the stock of her rifle into her shoulder and fired off a shot, then cocked the lever down and up to load the next cartridge into the chamber, and fired a second round.

Still it came—launching into the air toward her, teeth bared, its long ears flattened to its skull.

Too close to get off another round, she turned the gun and grabbed the barrel, swinging it like a baseball bat. She slammed the rifle against the creature's head, knocking it to the side, and then braced herself for the next attack.

Only the wolf never regained its feet. It twisted in agony on the ground as the silver load finally did its work. Poison gripped its body, causing it to convulse and forcing red-tinged foam to spill from its lips.

When it relaxed, expelling a final labored breath, the body transformed, shifting in a dark, blurred instant into a man.

The dogs burst into the clearing and circled the dead werewolf, whining and snapping, but never actually biting. Then Sam barreled out of the brush, coming to a halt as his gaze took in the scene in one sweeping glance. He bent double and rested his hands above his knees as he dragged deep breaths into his lungs. "Goddammit, Kate. When I tell you to run…"

She shrugged and pretended her own heart wasn't racing like a thoroughbred's.

"Well, he's dead, ain't he?"

He shot her a glare. "You know, Kate, you are one stubborn cuss."

She grinned and lifted a single eyebrow.

His gaze swept down her body. "Did he bite you?"

"Not so much as a nibble."

Danny raced up the arroyo and called off the dogs. "So do we bury him?" he asked, once he had them under control.

Kate shook her head and looked away. "The buzzards

have to eat, too."

* * *

Kate scraped the dirt off her boots on the edge of the stoop before entering Cass's kitchen. She gave a nod to the older woman who stood covered in flour up to her elbows, cutting biscuits from flattened dough. She held up the bird by its feet. "What do you want me to do with this?"

Cass grimaced. "Stick him in the pot. Gotta blanche that buzzard before I pull its feathers."

A large stock pot filled with boiling water rattled in the old gas range. Kate lifted the lid and dunked the turkey buzzard, feathers and all, into the pot. "If anybody asks…"

Cass held up her hand. "I know. It was an old damn turkey. Coffee's in the thermos. Help yourself."

Kate poured a steaming cup and flashed a smile, then tromped through the house to her office, avoiding the living room. She knew she was being a little cowardly, but she didn't think she could bear sitting in the living room with the families' quiet chatter surrounding her. Now that the ranch hand's bunk house had been subdivided into living quarters for the three families, she'd hoped for a little more privacy, but their noise and the sight of their haunted faces spilled over into her home as well.

So she'd settle down to her meal when it was ready in her office. The large dining room table would be crowded enough with everyone eating in shifts. Not that there'd be much reason for anyone to linger. Food was scarce. Their meals meager. Soon, they'd be forced to make another run for supplies. She'd been waiting for sunshine, but the unrelenting black sky kept them trapped inside the boundaries of the ranch.

At times, the weight of her responsibilities crushed her, making her feel overwhelmed and a little scared when she thought about so many people—especially the families—arriving at the gates. She feared she couldn't feed them, wouldn't be able to save them in the end. To protect her heart and her sanity, she avoided knowing them too well.

So Kate took her coffee at her daddy's big roll-top desk and eyed the silent radio, knowing she shouldn't turn it on and waste precious electricity. But dammit, this was her ranch house — her blood. Her men protected the people within Sanctuary.

Besides, this was their only link with the outside world.

She turned it on and let the old-fashioned transistors heat up, then turned the dial to tune into the band where she knew he'd be waiting. "This is KN5GST calling. The name is Kate. Anyone listening? Over."

A moment later, the whine from an engine sounded over the air. "This is AA3TZ. How are you, Kate?" he said, dropping the ham lingo.

Her hands clamped around the microphone as she held it, and she closed her eyes as his voice surround her like a soft, warm blanket. "Been better."

"Any breaches?"

"One got through today. I killed it."

"I'm sorry about that," he said softly.

She blinked — not because tears gathered in her eyes. Just dust. "It's okay," she said swiftly. "He was just another monster." She'd try to forget how young and vulnerable he'd looked, lying naked and bleeding into the dry dirt.

"Still carrying that antique gun?"

Kate's lips curved into a grin. What was it with men? Sometimes, Ty sounded a lot like Sam. "It did the trick."

"How many shots did you manage to squeeze off?"

"Two." She shivered, remembering just how close the wolf had come.

"Goddamn, Kate, what's it going to take to get you to be more careful?"

"I know what I'm doing."

"You give any thought to what we talked about

before?"

Kate shifted in her seat, uncomfortable with the direction he was going to take the conversation. "I have, but I don't know how we'd manage it. 'Sides, we have most everything we need here, at least for a while."

"Honey, you can't hold out forever. They can. Soon, you won't find enough gas pumps with gas in them or cars to siphon off to run your generator. Your propane won't last long with as many mouths as you're feeding now. What happens when you can't scavenge enough food to hold off starvation?"

Every word he said was true. Eventually, they'd all have to leave Sanctuary. But not now. She wasn't ready to let go just yet.

"Kate, the wolves are getting hungry enough to risk facing your armed men inside the game fence. When they're inside, you'll be the one who's corralled."

Kate knew in her gut he was right. But how could she abandon a hundred years of tradition—of McKinnons on Sanctuary ranch? "I don't have enough big trucks or men to protect a convoy for any distance."

"I've been thinking about that problem, and I might have a solution for you. Let me get back to you."

"All right." Her hands squeezed tighter on the mike. He'd pestered her about leaving, harangued her about her recklessness. Now, he'd say goodbye. Just like always. "You doing okay?" she asked, wanting to extend the conversation.

"I'm fine. Stay put tomorrow. I'll talk to you tomorrow night. Out."

She listened to the hum until it cut off, then turned off her radio, and sat back in her chair.

Ty Bennett. For the thousandth time, she wondered what he looked like. She already had a picture in her mind—tall, dark—shoulders wide enough to cry on.

She wished she could ask him, "What color are your eyes? Your hair?" However, while she'd poured out her worries over the air waves countless nights, he'd been reticent about giving her details about himself.

How she wished she could give his deep, rumbling voice a face. So she'd know him if ever they met.

But she'd never asked him personal questions. Never tried to let him know her interest. She wasn't very good with men. That part of her life had been stunted by "The Apocalypse" as everyone had started to call the last set of wars which colored the skies black and painted the weather cold.

Sam had been the only man around to hold her when she'd cried over her daddy's death. He'd also been her first and only lover, although a reluctant one. Older than her by more than ten years, he'd always felt guilty about taking her innocence, but she'd pretty much insisted.

Now, they occasionally came together out of need. While Sam held out hope that eventually she'd lean on him a little more, she wasn't in love with him, and he knew it. But she thought she might be falling on love with Ty—or maybe, the idea of him. Although they'd never met, her heart soared at just the sound of his brusque voice.

As always happened when the shadows outside lengthened and the long night stretched like an endless road, she wondered how different her life might have been.

The ignition of a dirty bomb in D.C. started the last war. The enemy hadn't needed airplanes or to break into congress while it was in session. They'd sipped coffee in a Starbucks a block away from the capital when they'd detonated the explosive loaded with enough Russian plutonium to blow up a couple city blocks. U.S. retribution had been swift and a thousand times more deadly.

Winter hadn't come to them overnight. And at first, other than the devastation in D.C., the rest of the country went back to business as usual, occasionally glancing at the ever-darkening sky—not admitting the changes to the patterns of the winds or lack of rainfall. Crops failed. Potable water supplies dried up. Global warming became a non-issue as temperatures around the world cooled.

But if the initial fallout hadn't been enough to contend with, creatures that had lived millenniums in the shadows were freed to roam at will by a permanently overcast sky.

Sam knocked against the open door, pulling her from her memories. He strode inside and sat down in the chair beside her desk, raking a hand through his short blond hair. "Any news?"

She shook her head. "Same ole."

"He still tryin' to talk you into leaving?"

She kept no secrets from Sam. He knew about her obsession with the voice that waited in the darkness for her call. "Yeah."

"Maybe you ought to think about it," he said quietly.

Surprised, she gave him a sharp glance. It was the first time she'd heard that from Sam. Sanctuary was as much his home as hers.

"Want company tonight?" His brown eyes betrayed not a hint of hunger. But she knew he ached.

She was tempted. Sam was an attractive man with lean, strong body, but Ty's voice still reverberated around her mind, so she shook her head and glanced away.

His lips thinned, but he nodded his understanding, no trace of disappointment in his expression.

Feeling tense and little sick to her stomach, she almost wished he'd give her some hint of what he really thought. Sometimes, she even wished he'd insist on having sex, because she was hot for it. However, afterward he'd leave her bed with a haunted look in his gaze, and she'd cry into her pillow.

They were both unhappy and holding onto to something that didn't really exist. Loneliness was dealing their lifelong friendship a slow death.

Kate cleared her throat. "Who's on watch tonight?" she asked.

"Danny and Mr. Bates."

She lifted an eyebrow at the name of one of the refugees who'd arrived at the gates in recent weeks. "Does he know which end of a gun to aim?"

Sam's lips curled at one corner. "He wants to pull his own weight. He's been practicing."

"Don't give him any silver shot—can't afford to waste it in the dirt."

"We've got one more problem."

She drew in a deep breath, not liking the dread she saw in Sam's expression. "What now?"

"We need to make a gas run."

Kate felt her jaw tense and her spine stiffen hard as steel. "We can't wait for sunshine?"

He shook his head. "We have enough fuel left to run the generator for maybe a day. I'll take a posse into town in the morning."

Kate shook her head. "I'm going. I need you here, checking fences."

"Kate, now's not the time—"

"I'm going. Get a list from Cass of everything she needs. We'll make a run on the grocery store while we're at it. I'll be back by nighttime."

"Kate, you can't keep everyone safe."

"I'm a better shot than you. But the men, especially the new ones, listen to you. I need you here. I'll take Danny and Shep."

He stood and unbuckled his gun belt. "Take my pistol and leave that old antique with me in the morning."

Not wanting another argument, she held out her hand for the gun belt.

He dropped it onto her palm and dipped his head. "I'll see you in the morning."

Kate didn't watch him leave. She was already reaching for the kit in the bottom drawer of her desk. As everyone else hunkered down for a restless night of sleep, she pulled apart the pistol to clean the bolt, the chamber, and all its mechanisms.

The greatest gift John McKinnon had given his little girl was he'd taught her how to kill.

Chapter Two

Kate mashed her foot against the gas pedal, sending gravel spraying as she rounded the corner.

Danny, who stood behind the cab in the truck bed, pounded on the roof.

Beside her on the bench seat, Shep, her oldest hand and her dad's best friend, hadn't loosened his grip on the door handle since they'd entered the city limits. "Tryin' to lose that boy, Kate?" he asked, his voice deadpanned and his expression wry.

Kate grinned. "You know damn well street corners are dangerous places. We don't want to get ourselves a hitchhiker." She didn't worry too much about Danny or Shep. They all enjoyed the rough and raucous ride—a chance to shake the dust off their boots after weeks of confinement to the ranch.

It kept their minds off the sights they passed—the empty, windowless houses with their gaping front doors, the gutted shop fronts with their contents emptied onto the streets. What had once been a thriving little west Texas community had become a ghost town. No one but the criminals and the monsters lived in Tierney any more.

The grocery store loomed ahead. "Get ready to roll," she yelled out the window to Danny. "Got the grocery list?" she asked Shep.

The old man patted his shirt pocket. "Think Cass'd let me through the door without it?"

"Good. Danny gets the cart—he's fastest. I'll guard the door." She pulled up next to the front doors of the grocery store, slid from the seat to the pavement, and pocketed the keys.

Danny leapt from the truck bed and ran for the door with Shep on his heels.

While the men shouted to each other from deep inside the store, Kate glanced at the sky. Once again, God hadn't relented. The cloud cover was deep—angry, gray clouds slid quickly across the sky with the wind pushing them clear to the Gulf before they could drop rain. Worse, the cover permitted no sunlight to scare the nighttime critters into going to ground.

Kate pushed back the edge of her duster and tucked it behind the holster hanging from the gun belt she wore strapped to her waist at Sam's insistence. She walked into the store and straight up to the cashier's desk, doing her best to ignore the overpowering stench of rotting food coming from the produce section. She reached into the shelf above the station, rooting for a pack of cigarettes, but found none and cursed.

So she returned her attention to the front doors and kept track of the men's progress which she could judge because Shep stood at the end of each row as Danny ran down the aisles to fill one squeaking cart after another according to Shep's shouted instructions.

She glanced at her watch—fifteen minutes. Too long. "Time to wrap it up. We have to go, guys," she shouted. It really shouldn't take this long. There wasn't much left on the shelves. She glanced down and kicked a cockroach off her boot and squashed it with her heel.

When the men moved into the storage area at the back of the building, she tensed, listening for any signs of trouble in the back, any signs of ambush. Not until she heard the whirring of the cart wheels coming down the aisle again did she let out a relieved breath.

She ran through the entrance to stand guard over the truck while Shep and Danny emptied the contents of the carts into the truck bed—mostly canned goods and paper products. Everything else had been eaten by bugs and mice or was too rotten for human consumption.

"Any place else we need to stop?" Shep asked.

"Just need to get the gas."

The stacked five gallon cans in the truck bed represented their hope they'd find enough fuel to run the generator and give them precious light for a few more weeks.

"We'll head to the Exxon station," she said. "It's more open."

At the gas station, she pulled out the key to the underground storage tank Mr. Jeffers had left her when he migrated east, and while Shep lowered a garden hose into the well to siphon gas into the canisters, she again kept watch.

When he was filling the last of the cans, she heard the sounds she'd dreaded—vehicles coming down the road at a fast clip. "Load up, guys. We're done."

Shep pulled up the hose and quickly locked the cap to the well, then bounded into the cab of the truck with the energy of a man much younger than his sixty years. Adrenaline could do that to a man.

Kate peeled out of the parking lot, heading back the way to Sanctuary, but as she'd feared, vehicles turned sideways in the road blocked their exit. She spun the steering wheel, running up over the curb to double back the way they'd come. "Don't you dare fire on them," she shouted to Danny. "If they shoot back, they could hit that gas. Let's find us a place where we can stand off."

The First Baptist Church was just around the corner and not a likely place for monsters to hide.

She ran up over the curb, all the way up to the front steps of the church, and everyone piled out of the truck and dove for the front doors as vehicles careened into the parking lot behind them.

"Shep, you check the back entrance," she shouted as she broke out a stained-glass window with her pistol grip. "Danny, you get up into the choir loft and keep watch from the upstairs windows."

They waited while vehicles circled the parking lot, effectively ringing the building. Whooping shouts rang in the air.

"How much ammo you got on you, girl?" Shep

shouted from the opposite end of the church.

She patted her duster pockets. "Enough. I don't miss much."

"Don't look like we need silver load."

He was right. What surrounded them weren't werebeasts—it was the lowest form of human life—those who preyed on the survivors.

"Well, this will be easy pickin's," she murmured and steeled herself for the coming confrontation.

Kate didn't wait to hear what they might say. The only thing they wanted was her—women were a scarce commodity on the frontier. She took a bead down the barrel of her pistol and squeezed off a shot through the windshield of a pickup, pleased at the splash of red that exploded against the glass.

Cool as ice, she chose another target, unwilling to let even a tremor of fear or regret ruin her shot—doing like her daddy taught her, pretending the men ducking behind their vehicles were just the paper targets she'd practiced on.

One. Two. Three down. Then Shep's shotgun exploded with a roar, catching a cry closer than she'd expected. Were they sneaking up on them?

"What do you see, Danny?" she shouted as she flattened her back against the wall next to the window.

"We've got maybe twenty of the bastards out there," Danny's excited voice echoed from above. "But they seem to be holding back now."

"Hello in there," a tinny voice said over a loudspeaker. "We don't mean you any harm. You had no call to fire on us. We were just...seeing if you needed help."

Kate gave Shep a skeptical glance. She edged closer to the window to shout outside. "Well, we don't. Why don't you move along?"

"Thought I saw a woman in there," the man said, the tone of his voice sly. "Honey, we can offer you better protection than an old man and a boy."

Kate's upper lip curled in a snarl. "Thanks for the offer, but we won't be stayin' in town long."

Laughter sounded outside, low and not especially amused. It had a dirty edge to it and made her skin crawl.

With the lull, she ejected her magazine and inserted a full clip into her pistol.

"It's gonna be nighttime soon," the voice outside said. "You really should find shelter. We have a nice place. Plenty to eat."

A sick knot formed in the pit of her stomach, knowing what the trade would be. However, she'd run up against their sort before and prevailed. The trick was to keep her wits about her. If she could just get a shot at the guy behind the mike...

A long silence followed. She darted a glance around the window sill and realized the attention of the men surrounding the building was on something in the distance. Then she heard it—engines, big ones, roaring their way.

Being the cowards they were, the gang bolted into their vehicles as quickly as they could and departed. Right behind them appeared a convoy of green camouflaged military vehicles. Hummers and large, canvas-topped transport vehicles with machine-gun turrets mounted on top.

Kate kept to the shadows while watching the long column of trucks come into view. "Shep, you see that?"

"Didn't know they were operating this far into the frontier," he said, coming up behind her to peek out the window. "Better stay inside 'til we know whose side they're on."

She expected the convoy to continue on past, but one by one they pulled into the church parking lot.

Kate held her breath, her heartbeat racing—the first suffocating wash of true fear pouring down her spine in an icy fall.

From the lead vehicle, a door opened, and a man dressed in blue jeans and a black leather jacket jumped from the cab to the hard pavement below.

Her first sight of him told her instinctively here was bigger trouble than she'd already faced. This wasn't the stupid scum she'd squared off with. He was a hundred times more intimidating.

For one, he was a big man. Taller even then Sam, his wide shoulders and muscled thighs bespoke of years of physical training. In close quarters, he'd be impossible to beat. She squeezed the grip of her weapon harder, already thinking where she'd have to place the first shot to bring him down quick.

The closer he strode, the greater her unease. Not only did he have the size to make her heart leap to the back of her throat, he moved with a rangy grace that said he'd be fast on his feet. His face with its square jaw and sharp cheekbones completed the portrait of an unstoppable man once he'd set his eyes on a target.

Now, she just hoped that dark, hard gaze never rested on her.

While she drew deep breaths to calm her racing heart and the tremor of her hands, an uninvited thought crossed her mind. If she weren't battling for her life in the middle of an Apocalypse, this would be the sort of man she'd want. Dangerous, brutal—sexy as hell.

But he was dressed in civilian clothes and riding in a military vehicle. Was he just the leader of a smarter band of criminals?

He stopped about twenty paces from the church doors and put his hands on his hips. "Kate McKinnon, are you in there?"

She jerked at the familiar deep tones of his voice. Her startled glance found Shep's.

His eyes were narrowed in his lined face, and he shook his head. "You know him? Might be some kind a trick."

"This is Ty Bennett."

Kate closed her eyes and sank against the wall, feeling like her whole world was spinning out of control. How could this be?

"Kate, the cavalry's here, sweetheart."

* * *

Ty held his breath as the slender figure descended the church steps. Although she was garbed in a long duster and wearing a cowboy hat that cast shadows over her face, he could tell a lot about the woman he'd come half the state away to rescue. Her slender shoulders were square, her chin held high.

The smart-mouthed woman he'd talked to endless nights looked brave — and brittle as glass.

The closer she came, the more his body tightened.

"She's prettier than I expected," Diego murmured as he stepped behind him.

Ty didn't bother to say he'd noticed, too. He'd already been fighting an unexplainable attraction to the sassy voice on the radio, but he thought she'd be older. The woman walking toward him was shaping up to be a delicious surprise.

When Kate stopped several feet away, he noted the edge of her jacket tucked behind her holster and the suspicion glinting in her eyes. A shotgun barrel poked out a window of the church behind her.

A smile curved one corner of his mouth. *Good girl.* Someone was watching her back.

Kate stood motionless, but her gaze swept his men as they dismounted their vehicles and waited beside them for direction. When her glance came back to him, her expression was stony. "You might have mentioned you were coming for a visit," she said, her voice tight.

Her husky inflection tugged at his cock. The game had begun.

Knowing she was easily riled, he decided to bait her. He didn't like her scared — angry, he could handle. He lifted one brow. "And I thought I told you to stay put."

Her gaze narrowed. "I don't follow orders very well," she said, her tone dead level.

Diego snorted behind him, and Ty knew his buddy was laughing his ass off.

Kate lifted her chin toward the convoy. "Now, a person might wonder how men such as you came into possession of military vehicles."

"A person? You wondering how, Kate?" he drawled. "Maybe I'm just a resourceful kind of guy."

Her nostrils flared, and her lips tightened. "And I'm just wondering what else you might be, Ty Bennett."

That's when he saw the hint of vulnerability in her gaze—and a glint of hope. This woman had lived a nightmare and needed what he offered worse than she knew. "Kate, we're ex-military living at Fort Davis in the Davis Mountains. Before things went to hell, we were part of a border patrol outfit—light infantry." Some of it was true. What he left out would have to wait until she knew him better.

Kate's lips relaxed a fraction. "Why no uniforms?"

"We were mustered out of the service when the post closed."

"They left behind functioning equipment?"

"They were in a hurry. Everything was abandoned. We've taken over the post."

"Is this everyone? All your people?"

"I left men behind to guard the post."

Her breath gasped softly. "Only men?"

He read her panic and decided to sidestep the issue for now. Concentrate on the pluses. "There's a sturdy fence, a mess hall, food in storage to last a large unit months, an artesian well…everything a community needs to survive. We have room for you and yours if you'll come. If you want to go on after that to one of the coastal cities, we'll find a way to make that happen, too."

"There are only half a dozen women at the ranch—

three are married," she said faintly.

"We won't take what's not offered." The quiet, firm tone of his voice was meant to reassure her, but he knew she'd seen too much to trust blindly. "The same deal will be offered to them—they can stay at Davis, with us, or we'll find them safe passage to the safe zones on the coast.

The safe zones. He couldn't imagine her giving up the wide open country for safety's sake—living with curfews, Marshall Law, and cramped living spaces.

Her jaw flexed, and she looked away. "So how'd you know it was me in there?"

"I sent out scouts in advance of the convoy. They saw you enter town, hit the grocery store like kamikazes, and then steal gas at the station. I don't believe another female in this area would be so brazen. We got here as quick as we could when those bastards chased you here."

She shot him a pointed glance. "Your timing was amazing." Again, suspicion colored her tone.

"Remember, I didn't expect to find you here. You were supposed to sit tight," he said, baiting her again.

Kate snorted. "Like I said—"

His lips twitched. "Yeah, I know. You don't follow orders well. That's gonna change."

Her dark eyebrows shot up.

Before she could answer the challenge he'd thrown down, he continued, "Katie, you can't stay in Sanctuary any longer. You know it. Those men inside know it. You're living on borrowed time until the werebeasts take down your fence."

"It's my ranch, my home," she said through stiff lips.

"Maybe someday you can come back to it. For now, you need to get yourself and all those people depending on you somewhere safe. I've brought the trucks and the men—we can get you out of here."

She drew a deep breath, and her hands clenched into fists. "Why, Ty? Why would you do this? You don't even know me."

He formed his lips into a lop-sided smile. "You won't just let me be the Lone Ranger riding to the rescue?"

"I don't believe in heroes anymore," she said, her voice thickening. She blinked against the moisture filling her eyes, her sorrow and disillusionment etched in her strained features.

Ty gave her time to get herself under control but didn't look away to give her any privacy. Every tear, every worry, every delight she held inside would be his. From this moment onward, he'd never let her hide.

"Fair enough," he said quietly, choosing his next words carefully. Trust would have to be built one stone at a time. "Would you believe me if I said I came for you?"

Her gaze raked him. "Are you talking a trade? Get my people out safely — for me?"

"If that's what makes you more comfortable with the whole idea."

"I just wanted it spelled out," she gritted out.

"So what do you say?"

"I say, I'll kill you if you're lying."

He suppressed a smile. "About the coming after you part?"

"No, about the part where you'll get my people out."

"Do we have a deal?" He held out his hand, knowing this was the moment when she'd have to place her trust in him and take her hand away from where it rested alongside her weapon.

Her jaw clenched, and she drew in a deep breath and slowly raised her hand.

He slid his palm along hers and let his index finger glide up to the pulse that throbbed at her wrist. It quickened the longer he held her hand, convincing him the attraction he felt was answered. "So where are we going to bed down for the night?"

Chapter Three

Kate felt the earth move beneath her feet—so shocking was the undercurrent of sensual promise in his question. She drew in a shaky breath. "We're not stayin' in town."

He laid his other hand on top of hers, enveloping her in heat that radiated up her arm and to places she had no business noticing when danger was still afoot. "My men need to top off the vehicles and find that crowd of troublemakers before we head out to your ranch."

"Fine," she said, her voice clipped. "We'll see you at the ranch tomorrow. I'll be sure to tell the men at the gates not to shoot you on sight."

His hands squeezed hers. "I don't want you heading out there on your own. The sky will be pitch-black soon."

"We're ready for any trouble." The only trouble she saw was standing right in front of her.

His eyes narrowed. "There's no need to take the risk. We're here to help. Let us do our job."

She slowly pulled away her hand. She couldn't think when he touched her. At least not about anything that made any sense. His broad frame and handsome face turned her brains to mush.

"Katie, you need any help out there?" Shep shouted through the window.

Still not willing to turn her back on Ty and his men, she shouted over her shoulder. "Everything's under control," she lied.

"We need to talk," Ty said.

"I agree. There's a gazebo out back on the grass."

"You really want to be out in the open for it?"

"Who the hell's gonna attack with the Army in the front yard?" The intimacy of four walls around them would be too tempting. She'd fantasized about him too long.

He drew a deep breath and signaled with a wave of

his hand for her to precede him into the church.

Accepting his direction meant turning her back on him and his men. But hadn't she already surrendered when she'd left the safety of the church? What chance did she really have if things turned ugly? Deep inside, she wanted to trust him. Wanted so much more.

This man had kept the hope for a better future alive in her heart for months. He'd made no promises and told her damn little about himself—but she'd held tight to the strength in his voice when he'd admonished her for being reckless, praised her for her courage, and comforted her all those times she'd felt so overwhelmed.

She'd wanted to turn over the reins to someone stronger and more capable. Well, here he was.

His body appeared relaxed, like he had all the time in the world for her to make up her mind. She wondered what he saw and wished now she'd at least run a comb through her hair before she'd bound it in her usual ponytail.

Her dad had always said she should go with her gut when logic failed. Her instincts told her he was a dangerous man—and she wanted him on her side. Whatever the cost.

If her body was only too happy to surrender, she was entitled to enjoy making "payment". She turned and led the way into the church, her heart skipping a beat when his hand settled on the small of her back. The pressure, even through her coat, thrilled her.

Shep awaited them, his rifle barrel pointing toward the ceiling. His eyebrows rose when he saw how close Ty stood.

"I know him, Shep. He's here to help."

He nodded and lowered his weapon as more men filed inside the chapel, but he didn't look happy.

"I'll have the men get the generator going and set up a perimeter defense," Ty said.

Another load off her shoulders. She glanced above to

the choir loft. "It's okay, Danny. You can come down, now."

Danny's face, brimming with curiosity, peered over the balcony. "You sure?"

"Yeah. I've been...expecting them."

Ty nudged her back, a reminder he wanted to talk.

"I'll be in the back," she said to Danny and Shep. "Take a load off. Looks like we'll be spendin' the night here."

She headed to the back of the church, hanging a left at the altar and striding into the corridor where the church offices stood vacant. The door leading to the lawn in back opened with a whine, and Kate stepped into deepening twilight with Ty right behind her.

Their boots crunched on the dry grass, adding to the crackling tension building in her shoulders and back. Ty was here. They were alone. What would happen between them? Would he insist on taking his pleasure now that the bargain had been made?

She wasn't sure whether the thought excited or appalled her. Sam had been her only lover, but not once in their years-long arrangement had she felt this sharp-edged excitement.

Mingled with anticipation was the fear she'd disappoint. Ty was so much more man than she was woman.

They climbed the steps of the gazebo, and she turned to face him. Shielded from any prying gaze by the lattice-board sides of the building and the dried vines clinging to the frame, they stared at each other for a long moment.

Now that they were alone, she felt more than a little unnerved by his dark, hooded gaze. She cleared her throat. "You said you wanted to talk."

His gaze bored into hers. "We should set some ground rules."

She nodded, her mouth suddenly dry. Rules? "For the trip?"

"For what happens between us."

A fine trembling started deep inside her. He'd shot straight past business into intimacy. "All right. Shoot."

"First, you tell me everything I want to know. No secrets."

"Will you do the same?"

"In time."

She snorted softly and gave him a derisive look. "I'm supposed to give you my trust, but you won't reciprocate?"

"It's a little complicated. There are things best left alone for now. Can you live with that?"

It was perverse, but the mystery surrounding him was a huge turn-on. "Depends."

He lifted one eyebrow in question.

"On whether you follow through with your promise to provide safe passage to the people at the ranch."

He canted his head and stared like he was trying to see inside her. "Don't you want to ask anything for yourself?"

She licked her lips. "I think I'm going to get it."

His lips curved, and his dark eyes crinkled at the corners. "I think you're right," he said, his voice a deep, smooth rumble—like a panther's purr.

Her cheeks burned beneath his scrutiny. "What else?"

"I'm in charge. No questions. When I'm not there, you'll follow my next in command."

Her teeth ground in frustration. "Will I have any say?"

"I'll listen. But I make the decisions."

"Will your next in command have power over me?"

"He'll give the orders, but you're mine. He won't touch you."

The way he said it, flatly like an already recognized fact, rankled while at the same time tripping a thrill that heated her body from the inside out. She didn't know how to respond.

"Does anyone else have a claim on you?"

The deep, dark texture of his voice upped the tension building in her core. "Why?"

"Just wondered if I might have a fight on my hands."

She shook her head, ready to deny, but remembered his warning about no secrets. "My foreman, Sam…he's the only one. Sometimes. But he won't interfere."

"When was the last time you slept with him?"

She jerked at the crudeness of his question and dropped her glance, unable to hold hers steady beneath his steely gaze. "Weeks, and we don't sleep together," she muttered.

"Take off your hat."

His tight, roughened voice drew her nipples instantly to aching points. She closed her eyes and took off her hat slowly.

"Your hair. Let it down."

Her fingers trembled as she fought the elastic band, but finally her hair fell around her shoulders. She knew it was longer than had been fashionable, but her dad had loved her ponytail and had tweaked it often.

She gave him a quick glance to gauge his reaction. The flare of his nostrils seemed a good sign he was pleased. Her hand rose to smooth down the flyaway strands.

He reached out and tipped her chin upward to study her features. "Green. I thought they might be."

"Do we still have a bargain?" she asked, trying to sound cool but knowing he heard the nervous quaver in her voice.

His response stole her breath away. He stepped so close the heat radiating from his body warmed the space between them. As she tilted back her head to hold his gaze, his head dipped, and his mouth covered hers.

Now, she'd been kissed plenty, but she'd never been devoured. He ate her lips, slanting over her mouth, sucking her lower lip between her teeth to nibble, and then sealing their mouths to thrust his tongue inside. He swept behind her teeth, stroked over her tongue, and curled his to tug and tease until she groaned.

Kate grasped the corners of his shoulders, holding on for dear life as he circled and prodded and told her without words how he'd fuck her. Hard, relentless— leaving nothing undiscovered.

She'd never known the likes of the lust that arose inside her—so strong her whole body shuddered with need. She closed the distance between them and pressed her breasts against his chest.

Ty's hands dropped from her face and parted her coat to reach inside. He smoothed around her waist to her back, and lower, to cup her bottom and draw her hips close.

His erection, thick and hard as a post, ground into her belly, building a fire that swelled her pussy and drenched her panties—she was more than ready to keep the bargain. *Now!*

He lifted his head and dragged in a deep breath. "I won't take you here."

"Why not?" she said, and glided her lips along his firm jaw.

"It's too open."

"Who's gonna watch?" God, couldn't he tell she didn't care? She nipped his chin.

"It's almost dark. The moon's rising."

"You think werewolves need moonlight to prowl?"

"I *know* they're more vicious when the moon rules them. We go inside."

Kate jerked away, and his hands fell to his sides. Maybe he didn't want her as much as she did him. Maybe he'd just been playing with her to see how far he could lead her? She drew the edges of her duster tight around her and swept her hat from the floor where she'd dropped it. She placed it on top of her loosened hair and gave him a look that anyone who knew her would say meant war.

"We still have a bargain," he reminded her.

"I still don't follow orders well," she said through gritted teeth.

"Like I said, I'm gonna take care of that. Let's get back inside. I need to check on the men."

Kate wiped her mouth with the forearm and cursed under her breath. Her lips still throbbed. Anyone looking at her would know she'd been kissed. She shook her head. Since when did she care? She'd been ready to fuck him where they stood.

Her body hummed with frustration, but she put one foot in front of the other, ignoring the moist heat between her legs and the man at her back.

* * *

Ty curled his hands into fists as he followed her inside. Frustration rode his cock still crammed behind his zipper. He was grumpy and aching, and the woman was a hard ass. *Christ*, how he'd liked to have laid her on the floor of the gazebo and rode her until she hadn't the strength to open her mouth again and argue.

Diego stood just inside the door, his face expressionless, but his eyes glinting with mirth. He sniffed discreetly as Kate passed and raised an eyebrow. "That was quick," he said, soft enough for only Ty to hear.

Ty growled and stomped past. Diego's soft laughter followed him down the corridor. A hum sounded from the distance, and lights flickered into life throughout the hallway and the rooms lining either side.

A glimpse of a couch in an open doorway to his right clinched it. He grabbed Kate's arm and swung her around, lifting her off her feet and into his arms. He carried her through the doorway and kicked the door shut on Diego's laughter.

"What the hell do you think you're doing?" she said from between tight lips.

A good fight or a good fuck was the only thing that would satisfy him now. That Kate would give him both only sweetened the need pooling in his groin.

He set her on her feet, knocked her hat from her head, and tore the duster down her arms. Then he stripped her gun belt from her hips and reached for the T-shirt hugging her slender curves. He pulled it from where it was tucked inside her pants and roughly shoved it up. Her arms remained at her sides, her expression sour as a bulldog's.

"We have a bargain," he reminded her.

Later, he'd tell her later he hadn't meant a word of his offer. He'd have helped her without the exchange of favors. Right now, he had to be inside her, fucking deep into her tight cunt, burying himself in warm, wet *human* woman.

She lifted her arms slowly, defiance riding the curve of her jaw. But her nipples told a different story. They sprang against the thin fabric of her bra, round hard knots he wouldn't ignore for even a moment longer.

With her arms and head trapped in her t-shirt, he ducked down and clasped one little bud between his teeth and bit softly, surprising a gasp from her. Then he sucked it through the fabric, pulling hard until it ripened further. He pulled the edge of the cup beneath her nipple to expose it and groaned. The hard, pink bud beckoned him, hardening and scraping his tongue as he circled on it.

She wriggled against him, struggling to free herself, and he let her nipple go to drag her shirt over her head. He broke the clasp of her bra in his haste to free her breasts.

They were small and round and tilted upward, the nipples like budding flowers seeking sunlight. He backed her to the leather couch and lay her lengthwise on it, then bent to sip at one breast while he palmed the other, squeezing.

Her legs moved restlessly, sliding sinuously on the leather, pressing together and apart. The aroma of her arousal scented the air, making it impossible for him to ignore the tightness of his jeans one minute more.

He stood and removed his jacket and raised his own t-shirt over his head, then reached for the button at the top of his waistband.

Her gaze clung to where his hands worked. Her

flushed face was tight, her lips swollen from his earlier kisses. He pulled down the zipper and reached inside his underwear to draw out his cock, sighing when cool air washed over it. Her gaze raked him. He couldn't wait to finish stripping and simply shoved his pants low enough to free his balls.

She sat up and swung her legs off the sofa and leaned toward him, her face level with his cock. He held his breath while she slanted her head and ran her tongue from the base of his cock and up his shaft.

He raked her hair with his fingers and guided her toward the head.

Her tongue curved and licked the underside of the ridge surrounding the crown— teasing strokes that had him flexing his buttocks to push his cock between her lips. She relented and opened wide, swallowing him whole.

He stroked inside her hot mouth, feeling the light scrape of her teeth and the soft suctioning of her lips as she drew him deeper.

He couldn't remember it ever feeling this good. Endless nights of stroking his cock inside his palm, of tamping down the memory of a woman's mouth sucking his cock to orgasm, had killed his expectations of ever knowing this kind of elation.

Wild, unfettered—hot as hell. But he didn't want to come in her mouth. Not the first time. He wanted to empty his balls inside her soft body. He pulled away and helped her stand.

Her eyes were bright, her cheeks reddened, and she reached upward to kiss his mouth while he shoved her pants past her hips.

"Sorry. I'll make it up to you later." He turned her, pushed her down, and bent her over the couch. "Gotta be inside you, Kate. Can't wait."

"Please hurry," she whispered.

He didn't know if she was telling him to get it over with or she was just as excited. He was desperate enough not to care. His fingers sought the moist opening between her legs and thrust inside.

Her inner muscles eased and clasped, urging him deeper. With her legs trapped in her blue jeans, she hiked her bottom higher — seeking a deeper penetration.

Ty slid his thumb lower and found the hard little knot at the bottom of her slick folds and rubbed it, pressing gradually harder as her breaths shortened, punctuated by thin, feminine moans.

Withdrawing his fingers, he positioned his cock at her entrance, watching the wet, swollen lips swallow the head as he pushed forward.

Kate's lean, muscled ass quivered, and she pressed her forehead to the cushions as she groaned. "God, Ty, fuck me."

Spreading his legs wide to straddle hers, he placed his hands on the sofa cushion and started to pump his hips slowly, working himself inside her tight cunt — cramming deeper into her moist, hot passage, one stroke at a time.

"Faster, please," she said, her voice tightening like the grip of her pussy on his cock.

Faster, harder, he thrust in and out, loving the way her cunt rippled inside, caressing his shaft as he fucked her. He grew more excited as other sensations built. Hot, humid heat. Pressure surrounding him, milking him. He pistoned into her, his balls banging against her clit. His breaths came shorter, his strokes sharper.

Her bottom slammed back to take him deeper, and more moisture drenched her channel, easing the friction and his movements as he pounded at her womb.

"Ty!" she gasped, then her whole body went rigid, straining against him, clamping hard around his dick.

She made it impossible for him to hold back one second longer. His balls erupted, cum exploding from his cock. He cried out, unable to temper the anguish that burned his throat. When the storm passed, he continued rocking against her, unwilling to leave the heat surrounding him and the soft ass that cushioned every stroke.

He leaned over her and laid his cheek against her shoulder while his heart and breaths slowed.

"You'll get my people out?" she asked, her voice muffled against the cushion.

The bargain. He snorted, too drained to laugh. The contrary woman was a single-minded little bitch. "Yeah, I'll take them to fucking China if you want."

Chapter Four

Even as she lay limp as a dishrag on the cushions of the couch with Ty blanketing her back, a niggling thought entered her mind—something wasn't quite right. She wondered if it was just her mile-wide pessimistic streak that wouldn't let her fully enjoy the moment.

Ty had been wild and forceful, everything she'd ever craved in a man. The bigger-than-life hero come to the rescue she'd always secretly dreamed of.

But she didn't believe in fairy tales.

She could have cried with disappointment. Ty was too perfect, too magnificently honed—too well-hung to be entirely human.

Was that it? Was he a *werewolf*? If he was and the men who followed him were cut from the same pelt, then they were a species of *were* she'd never encountered before. Those she'd observed appeared to prefer their wolves' coats. The longer they lived past their first shift, the more they craved the call of the wild.

But these men appeared too organized and comfortable in their human bodies.

Well, there was only one way to be sure, but how the hell was she going to get silver inside his body? Every person who stepped on Sanctuary was tested before entering. Could she wait that long and risk bringing the enemy to the gate?

His cock stirred inside her, reminding her of its delicious bite when fully erect. He'd worked his monstrous cock inside her slowly, crowding past her entrance, stroking so deep he'd banged against the mouth of her womb.

Her channel was already melting around him, and she stiffened her back, fighting the urge to let him fuck her one more time. So far, only her pussy had experienced any penetration—her skin hadn't suffered so much as a scratch. A woman couldn't be turned by fucking.

But she could be if she angered him enough to bite her. How could she test him?

Draped over the sofa, her belt buckle dug into her hip. It was a turquoise and silver conch, and the prong on the back was sharp. She'd used it before, but it wouldn't penetrate deep enough to kill him if he was a *were*. So how could she stick him and make it appear an accident?

She needed him relaxed, compliant—unsuspecting. There was only one way that came to mind.

Hell. Was she just looking for an excuse to have sex with him again? Was her mind still so muddled with his spicy scent and the fullness that even now stretched her inner walls? She could hardly think past the delicious ache.

She needed a distraction—for him and her.

"Ty," she said softly.

"Mmm?" he murmured against her shoulder.

"I think these jeans are cutting off my circulation. I need to get them off."

He groaned but lifted from her body, pulling out his cock slowly, but not before he glided back in one more time as though he hated leaving her.

Awkwardly, she rose and faced him, dismayed to find him pulling up his pants. "Um...I thought..."

He looked back at her, one eyebrow raised.

"But I was kinda hoping..."

A smile lifted one corner of his mouth. "I need a little time to recuperate, sweetheart."

Feeling a blush of mortification heat her face, she cleared her throat. "I was hoping I might help you with that."

Both eyebrows rose. "I see." He glanced at the door and lifted a hand to rub the back of his neck. Then he gave her a narrowed glance that dropped to her breasts and back up to her gaze. "I guess we have a little more time."

She toed off her boots and hurriedly pushed her jeans

the rest of the way down her legs, afraid he'd change his mind.

He stared as she finished undressing, his gaze zeroing in on her pussy.

Shifting apart her legs, she let him see the fluid dripping down her thighs. Seduction wasn't a skill she'd ever acquired, and she hoped she didn't look like a fool as she settled a hand on one hip and trailed the other up her belly to cup a tiny breast.

She knew she had to look like a half-grown girl—all angles and slight curves. Perhaps she wouldn't appeal to him at all now that he could see every one of her flaws.

But his jaw tightened as he watched her play with her tit, and his hand adjusted his cock inside his pants. She was further emboldened by the flush that lit his cheeks and the quickening of his breaths.

His hands dropped to the waistband of his jeans, and he slowly unbuttoned them. This time she was the one who couldn't look away as the widening placket opened to reveal his straining cock.

When she dragged her gaze up to his, her body started quivering at the smoldering intent she read in his expression. Taking a deep breath, she nonchalantly tossed her blue jeans to the sofa, careful that the buckle landed on top.

He continued the unaffected, but sexy striptease, tugging down his zipper and gripping his pants to shove them down his thickly muscled thighs.

As his still semi-erect cock lifted from a thatch of dark curls, her mouth went dry. Lord, he was beautiful. And the part of him that proclaimed him all male was especially so.

His long shaft was thick and straight. The skin stretched around it had a satiny sheen. The plump head was purplish, and all along the shaft were ridged veins that stood out against his flesh like those mapping his muscled arms.

Kate shook herself from her momentary awe and

licked her lips, trying to decide how best to seduce him. She had a job to do, but her body certainly didn't view it as work. It creamed with pleasure.

She stepped toward him in her bare feet and realized that even at 5'10", the top of her head could snuggle beneath his chin. Never before had she felt this overwhelmed by a man's height and breadth. She lifted a hand to the back of his head and pulled his face down for what might be their last kiss.

His mouth slid over hers, his lips sucking her lower lip between his teeth to nibble. Lord, she loved the way he transformed a kiss into a purely sexual act that reminded her of every place he'd already nibbled and sucked. However, she couldn't surrender to his seduction. She needed to be in charge this time.

Her hands pushed against his chest, and he relented, letting her step away.

She gave him an uncertain glance, noting the tautness of his jaw and the heat burning across his sharp-bladed cheekbones. Before she lost her nerve, she dropped to her knees in front of him and pushed down his jeans past his ankles.

He stepped out of them, and she stared at his feet for a long moment, willing herself to remember what she had to do. Then she turned her face upward.

Her cheek grazed his shaft, and he sucked in a deep breath.

So he likes that.

This time, deliberately, she rubbed her cheek up and down his shaft, then sifted her hair along it. Already, she noted the changes in his cock as it filled, hardening, stiffening, straightening until it raised high against his belly.

The satiny appearance of the skin didn't deceive—she closed her eyes as she caressed him with her face, breathing in his musky cum-drenched scent. But it was the steely muscle beneath that drew her lips to finally skim her mouth along his length, sucking softly as she made her way up one side then down the other.

Down to his balls. She cupped the heavy sac and rolled it in her palm, testing the weight. Tugging it gently, she smiled as she forced a gasp from him. She knew she was on the right track when his fingers threaded through her hair. He didn't force her direction, but the changing tension in his fingertips told her what pleased him most.

So she experimented, lifting the sac to lick behind his balls, suctioning on the soft, taut skin behind his scrotum.

His legs braced wider apart, and his thighs bulged as she scraped her fingertips up the inside of his legs. "Kate," he whispered.

She lapped his balls with the flat of her tongue over and over until a groan slid from his throat. Only then did she relent, sucking one hard stone inside her mouth.

"Christ, Kate!" His curved fingers bit her scalp.

With hers skimming his shaft, she tugged the ball with her lips while tonguing it inside her mouth. When she released it, she scooped both balls into the cavern of her mouth, earning a trembling that shook his thighs.

As much as she would have loved laving his balls longer, her own body urged her to hurry. Moisture trickled between her thighs, and her nipples hardened like diamonds, aching for his touch.

She moved up his shaft until she reached the head and opened her mouth wide to take it inside. Here, resilient softness responded to the pleasuring of her tongue. She rose on her knees to take the plumb-shaped crown into her mouth.

Placing both of her hands at the base of his cock, one atop the other, she stroked upward to meet her mouth as she went down on him, squeezing her hands hard around him while suctioning the cap.

Sam had showed her what pleased him, and she was glad the lesson translated so well to Ty. If she felt a moment's guilt for her enjoyment, she reminded herself, she'd never promised Sam a thing.

She chewed softly around the head of his crown and sucked again, pumping her hands on his shaft up and down, up and down.

"Kate, stop! Stop," he groaned.

Kate ignored him, not relinquishing her hold on his cock.

His hands slipped behind her nape, and he pushed her further down to take him deeper. His hips flexed, driving him against the back of her throat.

She gagged softly and then relaxed the muscles of her throat, to take him deeper, loving his helpless moans, but this wasn't going to get him closer to the sofa and her belt buckle.

She pulled back and lifted her chin to the sofa. "I want to fuck you, Ty. I want to ride."

He stared down, his chest and arms clenched, his breaths flaring his nostrils.

"Sit on the couch. I'm gonna climb on top of you."

He did as she asked, sitting with his thighs splayed to make room for his balls, and he held open his arms.

She stepped between his legs and then leaned to grab his shoulders as she climbed one knee at a time onto the couch. With his arms closing around her, she slowly straddled his hips, gasping when the ridge of his cock slid against her slick heat. She knelt, keeping high enough to feel the head of his cock nudge between her legs.

Ty latched onto one of her breasts, biting a nipple with enough force to set her trembling.

Her hands clutched the back of his head, urging him to suckle. Then she reached down between them and grasped the end of his cock and guided it to her entrance.

With one of his hands palming her tiny breast and the other clutching one cheek of her bottom, he helped her slowly sink toward his lap.

She circled to screw him inside, pressing downward then rising, pumping up and down to create the moisture and friction that would ease a deeper penetration. He was big, and her already tender inner tissues ached and burned. So she screwed him slowly until a wash of desire coated her walls, and she was able to take him deeper, her thighs straining, burning as she worked.

He let go of her nipple and both hands settled on her ass to help her lift and sink — deeper each time. He kissed her cheek and nuzzled her ear. "Baby, you have no idea how good this feels."

A final twist and her pussy met the root of his cock.

She paused, her breath coming in shallow gasps. She rolled her forehead against his, keeping her eyes shut tight. "And you don't know how full I feel — how..."

"Complete?" he whispered.

Kate nodded and opened her eyes.

His face was dark and tense — the same smoldering look he'd given her before that created a momentary thrill of fear. That look also ignited the hottest lust she'd ever known.

She leaned toward him and took his mouth in a wide-open kiss. Their tongues stabbed at each other, and their hands gripped and squeezed whatever they could reach.

His hands squeezed her ass in a bruising grip, grinding her hips forward and back so the crisp hairs of his groin scraped her delicate clit.

She moaned into his mouth and lifted again — up and down, harder, sharper. Her movements came faster, almost frenzied. The pressure inside her so great, the friction so hot, she couldn't control herself. She panted into his mouth, and her arms wound around his neck as she fucked him harder.

Then she was there — the blackness overwhelming her for a moment. She threw back her head and cried out as she rode his cock — now painfully hard and thick — her strokes pounding against his groin as she fed her ever-broadening orgasm. Her cries strangled in her throat as she was cast over the edge.

Ty held her until the trembling subsided. Her cheek was pressed to his shoulder as his hands stroked over her back, and she realized he was still hard as a rock inside her.

She lifted her head. "I'm sorry. I couldn't wait for you."

He snorted. "It was worth the show. But I thought you were doing me."

"I was. Sorry." She leaned back and grinned ruefully. "Give me a chance to catch my breath."

He kissed her lips, just a quick smack and grinned again. "Anytime you want, sweetheart, you can ride me like a bronc — take your pleasure off my cock."

Blushing, she laid her cheek back on his shoulder and found herself staring at her buckle nestled on top of her jeans. Christ, it was now or never.

She hated to ruin the mood and possibly incite him into violence, but she had to know. She reached over and grabbed it.

As his hand smoothed over her thigh, she jabbed the prong deep into the top of his hand.

He jerked away his hand. "What the fuck?" he said, between gritted teeth. "You trying to stab me to death with your belt buckle?" Ty's hand shot out and closed hard around hers, turning it to see what she clutched inside her palm, noting the blood on the prong of the buckle.

When his glare lifted to her wide-eyed gaze, he said, "If I'd been a fucking werewolf, what would you do right now?"

She lifted her shoulders in a shrug, pretending she wasn't afraid. "I hadn't really thought that far ahead."

His eyes narrowed and then he held out his hand. "Take a look. Satisfied? Not even a welt."

The bloody wound looked angry, but the skin around it showed no signs of allergic reaction. Her cheeks heated guiltily. "Well, I couldn't risk bringing you onto the ranch without knowing for sure."

"I understand that," he bit out, his face growing darker. "But you took a risk I'm not willing to forgive."

Impaled as she was on his body, she couldn't exactly make a run for it, so she stayed silent, not wanting to incite him further.

"If I'd been a wolf, right about now, I'd be ripping your throat out. Did you even consider that?"

She shook her head and swallowed.

"Tomorrow," he said, his voice deadly even, "you can test every one of my men, but for now there's the issue of how reckless you were and the chance you took. You need to think before you act, Kate."

She tossed back her hair. "I have good instincts. I go with my gut on most things."

"You belong to me now, and if there's one thing you're going to learn, it's to consult with me before you take off with one of your hair-brained schemes."

Hair-brained? Her back stiffened, and her chin rose. She resented his tone and the fact that he was pretty much dismissing everything she'd accomplished to this point. She'd been the one to lead the ranch hands. Her instincts and her will had kept everyone on the ranch alive and together. If he thought a little hot sex was all it was going to take to keep her in line…

But now wasn't the time to argue. The look on his face said he was through talking, too. "I don't know what you're thinking, but you're going to learn who's in charge here. If I have to fuck you morning, noon, and night to keep you complacent, I will."

She gave a short cynical laugh. "What? You think you'll wear me out?"

His hands closed hard around her hips, and he pulled her up and off his cock.

Before she sucked in her next breath, he took her to the floor and stretched over her, trapping her arms and legs with the weight of his body. With a darkening look, he burrowed his cock between her closed legs, and his hands tightened around her wrists like manacles.

With his first hard thrust into the narrow space he'd made, he gritted out, "Every word, every thought, every action. Mine." His cock crowded past her swollen lips and rammed into her cunt.

Even as her mind protested his heavy-handed tactics, lush, wet excitement exploded inside her.

"Say it, Katie," he growled.

She shook her head, not wanting him to find her an easy conquest—and needing more of his violence.

His hips powered against her, and she wished she could lift her legs and take him deeper inside her.

But he kept her trapped beneath him, unable to move. The only resistance she could manage was squeezing her inner muscles around him—but he couldn't be halted, and her grip only increased the friction.

"Say it."

She shook her head, not wanting to let those words slip from her lips. He'd have to try harder.

His mouth slammed down on hers, and his tongue stroked inside, matching the rhythm of his jerking hips as he drove into her, again and again.

Kate's breaths gusted in time with his thrusts, and her back curved to force him off, but she only managed to abrade her nipples against his chest, and she groaned.

He dragged his mouth away and nosed under her chin, scraping her neck lightly with his teeth.

She shuddered.

"Say it, Katie," he whispered into her ear.

With her legs closed and his cock squeezing between, she felt the fullness stretching her entrance, but couldn't get the length she needed, or encourage him to rub the delicious spot he'd found inside her.

His hips pounded at hers. "Say it, Katie," he rasped.

She couldn't stand it, couldn't take it one moment longer. She had to have him deeper. "I'm yours," she sobbed. "Please."

He halted abruptly, and one knee nudged between her thighs, then the other.

Katie quickly wrapped her legs around his waist.

He leaned up on his arms. "Play with your tits."

Not willing to argue when she was close to finally getting nailed the way she wanted, she lifted shaking hands to her breasts, spreading her fingers to let her nipples peek from between them.

His cock speared into her. "Pinch your nipples."

She lifted her hips to meet his next deep thrust and squeezed the tips of her breasts.

Apparently satisfied she'd do whatever he commanded, he lowered his body, trapping her hands between them. His hands slipped beneath her bottom to bring her closer still, and his fingers slid between her cheeks to trace her asshole.

Kate tightened in shock.

"You're going to take it," he rasped. "You'll take everything I give you." He lifted off her and rolled her to her stomach.

When his arm circled her hips to raise her bottom high, she rested her head on the carpet, surrendering completely to his will.

Her ass wasn't virgin. Sam had shown her that delight, too. But she'd never felt so much pressure as the broad head of Ty's cock pushed against her resisting anus.

His hands massaged and spread her bottom wider. Spit dripped between her buttocks, and he rubbed it around her hole then brought his big cock back to try to enter her again.

She couldn't help the whimper that slipped between her clenched lips. It was painful. He hadn't bothered seducing her asshole into relaxing its guard. But she was hot for it all the same.

His thighs snuggled up to the inside of hers. "It's gonna hurt a little."

She snorted. "Just fucking do it." Her words were

insubordinate, but her tone was thin and needy.

He pumped against her asshole, pressing hard, then backing off, before coming at it again a little harder.

Kate's back relaxed, and she willed her ass to do the same, gasping when finally he breached her hole, and his crown crowded inside her an inch.

Out again, and then deeper.

She sucked air between her teeth as her ring and inner tissues stretched beyond comfort to accommodate his girth. "Stop."

A sharp slap burned one cheek, and she reared up to aim a glare over her shoulder. "I wasn't saying no. Just wait." She squeezed around him, holding him back.

His low grown told her how much her tightness pleased him. But he lifted his hand and spanked her other cheek, the sting sharper this time.

She tried to hold back her moan, not liking the fact her body loved this further proof of his command, but he drove it from her throat with a succession of slaps that warmed her bottom and had her writhing on his cock in moments.

"Never tell me no, Kate," he whispered. "I can't be held off. Not when all I want to do is fuck you deep and hard and drink your cries."

She sobbed, her body shivering—goose bumps rising on her skin at the bleak, hoarse texture of his voice.

Slowly, inexorably, he eased his way with shallow thrusts and sharper slaps, until his cock filled her dark channel to bursting.

He leaned over her back and kissed her shoulder. "It's gonna happen fast."

"I'm ready." A shudder rocked her whole body. "*Fuck me, Ty*. Any way you want."

He rose up behind her, and his hands settled on her ass cheeks, gripping her hard, lifting them apart to make more room for him to drive closer. He widened her stance with his knees and then reached around her waist. His hands slid between her legs, and as he slammed his hips against her ass, he pinched her clit.

Kate screamed, unraveling in a shuddering, gasping convulsion.

Ty hammered his cock deep inside her ass, plucking her clit all the while until she couldn't take the sensations slamming through her body one moment longer. Her head and shoulder slumped to the ground while he unleashed a storm—fucking her soundly, grinding her knees into the carpet, scooting her forward with the brutal force of his thrusts.

When at last hot, burning liquid erupted inside her ass, Kate groaned and slipped into darkness.

Chapter Five

Even before he pulled his cock out, Ty was cursing himself and his lack of self-control. He knew he wasn't making the best of impressions on this infuriating woman.

She'd been reckless. Challenged his right to command her. His response had been swift, instinctive—and harsh. He'd wanted time to woo her before letting her see that side of him.

Kate McKinnon didn't understand the nature of the monster that had her by the tail—literally. He couldn't be led. Couldn't be *partnered*. It had to be his way for her own safety. For when he finally let her see his true nature, he had to be certain she'd never incite the beast inside him into violence. He might kill her.

When she'd stabbed him with the buckle, he'd come close to letting loose the beast. Quickly, he'd substituted one lust for the darker one—pushing her to the floor and mounting her, screwing her brains out.

But if the only way to get a handle on this woman was dominating her physically, sexually, he'd do it. A man had to do what a man had to do—especially if he wasn't entirely human.

She'd been clever to realize something was afoot. She'd just picked the wrong monster, and he wondered if she'd ever encountered his sort before.

"Did you really come to Tierney for me?" she asked quietly.

He lay on the floor beside her and pulled her into his arms, his belly to her back—perfect for him to continue groping her sweetly rounded breasts. He squeezed one small mound. "I couldn't leave you out here on your own."

"That's not what I meant. You got to the sex pretty damn quick—like you'd been anticipating it. I could have been eighty years old for all you knew."

"I knew you weren't," he said, rolling a nipple between his thumb and forefinger, hoping to distract her. "I did expect you to be a bit older."

"I'm twenty-seven," she said, a hint of gruff defiance in her voice.

"That old?" At her snort, Ty smiled against her hair. She was prickly as a porcupine. "Your dad died ten years ago. You were seventeen?"

"Yeah."

That shut her down quick, but he needed to satisfy his curiosity about a couple more things. "When did you and Sam become lovers?"

Her back stiffened, but her nipples flowered against his palm. "Ten years ago."

Ty could see how it had happened. She'd been young and alone when her father was killed—in need of comfort. Sam had been her rock.

Ty could understand it, and part of him was glad she'd had someone to turn to, but he was already predisposed to hate Sam's guts. "How's he going to take it? Your being with me."

Her answering sigh had him tightening his hand on her breast, but he forced himself to relax.

Finally, she drew a breath, and said, "I'm sure he'll be disappointed, but I've never led him on." She turned in his arms, her gaze studying his face. "What about you? Have you ever had a relationship?"

Wishing he'd turned the light off, he shuttered his expression. "None that ever mattered. I went into the service pretty young and moved around a lot."

Her eyebrows drew together. "Well, that tells me a lot. You want the down and dirty on me, but you won't share."

Ty frowned back, thinking he'd have been better off never opening this can of worms. He hated talking about his past. Hated even remembering he'd had a life before Davis. Choosing his words carefully, he replied, "I spent some time in the Middle East on my first tour. By the time I made it back, all hell had broken loose here. There was never time." He picked up a loose curl of her hair and teased her nipple.

Kate's breath caught. "Why are you ready now?"

How could he tell her the truth? He needed sex almost as much as he needed sustenance—and the two were closely intertwined. He chose not to answer. Instead, he hooked his arm around her waist, bringing her body flush with his. "I need to check on my men."

But he couldn't let her go. Not yet. Her warm, lithe body hummed with her quickening heartbeats.

Kate slid her thigh over his hips and pressed her sex against his cock. "This is all you came for, isn't it?"

Ty met her glance, but rather than giving her the words she wanted, he kissed her, sliding his mouth over hers. To shut her up. Not to tell her he already suspected he'd just been kidding himself.

He needed more than her warm body and the brilliant life force that filled her. If he'd been anywhere near ready to admit it, he might have said he'd loved her just a little bit after sharing those nighttime conversations that had left his body aching and his heart...opening.

When her hands once more surrounded his cock, he groaned and dragged his lips away. "Save that thought for later." He eased away from her body and stood, picking up his clothing from the floor, never allowing his gaze to return to her slender form.

He dressed in silence, wincing when he closed the zipper over his swelling cock. From the corner of his eye, he watched Kate sit up and grimace.

"I'm a mess. I can't dress until I clean up." She gave him an accusatory glance that told him he'd better do something about it.

Rummaging through a tall file cabinet, he found a pristine altar cloth and held it out to Kate.

"You've got to be kidding," she grumbled, but swiped

it from his hand, and gave him a pointed stare.

It took a moment for him to realize she wanted privacy, and he tightened his lips against a smile. After all they'd shared, she could still be embarrassed? "I'll leave you to dress," he murmured and let himself out of the office.

When he stepped into the hall, he found Diego leaning against the wall, smoking a cigarette. He straightened and gave him a sly look. "I would have tied her up. She's going to be a problem."

Ty snorted. "Let's just get inside the ranch first. Did they find those guys?"

Diego nodded. "The team shouldn't be hungry for a while. We saved you a snack."

* * *

Kate walked down the aisle between the pews. Many toward the end had been shifted against the walls. Army cots had been assembled, and several of the men Ty had brought lounged in various stages of undress.

Shep sidled up to her, eating from an opened can of beans and eying the men around them with suspicion. He glowered when he caught her eye. "You sure about these guys?" he said, under his breath.

"I stabbed Ty in the hand with my belt buckle." She shrugged, fighting the blush that burned her cheeks. "Nothing, not so much as a welt."

Shep's narrowed gaze swept over her, and Kate's blush deepened.

Danny strode toward her, his gaze sweeping from her unbound hair down her rumpled clothing. He gave her a pointed look, and Kate knew he disapproved. His loyalty lay with Sam.

She lifted her chin, daring either of the men to say a word.

"Missy, I hope you know what you're doing," Shep muttered.

Her throat tightened. She'd known them all her life,

but this wasn't something she was willing to talk to them about. She shrugged. "Not really. Not yet. But I need to find Ty so I can get a few things cleared up." And this time, she needed to make sure their conversation didn't involve hands and lips, or she'd never get to the bottom of it.

She found him standing in the darkness on the front steps of the church, talking to the Hispanic man she'd seen with him earlier. They both grew silent as she approached.

She ignored the other man, turning her back slightly to him as she faced Ty. "I thought we might talk about what's going to happen tomorrow."

Ty nodded. "Let me introduce Diego Salazar," he said, tilting his head toward the dark-haired man next to him.

She didn't like really want to meet him. Something about the way his gaze slid over her body, made her feel like she was the butt of a joke and only he knew the punch line.

Kate returned his stare, taking in his darkly tanned skin, black hair, and Spanish features. Too handsome for her to trust or even feel comfortable standing beside.

"Diego's my next in command."

Her back stiffened, but she nodded, reluctantly acknowledging the introduction. So this was the man Ty wanted to command her in his absence? When Hell froze over!

Diego lifted one sardonic eyebrow as though he could read her irritation. The slight smile curving his lips infuriated her.

Kate lifted her chin and glared.

"You two know each other already?" Ty said, a hint of laughter in his voice. His arm slid around her waist, and he leaned to whisper in her ear, "He'll grow on you. Promise. I only want to kill him twice a day."

She snorted and drew away.

"There's not much left to discuss," Ty continued. "When we get to your place tomorrow, we'll need everyone to pack up their belongings, and we'll load them all into the deuce-and-a-halfs."

Kate stared at him blankly.

"The transport vehicles," Diego murmured, his deep voice a silky murmur.

"We'll leave so soon?" Kate asked, feeling suddenly cold.

"It's not safe for you there, and you know it, and I didn't like leaving a skeleton crew behind at Fort Davis. How many people do you have now at the ranch?"

She shivered, fighting the urge to offer a protest. Ty was right. Much as she hated the thought of leaving Sanctuary ranch, she had to. She drew a deep breath and dropped her gaze as she forced herself to count. "I have my foreman and six ranch hands. Three families—thirteen total there. Another nine stragglers who showed up at the gates." Her voice grew fainter toward the end, and she realized she was close to tears. *What the fuck?* She never cried. "Oh, and Cass, the cook." Wishing she'd never sought him out, she half-turned, ready to escape back into the church.

"Do you have horse trailers?" Diego asked.

"I have three—big enough to load all the horses." It hit her then. She raised her gaze to Ty. "I won't be able to bring my cattle will I?" *A McKinnon without a ranch or a herd.*

"No," he said quietly.

She nodded, pretending to take it all in stride. "I'll have to leave them on the open range to graze," she said faintly. They'd be fodder for the wolves. Feeling chilled to the bone, she asked, "How long will it take us to get to Davis?"

"About ten hours. We'll leave in daytime—lowest wolf activity."

"So we'll spend one night at the ranch, then leave the next morning?"

He nodded.

"And when we get to your post, what happens?"

"There are officer billets standing empty. The families can be split out there. They'll be comfortable, but there's no running water. They'll have to use outhouses and get their water from the central well. The single men can bunk in one of the barracks."

"What about the women?"

She didn't miss the charged glance he shared with his next in command. "We'll see what arrangements they prefer when we get there."

Kate nodded, once again going with her gut to trust him. She wanted to ask where she'd stay, but he saved her the embarrassment.

"We'll have our own quarters off the operations building."

While she stood beside him, his hand rested on the small of her back, his thumb circling. It probably wasn't even something he was aware of doing.

But she noticed. She'd never considered herself an affectionate person. She and Sam had kept their relationship pretty much under wraps for years. The few gestures of affection they shared were relegated to the bedroom.

But when Ty slipped his arm around her shoulders while he continued talking to Diego, she leaned into him and slipped her arm around his waist.

His answering squeeze warmed her.

How had she come to crave his touch so quickly? She hadn't the example of a mother and father sharing physical affection, her mother having died shortly after she was born. Her father had raised her the best he'd known how, but his was a gruff sort of love, and he hadn't known exactly how to raise a little girl. She'd known he loved her with the obvious care he took with her education and the pride he displayed with her accomplishments, but he hadn't been easy with physical signs of love. A kiss had been a rare thing.

Ty's hand came up behind her neck, and he tilted back her head. "Why don't you go ahead and get some shut eye. I'm going to make the rounds and make sure everything's closed down tight for the night."

"You don't want company?" she asked, not caring that the other man listened to their conversation.

"Tomorrow's going to be a big day. Get some rest. I'll join you in a little bit."

She understood he probably wanted to talk privately with Diego and his men. She wished he were more open, but again, her instinct told her he was there to help. She knew there was something they weren't sharing, but she was tired. She'd worry about it tomorrow. For tonight, she'd lay her trust in his hands. She glanced at the parking lot and realized with a start that the pickup with the body slumped at the wheel — the one she'd been responsible for — had been removed. His men had been busy with cleanup, although she wondered why they'd bothered.

Other than the drying pools of blood on the ground, all other signs of the earlier battle had been removed.

"I'll see about cots," she said quietly.

Diego shouted over his shoulder to the men inside, "Don't bother bringing a cot in for Ty. He's found something soft to sleep on."

Kate fumed, really beginning to detest Diego. The way he looked at her with dark amusement gleaming in his eyes annoyed the hell out of her. He could mind his own damn business.

She escaped into the pastor's office and closed the door to the noise of the men's laughter. Hanging her hat on the doorknob, she removed her coat and gun belt, and dropped them on the desk. Then she sat on the edge of the couch and removed her boots. She laid down fully clothed and pulled her coat over her to chase away the chill in the air.

Strangely, for the first time in longer than she could remember, she fell into a deep dreamless sleep.

* * *

Ty stalked through the darkness toward the man kneeling in the center of a ring formed by his soldiers.

The man smelled of sweat, sharp and acrid despite the cold — and fear.

And well he should.

"He was their leader," Diego murmured. "The smartest among them. He ran."

The man stumbled to his feet, whimpering. "Please. Let me go." He reached out a hand.

Ty knew he couldn't see a thing. So thick was the cloud cover that the full moon above it was completely shrouded in darkness. He strode toward the man and reached behind his head to grasp his thick hair. He pulled him close, grimacing when the man released urine that leaked down his pants leg and filled the air with the sour odor.

He leaned close to whisper in his ear. "Say your prayers."

"Make me one of you. Please," he begged, his breaths hacking with his sobs. "I don't wanna die."

"You frightened my woman. Why would you think I'd spare you?"

The man trembled like a leaf on a windy day. "I didn't know... I wouldn't have hurt her. I swear, I'm sorry."

Ty jerked back his head, baring his throat. "You're gonna give me a bellyache, aren't you?" He shook his head, letting loose his beast with a roar and bit deep into the man's throat.

Blood surged inside his mouth — rich, young, but tainted with the sour bite of alcohol. The man struggled, a gurgling sound issuing from the gaping wound in his neck.

When at last he quieted, Ty released him, letting him drop to the ground. With his bloodlust sated for the moment, he threw back his head and howled.

* * *

Ty found her sleeping on the sofa, fully clothed and unaware someone watched. He doubted she'd slept so soundly in a long time. Satisfaction warmed his heart—she felt safe. This was one thing he could give her.

Only with a full belly was he able to stand being this close to her. Even now, his hunger rose thick to choke the back of his throat. Soon, he'd have to taste her sweetness.

He woke her and pulled her up, then lay on the sofa, and dragged her body over his.

Her legs intertwined with his, and she sighed, murmuring sleepily as she fell quickly back to sleep with her head resting over his heart.

Ty gritted his teeth against the urge to rut against her. His cock was full to bursting, but he embraced the ache, thankful he'd finally found the woman he thought might be strong enough to be his mate. She'd taken his rough loving, even reveled in it. When the time came for a deeper, harsher joining he knew in his gut, she'd survive.

Holding her, *breathing* her in, felt natural and right. He willed himself to relax. With his hand settling on the curved small of her back, he, too, fell into a deep slumber, lulled by the soft, warm breaths that gusted against his chest and the steady beating of her heart.

Tonight, he'd let her rest. If he could stand it.

Chapter Six

Kate awoke to find herself pressed against the back of the sofa as Ty rolled out from underneath her. Just as quick, she felt her jeans give at the waist and heard the zipper rasp as he yanked it down. He quickly peeled her pants off her legs.

"Ty?" she asked, knowing what he intended since he left her top completely alone.

She quickly found herself, sitting at the edge of the sofa, her legs draped over the tops of his shoulders.

The inky blackness that surrounded them leant a feeling of unreality — like she was dreaming. The sounds of his breaths and the creak of the leather beneath her bottom seemed louder, filled with a ripening tension that brought her past dreamy pleasure straight to the blackest, hottest sense of eroticism she'd ever felt. Fear heightened her sensitivity so that when his thick thumbs parted her outer lips, she jerked and released a startled cry.

"Ty?" she repeated and reached between her legs to grab his hair. "Talk to me."

"Can't. Have to taste," he said, his voice so gravelly it was almost unrecognizable.

"Jesus," she gasped when his tongue, strangely wide and roughened, lapped between her legs from asshole all the way up to her clit.

When he repeated the action, again and again, she moaned, sure she was going to burst out of her skin she was so aroused.

Hot, thick cream gushed from deep inside her, and she arched, digging her heels into his back.

His hands gripped her hard, holding her hips steady as he growled and lapped the liquid pleasure smearing her thighs and his face. His tongue tunneled into her, twisting to reach as far as he could, seeming to search for every drop her body offered.

Kate gripped his hair hard and tilted her hips to grind her pussy into his face, wanting him deeper, needing his attention on her hardening clit. Her belly trembled, and her thighs widened — splaying to give him better access to every part of her that ached.

When one thick thumb sank into her ass, she keened long and loud. "Ty, oh God. Please. Suck my clit."

Instead, fingers, thick and calloused, crammed into her cunt, fucking in and out, twisting to screw her hard.

Ecstasy slammed through her, gripping her body in a convulsion that shook her belly and thighs and had her whimpering endlessly as it built.

When at last his lips closed on her clitoris, and he sucked — air whooshed from her lungs and her back shot off the sofa as a pulsing coil of heat tightened her womb. She rode his mouth and fingers, tightening and slackening her inner muscles to hold onto the rapture a moment or two longer.

When his mouth moved off the throbbing knot, she sighed in relief and slumped against the cushions as the aftershocks rippled through her vagina. He lapped her like a cat — rasping, soothing motions now — licking over her swollen lips and clit, delving to either side to trace the crease between her thigh and her pussy.

Her pulse throbbed against his tongue where he paused at her inner thigh, licking until the spot burned then grew oddly numb. A faint pricking sensation registered on her mind a second before she was thrust suddenly back into the maelstrom — her body awash with another deepening orgasm.

All the blood in her body seemed to flow toward her cunt in a rush, drawing to the spot where he mouthed her inner thigh. Hot and cold all at once, she writhed as his fingers thrust deep inside her ass and cunt. Her inner muscles clamped hard around him, milking him — lush, wet sounds quickening to the rhythm of his strokes.

Beyond words, almost beyond breath, her fingers

clawed at his hair as her body undulated, riding out the storm that never seemed to wane.

He groaned, a deep, guttural sound she echoed as she flew out of herself, rushing headlong into the darkness.

* * *

"It was too soon, *amigo*," Diego said quietly, as they sped up the long gravel road.

Ty glanced over his shoulder to where Kate sat huddled in the back seat of the Hummer, sleeping despite the rough ride. The dark purple crescents beneath her eyes bespoke of exhaustion and blood loss. "*Creo qué sí*. You're right."

He damned himself for his selfish act the previous night. He should have slept with the men inside the church rather then succumbing to the delicious temptation she embodied. With her warm body wedged close to his and her heart beats thudding steadily against his chest, he'd been driven slowly mad, until he'd broken the vow he'd made.

He'd promised not to take what wasn't offered.

That morning, Kate seemed unaware he'd crossed that line. Sluggish, she'd put her fatigue down to too little sleep and too much sex. She'd roused only long enough to see them all through the gate. Thankfully, his men had kept Shep and Danny busy long enough for Ty to bundle Kate into the lead vehicle without them realizing anything was amiss.

"That's one helluva fence," Diego said, eyeing the 12-foot tall game fence with the barbed wire coiled on top like makeshift concertina wire.

"Maybe she didn't need us so badly after all," Ty murmured, not sorry one bit they'd made the trip. "Maybe we'll find you a girlfriend, too."

Diego gave him a sour look, and Ty laughed. Diego's cynicism regarding the opposite sex was a longtime source of humor for the team.

Finally, the ranch house and outbuildings came into

view. He blew out a breath, surprised by what he saw. Despite the chaos that reined in the world beyond the fence, here, everything seemed well-tended— whitewashed, nothing out of place or order.

"Nice operation," Diego murmured. "No wonder she didn't want to leave."

Ty echoed the sentiment in silence as men poured out of the buildings.

Hands stood beside the corral and barn door and perched along the front porch, well-oiled weapons glinting at their sides or in their arms.

He approved.

He turned in his seat. "Kate, honey, wake up. You're home."

* * *

Kate held a steaming cup of coffee between her hands and breathed in the aroma. Finally, she felt like she was perking up. She sat on the railing, eyeing the loading of the transport vehicles.

The families tromped in a steady trail back and forth to the vehicles with their meager belongings. Even the children came with boxes of their toys for the journey. Watching their excitement, Kate felt the weight of her responsibilities shift off her shoulders. She'd done the right thing for them.

Boot steps clomped on the wooden porch, and she stiffened. Without turning to see who it was, she knew Sam had joined her. All morning long, she'd acted like a coward, retreating behind the excuse of overseeing the introductions of Ty's men and her people, taking part in the discussions with the families to help alleviate their fears of the coming trek westward to the Davis Mountains.

"Kate," he said, "you happy with your choice?"

She swallowed against the lump forming at the back of her throat and turned to face him, setting her coffee cup on the railing. "Yes, Sam. I'm sor—"

He shook his head. "Don't. I'm okay. It's not like we

ever made any promises."

It was hard meeting his gaze. His eyes were moist, but a slight smile curved his lips. He looked sad but resigned.

"You know I love you," she said.

"And I love you. I only want you happy."

He held open his arms, and she walked into them, wrapping hers around his waist. They stood like that for a long time.

"I'm not going with you, Kate."

"What?" she drew back, staring in shock at his handsome face. "Sam, you can't stay by yourself."

"Shep and Danny, and a couple of the new men, are staying, too. We'll take our chances here."

She wanted to argue with him, rail at him for being foolish, but she recognized the stubborn set of his jaw. She could have been looking in a mirror. "Then she's yours. Sanctuary is yours now."

"Come back when you can," he said, his voice rough.

She nodded, tears blurring her eyes, not knowing what the future might hold for either of them.

The front door slammed, and Kate turned to the sound. Shep stepped out onto the porch, his gaze hard. "What hand did you say you stabbed?"

It took her a moment to understand what he asked. "Are you talking about Ty?" she asked, feeling uneasy at the way Shep's lips thinned. "His left one, why?"

"Not a mark on him. I looked just a minute ago. Somethin's not right."

Kate stiffened, feeling like the other boot had finally dropped. She hadn't paid any attention, but she also didn't recall seeing even a scratch on the back of his hand that morning.

Shep and Sam drew their weapons, and Sam signaled to one of the hands who sat astride the corral fence. He jumped down and strode toward them, his hand already going to the gun strapped to his thigh.

Kate followed suit, knowing where her duty lay, even

as her stomach plummeted. She tucked her coat behind her holster and stepped off the porch toward the men loading the vehicles.

Diego watched them approach and murmured something to Ty, who turned slowly to face Kate and her cowboys.

His gaze swept down to the gun her hand rested beside before coming back up to meet hers. "Something wrong, Kate?"

"Your hand," she said, keeping her voice dead even. "You healed really fast."

He nodded slowly. "I've got a great metabolism. The only problem is it needs blood to fuel it."

Shep sucked in a breath. "Vampires."

Kate felt as though the ground buckled beneath her feet. "What? They're real?" Then she remembered the pricking sensation she'd felt the previous night when Ty had gone down on her. She stared at him for a long hard moment. "You said you'd never take what wasn't offered," she said, hating how hoarse her voice sounded.

Ty's jaw flexed, but he didn't respond.

"Nothing's changed, Kate McKinnon," Diego said. "We're not the bad guys. You are still under siege. We've come to help."

"For what price? Our blood?"

"Only if it is offered," he said, the Spanish inflections in his voice more apparent as he enunciated each word precisely.

Kate snorted and gave both Diego and Ty a disbelieving glare.

"Does this mean we're not going?" One of the women said, her arms filled with pillowcases of clothing.

"Ma'am, you'd best get back inside the house," Sam said, never taking his gaze off Ty and Diego.

Ty reached toward Kate. "We need to talk."

She drew her gun in a blur of motion. With her thumb, she clicked off the safety. "Don't ever come near me, again. I want you gone."

Ty started to step forward, but Diego's hand landed on his shoulder. "Not now, Ty. The children are frightened."

Sure enough, several sets of round-eyed stares peeked around the corner of the truck.

Just as Kate was about to ask Sam what they ought to do next, the radio clipped to Sam's shoulder squawked, "Sam, we've got another break along the southwest fence!" Danny said, his voice shaking with excitement. "And it looks like we have a whole goddamn pack headin' toward the herd."

"We gotta saddle up," Sam shouted to the men running from the barn. To Ty and Diego, he said, "This ain't over. Kate, you comin'?"

"Damn straight!"

"That's bullshit, Kate!" Ty shouted, his fists curling at his sides. "Let me and my men handle it. We're better equipped."

"My men are out there. I'm not sitting on my thumbs."

Ty glared at Sam. "You gonna let her ride into danger, again? Let me do this."

Sam gave Kate a quick questioning glance. At her nod, he tilted his head. "Have at it, soldier boy."

Ty blew a loud whistle between his teeth, and his men came running. In minutes, the Hummers were filled with his men, one standing in the gun turret mounted atop each vehicle.

Kate watched their trail of dust for a moment and then gave Sam a narrowed-eyed look. "You just gonna stand by and let those wolves eat their way through your herd?"

Sam's lips curled upward at the corners. Over his shoulder he shouted, "Saddle up, boys."

In minutes, Kate was spurring Lucy Lu across the wide open fields, heading to the wooded southeast corner of Sanctuary with Sam, Danny and his dogs, and two more hands at her sides. This was something she understood, something she was good at—the hunt stirred her blood and filled her thoughts so she didn't have to think about Ty and his "Band of Bloodsuckers".

Ahead, they heard the rapid bursts of automatic weapons firing in the distance.

At the edge of the woods, Kate reined in and looked to Sam. "They're going to drive the wolves towards us and into the brush, unless we can force them back their way."

Sam nodded. "Danny, send out the dogs."

Danny pointed into the tangle of brush and trees, and the dogs took off, whining and growling as they began to hunt. The cowboys separated, putting ten foot of distance between them to cover more ground.

Kate urged Lucy Lu to follow, ducking beneath low branches but following at a fast clip, keeping the sounds of the dogs just ahead of her. This deep in the brush, they'd not cross paths with the vampires in their vehicles. Perhaps, they could chase the wolves from the brush into their path and let the soldier-boys take it the rest of the way. They seemed so eager to prove they were there to help.

Kate and her horse entered a clearing, and she pulled back on the reins. Lucy Lu's ears were pricking back, and her flanks quivered with her fear.

The dogs suddenly sounded louder, and that was when Kate heard deeper growls and saw blurs of gray fur as wolves burst from the brush and leaped into the air toward her horse.

"Sam!" she shouted, slipping her boots free of her stirrups when Lucy Lu started to go down. She kicked away from her horse, firing her pistol at the beasts as she fell back to the ground.

Wolves snapped at Lucy Lu whose high pitched whinnies tore at Kate's heart, but she had her own problems. She scrambled to her feet while two wolves circled her, tightening the circumference with each turn.

She had three silver bullets left before she'd need to reload. Each shot had to count or she was dog meat.

Danny's dogs hurtled into the clearing, biting at the flanks of the wolves savaging her horse but never letting the beasts' muzzles near their own hides.

"Kate, hold on!" Sam shouted from astride his bay as he rode in with his gun drawn.

Kate couldn't take her eyes off the wolves closing in on her. If they'd only pause a moment or move in a way she could predict where they'd be the next instant, she could risk a shot. But she stood, turning in slow circles, her gun pointing outward but close to her body so they couldn't knock it away.

Her heart raced, and her breaths shivered as she clamped down on the fear that threatened to seize her muscles. She needed to remain steady, sure — needed like she never had before to hit every target.

One bite and she was a dead woman. If the wolves didn't kill her, one of her men would have to — those were the rules.

She'd shed buckets of tears over her father's death, but she'd understood why he'd stuck his pistol in his mouth and pulled the trigger. He'd done it to save her. She'd demand no less of herself.

Danny broke into the clearing and took aim at the wolves covering Lucy Lu.

"Kate, I'm going to try a shot. Don't move too sudden," Sam said, sliding from his saddle. He raised his weapon and sighted down his barrel.

But Kate had to turn to keep both wolves in sight. Suddenly, one lunged inside the circle, and she jerked off a shot, missing the cur who quickly returned to circling her, its fur raised in hackles on its back and its fangs bared.

Devils! Hell's spawn! She hated and feared these creatures. And she didn't care that most of them hadn't entered their present state willingly — they earned demon's souls the first time they turned their appetites toward a human.

"Dammit, I can't get off a shot. I'll hit you," Sam said, his voice tight with fury.

"Take it, Sam. Better a bullet than a bite. Do it," she commanded.

A gunshot rang out; dust lifted as it burrowed in the dirt at her feet. As if the shot was their signal, one wolf turned to Sam, and the one remaining faced off with Kate.

She stared it in the eye, knowing even if she could get off a shot, it would be too late. At that moment of clarity, she pulled back her trigger.

The beast leaped, the shot hitting it dead center in the chest, but his momentum set him on a path to take her down.

She braced herself, but a movement crossed the edge of her vision—a blur so fast, she couldn't understand what she was seeing.

Something knocked the wolf aside.

When it rested on top of the wolf, holding it down as the silver worked its poison through the beast, Kate blinked and found Ty braced over it, his chest heaving and his arms bulging with effort.

Kate swayed on her feet and caught herself before she crumpled. A quick glance around the site and she saw more soldiers spilling into the clearing, blasting the last of the wolves into oblivion.

Sam stared at her, his arm dangling by his side with his weapon pointing toward the ground. He drew a deep breath. "You all right?"

Kate nodded and swept her gaze from head to toe over him. "You?"

"Not a scratch." His lips curved upward. "Damn, but that was close."

Relieved they'd both been spared a bullet that day, Kate settled her gun into her holster and turned back to her horse, lying in an ever growing puddle of blood. Lucy Lu's sides billowed.

As she came around to the horse's head, Kate saw the deep gashes beneath her throat.

Her horse was dying.

Kate dropped to her knees beside her old friend and smoothed her hand over her muzzle, not caring that tears tracked down her cheeks. She knew what had to be done, but she couldn't let go.

Her daddy had helped her train the horse, spending endless hours watching them ride in circles around the corral. She leaned close and kissed her and looked into her wild, brown eyes. Then she drew her gun from its holster.

"Baby, let me do it," Ty said, kneeling beside her.

She gave a savage shake of her head and leaned back to place the muzzle of the weapon to Lucy Lu's head. The shot dulled Lucy Lu's eyes in an instant, and Kate dropped the gun in the dirt.

Strong arms closed around her, and she turned to snuggle her face in the corner of Ty's shoulder. Sobs tore from her throat, tears flowing to wet his t-shirt, but he held her as they knelt in the dirt, crooning nonsense into her ear and rubbing her shoulders and back.

"Kate."

Sam's voice broke through her pain-filled haze, and she drew back to look over her shoulder.

"Look at his face, sweetheart."

Kate lifted her gaze to Ty's face and gasped. His handsome features were a gruesome mask—heavy, protruding brows, fangs curving over his bottom lip. Even his dark eyes were changed—narrow, vertical slits against gold disks. A monster held her inside the circle of his arms.

That he hadn't traded his mask for his human face told her something—either he was still too caught up in the moment, too angry to remember...or he wanted her to see the real him.

The longer he held her stare, his chest barely lifting with his shallow breaths, the surer she became it was the latter. She lifted her hand and traced the shape of his heavy, hooded brow. "You aren't ruled by the demon inside you. Not like them. I understand now," she said quietly.

The bony mask melted, reshaping into his strong, sharp-edged features. "I'll understand if you can't accept that part of me. I'll still take you and yours to safety."

Her hand crept from his shoulder to his nape, and she grasped his hair to pull him closer. With her lips a breath away from his, she said, "I'll take all of you, Ty."

* * *

For Ty, her kiss felt like absolution—a purifying burst of heat that cleansed his soul. He wrapped his arms around her and slanted his face to deepen the kiss. When they came up for air, he realized they were still sitting in the dirt beside her dead horse.

He pressed her face to his shoulder. "Don't look. I'm going to take you back home."

A trembling shook her slender frame, and she ducked her head. "Sorry, I'm such a wimp. I always feel like this afterwards."

He shared a smile with Diego. His aftermaths usually involved breaking something. Tears, he'd learn to handle. "It's okay," he said and kissed her hair. "You can lean on me." He started back down the trail to his Hummer, but Sam Culpepper stepped into his path.

Sam's gaze fell to Kate snuggled against his chest, and his jaw tightened.

Ty gave him a moment to accept her choice and then stepped forward, forcing the other man to make up his mind quick how he wanted to handle it.

Sam stepped back and turned away. "Gather the horses, men. Let's ride back to the house."

* * *

Kate hefted her suitcase onto the rear of the transport, surprised when hands reached around her to help her. "I can manage this myself, Ty."

"I know. I want to help."

She let go of the case and stepped away, turning for a final glance at the ranch house.

Sam stood on the porch with Shep and Danny beside him. They'd already said their goodbyes, and she was through crying. She gave them a little wave and headed toward the Hummer at the lead of the caravan.

"You know," she said over her shoulder, "I'm not going to let you fight all my battles."

"I had a suspicion you'd be stubborn," he said, his voice a sexy rumble, closer behind her than she'd thought.

Her mouth stretched into a grin. Their easy banter helped. As she'd packed a few precious photos, the clothes she'd need, and loaded the few horses she knew she'd want to bring along, she realized that while she'd miss her home, excitement stirred inside her.

While Ty stowed her daddy's gun beneath the seat, she glanced around her one last time. "I love you, daddy. Watch over Sam," she whispered.

With Ty's hand at her elbow, she climbed into the passenger seat and faced forward—toward new life. One she was finally ready to embrace.

Dark Heat

Leigh Wyndfield

Leigh Wyndfield

Chapter One

The blood-red, heavy velvet on the walls made the massive throne room seem stifling. The bold, swirling pattern on the hard tile beneath her knees bit into her skin through her healer's robes, adding to her urge to leap to her feet and run. But it was the man Caelan prostrated herself before who had all her attention, even as she tried not to stare at him, fearful of drawing his notice.

No matter what the consequences were, she couldn't lie. She could, however, evade the question with other truths. What mattered were the words that left her mouth. This gift, which had saved lives in the past, now led her into a situation where her own was in jeopardy.

Whatever she said, she would either betray her only friend or enrage her King.

Caelan bowed her head deeper, hoping to delay the inevitable, knowing King Useph wouldn't hesitate to crush her if he suspected even a fraction of how much she really knew.

To her left, Brianna sobbed silently, her body shaking, blood sliding down her cheek, along her chin to puddle on the skirt of her golden angel's gown. During her beating, her kind blue eyes had filled with anger and a stubbornness Caelan would never have guessed possible in her sweet, gentle-natured friend. As delicately beautiful as Brianna was, as fragile as she appeared, even after they'd terrorized her, she had lied.

"You dare to defy me. <u>Me</u>, your King!" Useph had been their friend long ago. The three of them, all related through the vagaries of noble birth, had grown up in this castle together, running wild, playing in the gardens and laughing together. In the five years since he'd ascended to the throne, he'd turned from a lost, gentle boy into a power hungry ruler Caelan didn't even recognize, crushing anyone who got in his way.

Righteous anger marred his handsome face, but it was the fisting hand on the arm of his throne chair that had everyone in the room flinching.

His calculating gaze swooped down on her. "But you, Caelan, you cannot lie." His voice turned knowing, dripping like honey, his eyes full of satisfaction.

No, she couldn't lie. Falsehoods of any kind eroded her ability to heal. There was a reason her magic was called Speaking. She healed with words, a gift bestowed by the Goddess at her birth. If she lied, her words lost their power. So she would not lie. But that didn't mean she had to tell the complete truth either. "Please, Sire, I have never seen Brianna with him."

And that was true. She'd never actually seen them but knew without a doubt that they'd been together. Brianna had told her they'd spent the last month lying in sunbeams and laughing. And Radley's face, as Caelan shoved him aboard a ship to safety that had left port only hours before Useph had them dragged to the throne room, had been filled with grief only a lovesick fool could experience. They'd been playing with their very *lives* and they'd known it, yet they'd fallen in love anyway. And their foolish behavior now involved Caelan, putting her in a position where she risked her healing power.

He's on the edge, Caelan. Keep your head down, your voice respectful. Don't anger him, or he'll lash out at you with more than a fist to your face. You just need to make it through this interview unscathed. He won't kill Brianna. He loves her; he always has.

Useph settled back into the plush, red silk of his ornate throne chair, stretching his legs out in a deceptively lazy action. "You have never seen them together. How carefully worded, Caelan." He tsked. "So *close* to a lie."

Caelan reeled in her temper. She could not, *not*, treat him with anything but the utmost respect, or he'd go into one of his rages. He'd be sorry later, but if he killed her, the damage would be done. "Carefully worded or not,

Cousin, I am telling the truth."

"If you are so insistent on hiding Brianna's secrets, perhaps you would like to take her punishment as well. Cousin." He spat the last word, obviously displeased that she'd called attention to their family connection. Leaning forward, he stared at Brianna while drumming ring-laden fingers on his knee. "Would you let your best friend take your punishment to protect your lover?"

Brianna pulled her chin up, her eyes briefly begging Caelan's forgiveness, then her face turned hard. "I am not Radley's lover, my King, so I cannot tell you where he has gone."

Radley, a common soldier, a farmer's son. And the love of Brianna's life.

In the shadows behind the throne, Useph's advisor, Sneed, snorted in disbelief.

Brianna glared at Sneed with a contempt they all might feel, but no one dared to express. "If you punish Caelan because of your incorrect suspicions, her blood is on your hands, not mine."

Caelan barely stifled her moan. Had Brianna's love for Radley turned her insane? Was she mad? She must be to bait Useph like this.

Only by denying it and sticking to her denial can she save Radley's life. Useph had promised her lover's death, but Radley had disappeared. Their King knew Radley could not have escaped the castle unless someone aided him. The magical locks surrounding the area Brianna had been seen in could only be opened by those who had been blessed in ritual.

Only one person could tell him what he needed to know, and Caelan knew it would take luck she'd never had to keep that knowledge to herself.

She just wished Brianna hadn't fallen in love in the first place. No man was worth risking your life for under any circumstances. Why did first her mother and now Brianna have to make that mistake?

Useph lunged to his feet. "Don't you *dare* talk to me like that!" In two steps, he was before Brianna, the crack of his open palm on her face ringing through the room.

Caelan kept her head bowed, trying not to flinch. Her heart ached for her friend, but she didn't want to be caught in the middle of this battle. She was a peacemaker and had never been one to flaunt the rules or engage in confrontation. Her only mistake had been to help a friend in need.

In a moment of panic, she'd let Radley out of the castle and bargained with a boatmaster to secure him a space on a schooner setting sail for the New Worlds. Caelan had broken the rule she'd lived her life by, and now the consequences could be deadly.

"Your chaste body was intended for a marriage alliance and well you knew it, Brianna. Yet you sullied yourself like a whore with a farmer's son." Useph trailed a gentle finger down her face, shaking his head as if he was saddened by her behavior.

But Caelan had long suspected that the King had put off marrying Brianna because he wanted her for himself.

"Did you think that my love for you would keep you from feeling my wrath? Did you think you could do whatever you wanted because I've always wanted you?" His hand snarled in her hair, viciously yanking downward until Brianna fell to her knees before him. "I will kill your lover when I find him. You let him out of the keep, Bree. You helped him escape," he murmured so softly that Caelan could barely hear the words from where she knelt.

"No," Brianna moaned, and Caelan could tell from the agony on her face that she'd finally broken. Tears and blood ran down her face, mixing into a pink rain. Her body shook uncontrollably with fear. "I didn't let him out. I didn't unlock the door."

Caelan dropped her head into her hands. *She's scared. She's thinking about the time we saw the King beat one of his commanders.* The beating had gone on and on, until it was too much to endure. The sound of Useph's fists, then the whip Sneed had so helpfully provided, the spray of blood, the never ending cries the commander had uttered, pinned upright by his arms between two of his own soldiers. Until his face had turned to just a slab of meat with little specks of bone poking through. He'd lived—Caelan had been able to save him—but the ruined shreds of his face still made her stomach clench a year later.

And all that had only been over an order not being followed with enough speed. The commander's sin was not nearly as monumental as Brianna ruining a potential marriage alliance that would bring untold wealth and power to their country.

"If you didn't let him out, who did, Bree?" A stolen glance at Useph showed his long brown hair had shaken free from its queue by the force of his words.

"No—no one."

"She lies," Sneed scoffed. "Radley can't let himself out. He hasn't gone through the Keep Ritual."

"So who helped you, Bree?"

Brianna whimpered, crumpling in on herself.

"Shhh," Useph whispered. "Calm yourself." He dropped to his knees and cuddled her close, rocking her a little. "I need to know where he's hiding, Bree. Once I kill him, everything will be all right again." He pulled back to cluck her under the chin. "Just tell me where he's gone."

"I don't know. I swear it."

"She knows," Sneed snarled, pointing a gnarled finger at Brianna.

"I don't think she does, Sneed. I don't think she knows where he's gone." Curling a lazy finger around one of Brianna's curls, he stared off in space for a moment while Bree sobbed great tears of pain and hopelessness.

Standing abruptly, Useph dumped her on the floor and turned in half time. "Who knows all her secrets, Sneed?"

"Who, my liege?" Sneed asked promptly, ever there to

play the lackey.

"Why, her best friend and constant companion, of course. And to make things even more convenient, the only person in this whole castle who cannot lie." He crossed the room and stopped so close Caelan could see small drops of Brianna's blood on his otherwise perfect leather shoes. Feathering a finger along her cheek, he whispered, "And you will tell, Cousin. You will tell me where Brianna's lover is hiding."

The turn of events had Caelan gasping for breath. Nausea welled up, her stomach, twisting so sharply she would have burst into tears and huddled in a ball on the floor if she didn't think that would anger Useph more.

Instead she closed her eyes, trying to form the prayer that might call the Goddess. She didn't expect to be answered. Her deity was always so close when she healed, but in other parts of her life, the Goddess had gone silent.

Behind her closed lids, Brianna's shining face greeted her. "I love him, Caelan," she'd whispered months ago, sharing her precious secret, unable to contain her joy. "He's so gentle and sweet. And he loves me in return. He doesn't just want to possess me for my beautiful face, but really loves me, Caelly."

Caelan had tried to warn her, tried so hard to talk some sense into Brianna, but love clouded the air, making reasonable, well-thought-out actions impossible.

"Caelan, I'm waiting for the truth," Useph said, the sharpness of his tone saying he wouldn't wait long. He confirmed it by whispering, "You have until the count of five to tell me, or I'm throwing you into The Abyss."

"Please," she begged. Could she say the words that would lead to Radley's death? Could she live with that on her conscience?

Yet the dungeon below the castle—called The Abyss because people went in but rarely came out—scared her worse than anything. A deep pit carved into natural caves where people could only leave if the jailors hauled them up by ropes tied around their waists. She would be a lamb to the slaughter.

Anger crawled up her body and almost shook free a set of words she could never take back. How dare Brianna put her into this position? For that matter, how dare Useph? She was a healer. She'd just wanted to help when Brianna had come to her in tears and panic with the news they'd been seen.

"One," Useph said gently.

"I am your Speaker, King Useph," she reminded him in desperation. "I'm valuable to your household. Please do not do this to me."

No emotion passed his face at her plea. "Two."

In the background, Sneed sighed. "If you can't control two girls, Useph, how can you control a kingdom?"

"Do you think I won't do this?" Useph fisted his hands in her healer robes and hauled her to her feet. "Three."

"You will. You will. I know you will," Caelan said, rushing to reassure him.

"Tell me, Caelan."

If she told, she would save herself from the torture she knew was coming. But how could she live with herself if her words lead to someone's death?

"Four."

"Oh, Goddess," she whimpered. She couldn't tell, couldn't leave anyone in Useph's hands. She could only refuse and hope Useph came to his senses before his punishment killed her. "I cannot."

"Five." Useph let her go so abruptly she tumbled backwards, falling onto her bottom, pain shooting up her spine. "You leave me no choice. Guards, take her to the dungeon and ask her tomorrow and every day after that if she's ready to tell where he's gone."

Two men grabbed Caelan's arms.

"I'm sorry. I'm so sorry, Caelan!" Brianna sobbed

from where she sat crumpled and broken on the floor.

"So am I, Brianna," she said, right before the doors to the throne room closed behind her, maybe forever.

***

The rope around her waist bit deep as the guards lowered her into the murky darkness of The Abyss. For a moment, everything went black as her eyes struggled to adjust, and all she had to focus on was the overwhelming smell of unwashed bodies and the reek of desperation. Shouts filled the air, the words unintelligible as voices echoed around her. The guards had taken pity on her, tossing in the day's bread before lowering her down, and it sounded as if a battle was being fought below her.

The ground arrived without warning, jarring her body in a sickening jolt. She didn't want to untie herself, but the guards had promised to cut the ropes if she didn't untie them herself. With shaking hands, she undid the knots. Then as fast as she could, she crab-walked back into the shadows, her breath high in her throat as the fear washed over her, not stopping her scramble until her shoulder hit the cave wall.

Around her, the prisoners fought for half-loaves of bread with a fierceness that told her food was scarce.

It took her only a heartbeat to realize she might not survive the night. The dank, slimy darkness was broken only by a series of torches lit at intervals around the main cavern. Numerous bodies filtered through the murk, although a large majority of the prisoners were currently fighting in the middle of the cavern for their rations.

The torchlight danced as a chill wind whipped by, giving her a sharp warning of doom. The series of caves were inescapable. Once a month, the King sent down a patrol to make sure none of the small fissures that supplied ventilation had widened into an escape route.

But ventilated or not, Caelan wanted out. Within ten feet of where she huddled by the wall, a man the size of a troll smashed a smaller prisoner's head against the rock floor, then took the bread from his grasp. Groups chased people into the darkness. Shouts and cries of pain filled the air. A metallic tang of blood wafted past her on the icy breeze.

Twenty-five feet above her head, the grate shut with a clang, locking her in with a finality that drove terror through her veins. She had to survive a day.

A sob of panic tried to climb up her throat, but she tamped it down. She'd stay right here, near the grate, hiding in the shadows. She wouldn't move a muscle. Then tomorrow, she'd tell Useph anything he wanted.

If she was still alive.

"Well, well, well, lookie here," a voice said in the darkness, the words filled with anticipation and excitement that had Caelan's stomach twisting with a new surge of fear. "Fresh meat." She could only see his outline but thought it might have been the small man whose head had been smashed against the ground for his bread.

Using the cave wall for support, she pushed to her feet, her legs wobbling so badly, she almost fell down again.

"Hey, Rolf," the man shouted. "We've got a fresh woman!"

Almost as one, prisoners stopped fighting and turned, the action in slow motion as if they couldn't believe their good fortune.

The men shifted to let a tall, lanky shadow swagger into the torchlight. "Don't worry, boys. All of my followers will get a chance at her." In the dim half-light, Rolf appeared to be the Harbinger of Death, a childhood nightmare come real.

He smiled, a feral show of teeth.

His evil grin broke something inside her, goading her into a panicked dash, like a baby bunny before a rabid wolf. She ran from him, without thought, without planning, just an instinctive sprint for her life away from the thing which terrified her.

Fast as her shaking legs could take her, bounding over the uneven ground, pumping her arms for more speed.

She realized immediately she'd made a mistake but didn't stop. Couldn't now. Men who hadn't yet seen her swarmed in pursuit, her flight drawing their notice. Worse, she was in their territory, completely lost in the murky gloom.

She'd heard whispers when she was a child of drop offs where a prisoner would fall forever. One glance over her shoulder had her wishing for death. She had a trail of fifteen men behind her, their faces twisted in the dim light.

Run, Caelan. Run. Falling down a pit forever would be better than what they have in store for you.

She rounded a corner at a speed she'd never achieved in her life.

And ran straight into a dead end.

Spinning to face her death, she backed into the wall, only the sound of her own harsh breathing filling her ears.

It was darker here, the air a gray sludge, the room filled with frightening shadows.

The men formed a half circle but for some reason held off from bringing her down. She had no idea why they hesitated but tried to calm her chugging breath enough to think.

"Come here, girlie," Rolf coaxed in a parody of a gentle singsong. "I promise you'd rather be with us than him."

Him who, she wondered, inching along the wall to put a large rock between them. It wouldn't give her much protection, but she was out of options. *Fight for once, Caelan. If you're going to die anyway, die with blood on your hands and a snarl on your lips. What has being the peacemaker ever bought you anyway?*

"There he is," someone hissed and as one, the group shifted back a step.

Caelan tried to figure out who they were talking about, but she was alone on this side of the cavern. She had to put herself behind the slight safety of the waist high rock. The wall dipped behind it, folding in on itself, giving her a place where she'd be surrounded by stone on three sides.

Sliding into the crevice, she kept herself facing the men, feeling for the wall behind her with her hand.

Except she didn't feel a wall anymore. She felt the strong planes of a man's tight, flat stomach. He towered over her, his body a massive presence, making the man who looked like a troll earlier seem small now. Whoever stood at her back was a giant among men, certainly much bigger than her own five feet, three inches.

A strange premonition blew through her, a tingling running along her skin, her breath hitching in her throat.

Once, when she was a small child, the cook had told her a story about a young man who made a deal with an evil spirit to save himself from death.

Caelan knew in that moment that she'd only live to see tomorrow if she could convince the giant at her back to save her. Her pursuers were clearly scared of him. He might end up being a monster, but there was only one of him and fifteen of them.

But what could she use to pay for his protection? She only had her healing skills and her body to offer, and she doubted he was injured. Well, she'd been married, her arranged husband dying in one of Useph's endless wars soon after they'd wed. Her body had felt the weight of a man before, and while she found the act unpleasant, she wouldn't die from having sex.

Girding herself, she kept her eyes on the half circle of men and whispered, "My name is Caelan, and I'll trade you anything you want for your protection."

Chapter Two

Garron inhaled the woman, closing his eyes as he enjoyed the scents of freedom. She smelled of herbs and fresh air, just washed clothes, and petal-soft skin. His whole body tightened so sharply, he could barely focus on the swarm of Rolf's band of thieves and cut-throats.

"What could you possibly have to trade me that I would want, Caelan?" Her name rolled off his tongue, his fingers itching to see if she felt as wonderful as she smelled.

Part of him kept an eye on the men before them. Rolf ran the dungeons, but he hadn't challenged Garron since their skirmish a week ago. Garron still had an open knife slash that wouldn't heal, a memento from Rolf's blade. The wound had become infected, red streaks running up and down his thigh, but there wasn't anything he could do about it here in this hellish pit.

"I am a Speaker," she whispered. "I could heal for you."

Did Speakers sense an injured man's wounds? He didn't think so, but otherwise why would she offer to heal him? Then he realized her voice had been more hopeful than sure.

She still hadn't turned to face him, and he wondered what face went with the low alto voice that had shivers racing along his body.

So she didn't just smell good but was smart as well, somehow figuring out that he was the lesser of the two evils without even seeing him in the light. Garron's very name meant protector, not that he'd been anyone's guardian since Sneed had thrown him into The Abyss.

Unable to resist, he feathered his finger along her neck, the gentle contact drawing a shiver from her in response. She was as soft as she smelled, and he wanted her.

What was he thinking? He'd almost tunneled out of the caverns. The last thing he needed was a woman slowing him down or distracting him. He had three nights before Mabon. Three precious nights before he died.

"I don't need healing." That wasn't a lie. The moment he touched her skin, his brain had stuttered to a stop. He needed her, not healing.

One thing was for certain, he wouldn't let her end up in Rolf's slimy hands. Rolf was a sadist. No, best that he keep her close to him. He'd just make sure she didn't risk his escape.

"Then the only thing I have left to offer is my body," she said the words with force, her chin tipping up in defiance, sending a fireball of desire shooting through his veins.

Shocking himself, Garron heard himself reply, "We have a bargain then." His hand curled itself around her stomach on its own accord. He enjoyed the brush of the soft cotton of her dress, even as his mind decried his actions. He wasn't going to take any woman this way. She was desperate and offered him sex only as a way to live. He wouldn't be a Protector if he took advantage of her like this.

Maybe it was time for him to just accept that Garron the Protector was gone forever. The fact was, he wasn't the same man he'd been six months ago when Sneed had tossed him into The Abyss without a trial, without even a hearing.

He'd killed people and would kill more to save himself. In fact, he would have killed Sneed if a routine guard patrol hadn't been running a few critical moments early. Garron the Protector had been replaced by this man who was bending down to run his tongue along a desperate woman's neck.

The flavor of herbs and healing exploded into his mouth, wrenching a moan of pure lust from his lips.

As much as he wanted to stop, he knew he wouldn't

give the little healer up. No, he rationalized, if he left her unprotected, she'd last only moments before Rolf and his men had her under them. Better him than someone who might very well kill her.

"My protection for your body." Tilting her head back and to the side, he leaned over her shoulder to rest his lips against hers, the chaste kiss so erotic, he felt a growl building inside his chest. Unable to stop himself, he had to tell her exactly what would be between them. "For every day you are here, you will lie below me, screaming in pleasure while I bring you over and over again," he whispered, pulling her back into his hard cock, accepting this as the sign that he'd finally lost his humanity... and possibly his mind.

***

Caelan closed her eyes and participated in the kiss that sealed the bargain between them. It wasn't unpleasant, gentle for all the crassness of their bargain. His lips were soft compared to the rock hard muscles in his body, which circled around her in a protective shield.

When she'd married Zant, she hadn't known him well, only seeing him from a distance during castle celebrations. Zant was good-looking and cruel, enjoying the spoils of his position as one of Useph's right hand men. He'd been a rough and brief lover, preferring to spend as little time on the act as possible. He'd never kissed her like this, not once.

The arm at her waist tightened to bring her buttocks against his large, hard erection. She curled trembling hands around his rough, scarred fingers, trying to shake free from the daze that had settled over her. If it was from the terror or her position, or the odd hum of need swimming inside her, she didn't know.

It's only for one night. Tomorrow, you'll tell Useph everything he wants to know. You can do anything you have to do to last the next few hours.

His lips ate at her mouth, sending her head spinning

as she turned into his arms to better receive his kiss, the scent of powerful man swirling around her. Zant had been powerful, too, one of the top men in Useph's army, but there was something about this man that was different. A swirl of magic touched her skin, coming from inside him.

And then she knew. He carried the gift of Battle Shout, a power similar to Speaking except it rendered the other soldiers on the battlefield temporarily disoriented and terror-filled, ensuring victory for the Shouter.

She'd once been close to a man who carried it and had felt an odd attraction of her ability to his, the twist in her belly matching the twist she felt now, except it hadn't been this intense. Speaking healing words was, some said, the other half of the same power as Battle Shout. Two sides of the same coin. The ability to terrify and the ability to heal.

"Damn you, Garron! We saw her first!" Rolf snarled, bringing Caelan back to reality with a smack. Somehow she'd forgotten her pursuers, forgotten everything but the man kissing her.

She tried to move her head away from the kiss, but Garron pinned her with his other hand.

"Follow my lead," he whispered into her mouth.

Nodding once, she grasped his arm for balance, pressing into his body for support.

"If you want her, Rolf, come get her." Garron's voice came out as a dangerous hum that raced over Caelan in a physical swipe. Magic twirled through the words, reinforcing her suspicions that he had power.

Rolf took one step forward and then hesitated. "There are fifteen of us and one of you. We can take you down easily, and this time I'm not letting you live to challenge me again."

A low growl began in the center of Garron's body, and instinctively Caelan knew this was how he called his magic. Instead of driving her away, it made her cling tighter.

"Goddess," she whispered, her own healing power

169

pooling in the pit of her belly, the slide like a fresh mountain stream through her veins, coming more easily than it ever had before.

Garron's growl turned into a purr. His lips landed on hers, and without understanding why she did it, Caelan pushed her power into him. Zant had once told her kissing her was unnatural, the magic that shimmered below her surface repulsing him. Garron didn't pull away. Instead he drank deeply, accepting her as no one had ever done before, the low growl coming out as a sound of need.

Then he ripped his lips from hers and spun her behind him, leaving her disoriented and weak.

"Come fight me, Rolf!" he roared, the lash of his words ripping through Caelan's body like the slash of knives, wrenching a whimper from her throat. She covered her ears with her hands, trying to keep her eyes on her enemies. Above the pain, she felt the need to fight, to rend and tear and triumph, something so foreign to her, it left her breathless.

Rolf staggered back, gripping his chest as if he'd truly been slashed. The men at his back screamed in terror and scattered, one running the wrong direction straight into the cave wall.

Caelan knew being behind Garron had saved her from the worst of the pain. She buried her face into his back and gripped his tattered shirt in both hands, holding onto the only thing that could save her in her reeling world.

"This isn't over, Garron," Rolf snarled.

"We can end it now," Garron said, the words spoken in a dangerous murmur that echoed through Caelan's body.

"I'm not going to attack you here. Oh no. I'll kill you when you least expect it." Rolf's voice faded as he backed from the cavern. "Never stop looking over your shoulder, Garron. You never know when I'll be there."

Goddess of All Things, please save me from this place. I swear I will spend my life in worship of You if You keep me alive until tomorrow.

As usual, only silence greeted her prayers. The Goddess had long ago stopped speaking to her as She once had — before Caelan's mother had disgraced them all.

Caelan had once thought she'd become a member of the Temple, leading a quiet life of reflection and communion with the Goddess, but when she'd turned thirteen, her mother's sin had caused the Goddess to go silent, taking from Caelan all but her power to heal. Gone were her visions of the past and future. Even her ability to know if people lied had vanished.

For a brief moment, Caelan wondered if giving Garron her healing power to use in battle had been a perversion, but then she discarded the thought. If the Goddess didn't want Caelan using her ability in that way, why would She allow the exchange to happen?

"He's gone," Garron said, stepping away so fast, Caelan stumbled. "Follow me."

Dropping onto his hands and knees, he crawled through an opening she hadn't even noticed nestled in the depression in the wall.

Caelan swallowed past the hard lump of fear lodged in her throat, wondering how her whole life had turned upside down. Just yesterday, she'd been tending her herb garden and seeing a steady stream of sick from the village surrounding the castle. Now she stood in the gray darkness, having given her word to sleep with a man to save her life, while the chill air whistled by her in evil amusement.

Somewhere behind her, a prisoner screamed in agony, a long wail that bounced along the walls and raked claws of fear into her spine.

Caelan dropped to her hands and knees, scrambling down a short, sloping passageway, only to pitch face first into a small cavern.

Her hands had barely touched the floor before Garron caught her. "Watch the drop," he growled.

Instead of her usual reaction of fear, Caelan felt something else swirl inside her. It was as if all her fear had been used up, leaving her with only rage and anger. "How can I watch the drop if I don't even know it's there?"

Surprisingly, he didn't flinch at her sharp tone.

Setting her on her feet, he placed his hands on either side of the rock wall behind her and leaned in until she could almost feel his nose touching hers. "You can stay here for as long as you fulfill your end of the bargain, but you'll live by my rules and take my orders."

She glanced around her. Here turned out to be a five feet round uneven circle of a space that stretched up enough to give them room to stand, two small holes in the ceiling filtering in a dim light.

"I'm not sure that was part of our deal." She studied the layout with deliberate slowness, scanning the room around him just to be difficult. On one level, it puzzled her. She'd always done whatever it had taken to smooth over and pacify people. Yet here she stood baiting the tiger, and it felt so very good. A strange euphoria washed over her, the feeling as addictive as it was insane.

"I never agreed to follow your orders," she said, letting her voice drop low into a sultry whisper. She always followed the rules, and she'd never purposely tried to interest a man, but something drove her to do both now. What had gotten into her? The large power gift she'd given Garron must have made her reckless.

He smiled, the action more felt than seen in the murky darkness. Rolling his head down in a deceptively slow motion, his lips brushed her ear. "You'll follow them or spend your time with me tied up, only let loose when I want your body."

His threat rang hollow, even though she had no idea why it should. He was a warrior, ready to kill her attackers without a pause, but she didn't believe for a moment he'd hurt her. "If you want this body to come to you willing and ready, then you'd better watch your step, Shouter. You're not the only person with magic here."

"No, I'm not." He feathered his lips up her neck, a slow exploration. "Your power tastes like honey on my tongue."

She tipped her head back so he could nibble his way along her jaw line, unable to stop herself, unable to stop him, unable to calm the growing need inside herself. In a moment of complete clarity, she knew she didn't *want* to stop it. For the first time in her life, she felt as if she could do whatever she wanted, be whoever she wanted to be. After all, in the light of day, they wouldn't even recognize each other, and tomorrow she'd be gone.

Scared little Caelan suddenly wasn't scared any more. What had he said to her? *"My protection for your body. For every day you are here, you will lie below me, screaming in pleasure while I bring you over and over again."* She planned to hold him to every word.

A voice in the back of her mind pointed out that she'd never had pleasure from a man before, wouldn't even know how to receive it. She told the voice to be quiet and slipped her hands under his shirt to feel his skin. It was warm and smooth, silk over iron. "You promised me pleasure in return for pleasure. Give it to me, and we'll talk about your rules."

"Mmmm…" He nipped her neck, the pain quickly turning into sharp desire. "I promise you'll be more than satisfied."

Standing on her tiptoes, she bit him back, hard, on his shoulder, marking him without breaking the skin. "I'll be the judge of my own pleasure."

"You want this rough, Caelan?" he growled, spinning her into the wall, his body following hers to pin her against the coarse rock. He was hard and ready, calling her bluff. "Do you?"

Fear twisted with the desire flooding her body, turning into a heady brew. Did she? Did she want him to be rough with her? She would never in a million years think she would, but the thought had her panting in need.

"Do you?" he whispered, a tingling puff of breath on her ear.

"No," she gasped, but part of her thought maybe she was a liar.

"Then I'll be gentle." He released her immediately, stepping away, leaving her feeling as if she just missed something that she might regret for the rest of her life. After all, she only had until morning, and she'd be gone.

"May I unbutton your dress?" In a flash, the aggression was gone, the purr in his voice returning.

"Yes." She realized she was still pressed against the wall, her body wanting his so badly, she couldn't seem to gather the energy to turn to him.

At her back, gentle hands slid buttons from their eyes, the action so slow and methodical, she had to stretch to release some of the tension. The motion screamed of her need, but she was too far gone to stop it. *It has to be the magic, his power matching mine. That can be the only explanation for this.*

When he had enough buttons undone, he pushed the fabric of her dress off her shoulders to pool around her waist and ran powerful hands in a long stroke down her bare back. His shirt rustled as he shrugged out of it, then his naked chest pressed against her skin, dragging a whimper from her.

"Oh yes. Perfect. I knew you were perfect the first time you touched me." His voice lapped against her naked skin, edgy and rough.

The words swirled inside her, lifting her higher, filling her with confidence the likes of which she'd never had before. This man, unlike any other man she'd ever met, wanted her badly. His huge hands shook as he caressed her skin. Maybe it was only the moment, or their power match, or just the surreal situation, but she knew she could do or say or be anyone she'd ever wanted to be here in the darkness.

Turning, she slid the dress all the way to the ground, standing unashamed in the half-light in only her underwear and shoes. "Am I perfect, Garron?"

He drank her in, stepping to the side so the slim light could touch her body. "Oh yes," he said with enough reverence that she believed him.

Her whole life she'd been happy to be a mouse beside Brianna's angelic face, fading into the background, but she wasn't going to be a mouse now. Not when this could be her only chance to be powerful.

Trailing a hand along his naked chest, she circled him. He stood perfectly still, the only motion the opening and closing of his hands as they hung by his side. Energy radiated from his body, as if she'd chained a tiger using spiderwebs, and it was only the tiger who kept himself from eating her alive.

When she stood behind him, she lowered her mouth to taste his skin, feeling as if she were queen and temptress all rolled into one.

Leigh Wyndfield

Chapter Three

Garron felt her lips brush his skin like the lightest kiss of velvet. With discipline he hadn't known he possessed, he let her set the pace, her hands skimming along his arms with hesitant boldness, as if this was the first time she'd been given free rein to explore a man's body. The thought helped him to stand still when he wanted to dominate and consume her.

In the dark half light, he closed his eyes, letting the feel of her open palms against his bare chest tingle through him.

She was small, a full head smaller and then some from him, and little, but he'd tasted her magic and knew she was powerful. And he didn't doubt she'd given him the boost he needed to Battle Shout as he had. He'd been fading since he'd come here, unable to spend the proper time in meditation it took to gather the power he needed to Shout. His soul had been withering and with it, his abilities.

When she circled him into the dim light, he slid the simple ribbon from her hair, spilling rich sable tresses down her back, covering high, firm breasts.

She studied him with a dazed look, as if she fought through a fog to find her sanity.

"Sharing power has made us need," he whispered, knowing he couldn't let her find her reason, or they'd both regret it. Or at least he would. He hadn't realized until this moment how much he'd missed by becoming a Protector.

Always traveling the back roads and shorelines, looking for thieves, cut-throats and pirates. Escorting mail caravans, keeping the peace in border towns. The Protectors functioned as a town sheriff, only over a wider territory. Who would ever want to marry a man who would be gone most of the time? He'd thought it didn't matter, that he didn't need a wife to be happy. But the notion of coming home every night to a woman like this, running his tongue over dusky nipples, feeling her power fill his body, had him reconsidering for the first time.

Dropping to his knees, he circled her ankles with his fingers, then trailed his hands up the side of her body. Over rounded hips, past her tiny waist, skimming his fingertips along her arms, he let himself enjoy the soft skin, making sure he didn't push too far, too fast.

She grabbed his shoulders as if she needed to steady herself, her hands spasming as his palms passed over her buttocks.

He gathered her closer so he could press his lips into her flat belly, licking the taste of woman off her skin to hold inside of him.

She still wore shoes and thin, cotton underwear. Unable to control himself, he nuzzled his face into her sex through the fabric, wringing a gasp of surprise or pleasure from her, he didn't know which.

He'd said he'd bring her pleasure over and over again, and he'd meant it. For some reason he couldn't understand, it was vitally important that when she looked back on their time together, the memory alone would have her shaking in need for him. It made no sense, but it was true.

He could smell her desire, taste her on the air around them. A fine tremor ran through her, bringing him immense satisfaction.

Holding her hips to keep her still, he buried his tongue between the lips of her sex, tasting her immediately through the fabric of her underclothes. Pure woman and lust exploded in his mouth, and, beneath that, her power swirled, teasing him into wanting more.

"Garron," she whimpered, running her hands into his hair.

"Come for me, fast and hard," he hummed into her sex, enjoying her jump of surprise as the echo of his voice teased her clitoris.

Her underwear was soaked through, so wet now, it was as if she stood naked before him. He wanted to give her a relief that would only spin her higher. So he licked her clitoris at a pleasure-bending pace, keeping the pressure hard and fast.

She bowed in his arms, arching into his hands.

Pausing, he stripped her bare, the delicate fabric ripping in his too-strong hands. He didn't care, and she didn't notice.

The moment his tongue touched her naked clitoris, she came, her moan filling the small space and his own body.

He didn't let her recover, climbing to his feet and picking her up easily as she crumpled. "You're not done yet," he informed her as she snuggled into him.

Setting her gently on his sparse bed, he stripped the rest of his clothes and stretched out beside her.

Before she could protest, he had her straddling him. "Ride me."

Confusion passed over her features. "I'm not sure…"

"I am," he said, not caring that he pushed her to a place she obviously hadn't been before. "Hold the base of my cock and work me inside you," he whispered, wanting her to do it on her own, but knowing if she didn't, he'd do whatever he had to do to be inside her.

Things had spiraled out of control, and she wasn't sure how it had happened. Her underclothes were gone, her sex soaking with spent desire, and she straddled a man she'd only met a few minutes ago. A man she'd shared magic with, a man whose mouth had been on her sex, giving her the orgasm she'd only heard about in whispers.

Meeting his intense gaze, she had a moment of doubt. Or clarity. She'd lost her mind when they'd thrown her down here. That had to be it.

He growled, the low noise stirring something inside her, then he reversed their positions, tumbling her below him. "No regrets," he ordered, and in one push, entered her.

Her mind fell away, filled only by the intense pressure inside her. He was huge, all over, and he wasn't stopping. "Garron," she whimpered, trying to back away, but she was pinned against the bed.

"Shhh," he whispered. "You can take me. Relax into it. Want it. We were made to match each other." His voice and power trickled over her, twisting her stomach with need.

Then he hilted, the tip of his cock tight and hard against her womb, the pain a strange kind of pleasure.

He brushed her hair from her face. "There we go. See? I told you we'd fit."

After his earlier command, his slow kiss confused her. He toyed with her lips, nipping and licking, touching his tongue to hers, encouraging her to participate with soft murmurs.

He was still huge inside her, but as they kissed, her body adjusted to him, the pressure turning from the edge of pain into pleasure.

She ran her hands across his short-cropped hair, enjoying the sensation of his scalp against her fingertips while her lips dueled with his.

Without warning, he pulled back and thrust into her, the motion small but sending a maelstrom of desire through her body. Pleasure exploded deep inside her core, had her mindless and arching.

Then it was just his cock and her desire, building, building. Everything else narrowed into this one thing.

"Come," he ordered from somewhere far away, the single word driving her higher.

Then his finger pinned her clitoris as he thrust and release exploded over her, lights sparking behind her tightly closed lids, her body jerking in time to his release.

* * *

He'd passed out, and it took him a long moment of

fighting to come back to the living world. Something had awoken him, he knew, but the hyper-instincts that had never once deserted him were locked away, put to sleep by the most intense sex he'd ever experienced.

Caelan lay half tucked below him, one leg between his, her flat belly beneath one of his hands, her cheek cuddled into shoulder. Her hair wrapped around them both, twining them together like gossamer chains.

"Garron," Danner whispered from the darkness, his voice more nervous than usual.

"I'm here," he murmured, pulling Caelan tighter into him, hoping they didn't wake her.

"Is somebody else here?" Danner's voice quavered, the last word breaking as if he was a boy turning into a man, instead of Garron's age of twenty-six.

Caelan stirred, coming awake below him. She stretched and let out a feminine sigh that was part satisfied woman, part protest.

"Yes." The thought of Danner seeing her naked body had Garron tugging a blanket over her. She curled into him in response.

"Well." Danner came forward in a crouch, his too-thin body shaking with a continuous shudder that never ceased. Garron had found him beaten and bloody the first day he'd arrived in the dungeons. From that time on, he'd protected Danner. In return, Danner procured items that shouldn't even be found in The Abyss. He was a master thief, laying his hands on just about anything they needed to tunnel out.

"I'd heard some whisperings that you'd stolen Rolf's woman." The censure in Danner's voice told how worried he was. He'd never come so close to questioning Garron before.

Caelan's eyes blinked open. "What time is it?" She sat up with a start, staring at the light streaming in from the ceiling, the blanket pooling to her waist. "Morning already? I have to go!"

He rolled her under him as fast as he could. "We have company, love," he warned, then pulled up far enough to slide a finger along the outside of her breast to remind her of her state of undress.

Her mouth formed an O, and she dragged the blanket up as far as the pin of his body allowed.

"Danner, this is Caelan. Caelan, my right hand man, Danner."

"She's not coming with us, is she?" Danner asked, his voice saying he hoped it wasn't true.

Garron studied the woman below him, watching her stare at the dim light filtering in from the ceiling. He'd spent his life making snap decisions. He was good at it, having an instinctive feel for when to trust people and when to be on guard. With her magic humming inside him, he wasn't convinced his thinking was as clear as it should be, but his gut said she belonged with them — with him. He sure as hell wasn't leaving her in the dungeons. The thought of Rolf's hands on her perfect skin made up his mind. "She's coming with us."

"Coming where?" she asked, her gaze meeting his. He wondered what color her eyes were. Something dark, maybe a deep blue.

By saying the words, he'd commit himself to them. He knew that, just as he knew he shouldn't trust her completely. He shouldn't trust anyone. "We're tunneling out."

"What?"

"And you're coming with us."

She shook her head, her eyes widening in panic. "No, no. I'm getting out of here. I have to go to the grate, and they'll haul me up."

"She can't leave, Garron. She knows our plans now!" Danner's panic filled the room. "She can't leave!"

Garron stared at her through narrowed eyes, wondering how someone could leave after only one night in The Abyss. It didn't make sense, yet he could tell she believed it. He couldn't let her go anywhere. Framing her face between his hands, he let his voice drop into a purr. "Hear me, Caelan. You're not going to the grate. You know our secret now."

* * *

Caelan gathered the blanket closer and tried to think, only half watching Garron shimmy into a tight set of breeches, the sight of his naked buttocks sending a spark through her that she ignored.

All her life she'd done the right thing. She'd played by the rules, taking the path of least resistance. But Brianna had embroiled her in something that risked her life and catapulted her from her safe world.

Yesterday she would have betrayed her friend and caused Radley's death. She would have done anything to get out of here. Had, in fact, done something she'd have never considered doing before when she'd traded sex for safety.

Resting her head back against the rough cave wall, she stared at the dim light filtering from two holes in the ceiling.

But Garron had changed all that.

Inside, she felt changed, stronger, more of a woman than she ever had before.

Garron was giving her options. He thought he could force her into going with him, but she was somehow certain that he would never physically hurt her. Whether he knew it or not, when she did things at his order it would only be because she wanted to do them.

The thought was so foreign that on some level, she blinked at herself in surprise, but for all the shock of it, she knew it was true.

In the middle of her intense pleasure last night, something inside had broken free. A piece of her had finally realized that she was more than a healer. She was a woman men would kill each other for, a woman who could make a giant, powerful man fall to his knees and worship her. The confidence that realization inspired left her reeling.

So what was she going to do now? She could make her way back to the grate and beg to be hauled up. If she did, she'd have to reveal where Radley was hidden.

Anger flashed through her. Why had Brianna taken a lover to begin with? Why hadn't she been content with her life and left things alone? Their lives had been destroyed for a man Brianna had only known for a few months.

Caelan had devoted her life to healing people, to preserving life. If telling Useph where Radley had gone would lead to Radley's death, then she couldn't tell.

And now she had options.

Garron prowled the room like a caged beast, a growl vibrating low in his chest. "You aren't leaving."

She studied his body, loving the way it flowed as he walked. As big as he was, he shouldn't have been able to move so gracefully.

"She can't leave, Garron. She'll give us away!" The squirrelly little man in the shadows finally drew Caelan's notice. His hands shook in sharp spasms, the huge cut of his clothes making him appear smaller than he really was. He stood hunched over, as if he tried to shrink into the darkest space.

"I thought it was impossible to break out of The Abyss?" Yet even as she asked the question, she realized Garron was a man who could achieve the impossible. He had the aura about him of someone who could accomplish anything.

"By Mabon, we'll be gone."

Their gazes met, and her stomach twisted with the thought of two more nights with their bodies joined.

She shook her head to clear it of his spell.

What would she do after she tunneled out? She couldn't show up at the front door of the castle and resume her Speaking duties there.

That stopped her for a second. What would she do? What *could* she do?

I'm still a Speaker. I can go to the farthest edges of the kingdom and become a healer in a small town there. How many times have I wished for that kind of obscurity? Stop being so afraid all the time and seize your destiny.

Squaring her shoulders, she made the hardest decision of her life. She wasn't going to take the easy way this time. "If you're tunneling out, I'll go with you."

Garron stopped, dropping his hands on his hips. "You will, will you?"

She nodded. "Yes."

* * *

Danner paused for the tenth time and leaned close to whisper, "I don't like it, Garron. Something's fishy. She didn't even bat an eye when you said we were tunneling our way out."

They'd put Caelan in charge of hauling the rock back into Garron's quarters, where it was rapidly stacking up against one wall. A month before, the hole to the outside was only the size of Garron's fist. Now it was almost wide enough for Danner or Caelan to slip out.

"She said she could get out through the grate if you remember. Why would she stay with us if she could leave?" Danner's hands shook as he wielded a small pick.

Garron had no answer. In fact, the more he dug, the more suspicious he became. She was beautiful. All that petal-soft skin might have clouded his judgment. "Take her place hauling then, and we'll keep her here where I can watch her."

Danner nodded. "Good plan." He slipped away.

If Caelan was a Speaker, she couldn't lie without poisoning her healing talent, just as he could not lie without diminishing his Battle Shout. He should just ask her about her change of heart. *But what if she isn't even a Speaker? What if somehow Sneed planted her here to trap me?*

It would be easy enough to prove if she was a

Speaker. He'd have her heal his leg after they'd finished digging for the day.

You've felt her power, Garron. You know she has it.

Still, to be positive, he'd have her heal him and keep her tight by his side until they escaped.

Chapter Four

Caelan held the bread Danner had given her, wondering how she would get it to her mouth since her hands were shaking like tree leaves in violent winds. Exhaustion crawled over her from first hauling rock, then actually wielding a make-shift pick under Garron's disapproving eye.

He was angry with her about something, although at this point, she didn't care what. Let him be mad. She wasn't in the mood to worry about it. Her stomach tightened with hunger pains so sharp, she almost doubled over with them.

Danner smacked a cup of water by her, his beady eyes squinting with suspicion.

"Thank you," she said, more to annoy him than anything else. She didn't like Danner, no matter how hard she tried. Of course it was hard to like someone who looked at her with suspicion and distrust.

Garron slipped down the tunnel from wherever he'd been and crossed to where she'd dropped by the dirt pile. She'd made it this far, hauling out their last load of rock and couldn't go any further.

"You're a Speaker?" Garron said, his voice coming out hard and tight.

"Yes."

He undid the laces at the top of his breeches.

Caelan blinked in surprise, then she became truly angry, the infusion of emotion giving her a much needed boost of energy. "If you think I'm sleeping with you, you are mistaken," she bit out, controlling herself from slinging her bread in his face. She was hungry. No matter how mad she was, she wouldn't lose her dinner.

He laughed, a harsh sound that carried with it an insult, as if he didn't want her anyway. "I need your healing skills." Then his breeches dropped, and he stepped close.

She could see red streaks of a building infection starting from a long slash on his leg even in the darkness. How she'd missed it the night before, she didn't know. Well, she did know. She'd been distracted by him, not that he'd ever be lucky enough to touch her again after the way he'd treated her all day.

The cut wasn't deep, the slash running along the outside of his thigh the length of her hand. But infection had set in, probably recently or he'd be dead already. She'd feel bad for him, if not for the fact she wanted to kill him herself.

For the first time in her life, she was too angry to heal.

Leaning back against the wall, she craned her neck to see his face. "Infection's eating your leg," she informed him.

"Heal it," he ordered.

"No." She was tired of everyone treating her as if she were a servant. Useph and Sneed and the whole castle never asked, they ordered. Never thanked her. She was sick of it.

"What?"

"I don't follow your orders, Garron." Using both hands, she took a bite of the most tasteless bread she'd ever eaten.

"You're saying you can't heal?" he asked, danger swirling in the low words.

"Of course I can. I'm just not going to heal *you*." She sniffed to make her point, then defeated the bold words by fumbling the bread in her shaking hands.

He dragged his pants to his hips and dropped to one knee before her. "Are you a Speaker?" He underscored the intensity of his voice by grabbing her chin. She would have been afraid if she wasn't so annoyed.

Jerking her head to the side, she narrowed her eyes. "Yes, but I'm not healing you until you apologize for how you've treated me all day."

"What?"

She didn't dignify him with an answer, instead picking up the cup to take a sip of water. The bread had dried her mouth to the point of pain.

Water sloshed over the rim, the action of raising her hand to her mouth too much for her arms.

Garron took the cup from her hands, then pressed it to her lips. "Drink," he said, his tone gruff, but the anger was gone.

She did, ignoring the intimacy of the action. Goddess, she was thirsty. She hadn't known how much until she finally had access to water. In four long gulps, she finished it.

"More?"

She nodded, realizing the shakes were as much from dehydration as anything else.

"Danner," Garron said, not taking his eyes from hers.

The cup was refilled instantly, and he pressed it to her lips, tipping it so she was forced to drink slowly. "Careful not to take too much too soon."

She slowed down immediately. How had she missed her own deterioration? She'd been obsessing about the man before her, that's how. And about the fact she would never be able to go home again if she left the dungeon through the tunnel.

As angry as she was with Brianna, she would miss her. They'd been inseparable since birth. And the villagers needed her. Although the new castle Speaker would heal them.

With the water, her hands calmed enough to allow her to eat without incident. Garron sat next to her with his own meal and silently insisted on balancing her cup. Somewhere during their interaction, Danner had disappeared to wherever it was he went.

Closing her eyes, she leaned back against the wall with a sigh, her earlier anger muted by the simple act of sharing a meal. "How did you hurt your leg?"

"Rolf stabbed me in one of our many skirmishes."

"It's infected."

"Yes."

She rolled her head to stare at him. "Drop your breeches, and let me heal it."

He smiled, the action slow and sensual, as if he was turned on by her request. "Anything for you, love." He climbed to his feet, his actions causing an answering twist of her stomach.

She snorted to break his spell, but her attention fixed on the muscled stomach that appeared when he shrugged out of his shirt. "It's your leg that is hurt," she said, but her voice had dropped an octave, her body shivering with a chill of desire and the need to touch him.

He hadn't bothered to lace his pants earlier, so he only had to push them down, but his hands started higher on his hips, the sweep of his fingers as they traveled down his hips catching her attention like a fish on a hook.

She couldn't have looked away if the castle had been burning above them.

He bent at the waist, slowly shedding his boots and pants then lay on his bed.

She feasted her eyes on him. Why not? He wanted her to look, had begged her to stare at him by disrobing in that manner.

Rising to her feet, she dipped a bowl of water and picked up the cleanest rag from the pile beside the bucket. Then she crossed to him and knelt.

Yes, she was still angry, but why should she stop herself from touching him? That would only be denying what she wanted, and she was done doing that.

First she bathed his wound, cleaning it thoroughly. While the Goddess gave her the ability to heal, the Goddess also gave her a mind, and her mind was constantly looking for ways to improve the healing process. By cleaning wounds before healing, she'd increased her success rate. She'd also begun to use herbs and other recipes she'd picked up from the villagers. If someone didn't believe in the Goddess of All Things, she couldn't heal them with the Goddess's magic. So she'd found another way to help them, enjoying the learning process as she went.

Now it occurred to her that she had the perfect opportunity to explore another method of healing.

When the wound was cleaned, she brushed her fingers down his huge chest, across his abs, skirting his sex, and made her way to his thigh again.

With hands now shaking with desire, she made up her mind to heal him in a way she'd only heard about in whispered conversations between the older healers. The thought lit her on fire inside. Legend said a Speaker could heal using her mouth on a man's body.

And if it didn't work, she could always steal his power as he had stole hers the day before and use it to heal him in the normal fashion.

Meeting his gaze, she debated asking or taking. His eyes burned with the same need that ate her alive inside.

Take, she decided.

* * *

He'd abused her all day for no reason. Now that he thought it through, it made no sense that he'd be suspicious she'd been sent to trap him. Sneed was a mastermind at planning and dropping a woman down into the dungeons wouldn't guarantee that she'd end up with him. A small voice in the back of his head whispered that she had come straight to him, but he shook it off. It was more likely that she'd have been snatched before she'd reached him. Sneed was too calculating to leave that up to chance.

Why can't she be who she seems to be?

Because she's too good to be true.

Soft hands drew his thoughts to the present.

Caelan whisper-touched her way down his chest, stroking down every plane as if she enjoyed the feel of him. She explored every rib, pressed both hands onto his stomach with a reverence that held him spellbound.

Pushing his thighs apart, she climbed between his legs. Then she dragged her hands down his hips, the action so sexy, his cock jumped in appreciation.

Meeting his gaze, she licked her lips, the gesture erotic and unsure at the same time.

Then she lowered her mouth to his thigh.

Magic swirled in the air, and he knew immediately she was going to literally kiss him better. He'd never had anyone touch him this way during healing, never even known it was possible, but he felt her power like the brush of a hundred butterflies on his thigh.

As she licked around the wound, healing magic tingled his skin, down the inside of his leg and up into his belly. He had to pull himself up onto his elbows to watch her, wanting to see what she did as well as feel it.

She worked along the edges of the slash, slowly softening the angry red, before finally breathing magic on the wound.

His back bowed with the intensity of feeling, the rake of desire running through his body making him cry out.

He couldn't take it, couldn't have her push her magic into his body and not touch himself.

Without conscious thought, he fisted his cock and began to pump in time with her mouth. Unlike the other times he'd been healed by a Speaker, there was no pain at all, just the most intense pleasure he'd ever felt.

He was going to climax. He had to stop, but her beautiful, magic-filled mouth went on and on, picking up speed, forcing his hand to move faster to keep up.

Then an intense orgasm roared over him, and he barely registered the fact that now her lips were circled around the head of his cock.

The relief only lasted seconds before he knew he had to have her again and again. Desire crawled through his insides on the heels of her magic, and he wondered if he'd ever stop needing her.

* * *

She'd done it! She'd healed him with her mouth, and for those precious moments, he'd been totally under her control.

Her sex was heavy and full, but power burned through her. Usually after she healed, she felt depleted and exhaustion tugged at her. But now she felt amazing. Garron's magic and seed filled her up, driving her higher.

Even in the darkness, Garron's gaze consumed her, the look on his face so starkly full of desire she couldn't stop the small, knowing smile that curved her lips.

He brushed a finger down her cheek in a slow caress. "You look like you've just become queen of the world." Sitting, he leaned close to whisper. "You should. That was amazing." He nipped her neck, sending shivers of raw desire through her body. "I didn't even know that was possible." He rubbed his hand down his healed thigh. "It's gone. Not even a mark left."

"I'd heard whispers when I lived in the Temple of the Goddess," she gasped, trying to think around the burn inside her.

"You lived there? With those witches?"

"Yes." She blinked trying to grasp that someone didn't have the utmost respect for the Council Mothers and their citadel. "For two years."

"My home town of Trayborne petitioned them for a healer we so desperately need, but each time we've been turned down." Anger and frustration filled the words. "The sick must travel a half day's journey to find help, but the Temple ignores our pleas."

Her heart went out for a town in need of a healer. "I'm sure they would have sent someone if they could." Healers weren't that scarce, though. "Where is your town?" Perhaps no one wanted to live there.

"On the western border, but the Temple has promised to provide a Speaker to all who ask."

He shook his head, then kissed her, as if he was done discussing the Temple. She was glad to leave the subject.

He tugged lightly on one of her aching nipples, making her whimper.

She caught his hand and pressed it to her breast, hoping to relieve the painful desire building there. "Please," she heard herself beg. The fire inside her ignited into an inferno, making everything else drop away.

He fought his hand from her grasp, then stripped her dress from her body.

She scrambled to help him.

Scooting back against the wall, he carried her with him. Then he held his cock in one hand while guiding her hips with the other.

She crested him gladly, the action of fitting him inside granting her huge relief. Closing her eyes, she arched back, digging her fingers into his shoulders for balance as she worked herself down his length in slow pulses.

When she reached his base, he stopped her. "Goddess, you're beautiful, Caelan. You look perfect when need for me fills your face, like a siren from tales of old." He dragged her forward for a mouth-eating kiss. "Are you? Are you a siren?" Pinning her hips so she couldn't ride him and find relief, he whispered, "Are you a woman who has to have a man inside her, or am I the key that has set you free?"

Part of her protested that he was blackmailing her for information she wasn't sure she wanted him to know, but another piece of her would do anything at that moment to find release from the fire inside her.

She sat on his lap with his cock deep inside her, the position putting her at his eye level. Grasping his head with both hands, she clenched him with the inside of her body, enjoying the tightening around his eyes that showed he was fighting the pleasure. "I never knew sex could feel like this, never knew it could be so amazing." To tempt him more out of his mood, she ran her tongue along his lips, pulling away when he tried to kiss her.

His hands loosened, and she rolled her hips to fit herself tighter against him.

Everything receded, leaving only their bodies and her intense desire.

She was more exposed than she'd ever been in her life. She should be running into the shadows.

Instead, Caelan let her body go, riding him at her own pace, letting her face show just how much she wanted him.

It felt better to ride him deep, so she shortened the movement into a tight series of thrusts.

Far away she heard him moan, but this wasn't about him any longer. It was about her bringing him, bringing them both.

She increased the pace, the ball of sensation tightening inside her, reaching a screaming pitch. Placing her hands on either side of his head for leverage, she pushed down as hard as she could.

Then relief burst over her, making her cry out in pleasure and agony. Magic swirled and mixed, his and hers, two sides of a coin fusing together to make something powerful and addictive all at the same time.

* * *

Garron woke wrapped around Caelan, their bodies tucked together, his leg nestled in between hers, his arm slipped below hers to rest on her stomach. He felt completely sated, the hum of desire still riding under the surface, but muted and content, like the purr of a kitten.

Staring up at the cracks in the ceiling that let in the red of the rising sun, he stroked a lazy hand along the beautiful skin of Caelan's back, enjoying the feel of her under his fingers. Satisfaction streaked through him when she arched, the action saying clearly that she took pleasure in him as much as he did her.

Lying there, enjoying the moment like none other in his life, he realized he'd made a mistake. Before he'd ended up in The Abyss, he'd created a life that allowed him the freedom to do as he pleased without worrying about the limitations of his power. He couldn't lie, or he'd lose his ability to Battle Shout, so instead he'd kept all relationships on the surface, building a wall no one dared to climb, even the women he'd bedded.

But somehow, with Caelan, he'd forgotten about the wall, hadn't, in fact, even remembered it in the heat of their sexual explosion.

Before he'd never experienced this feeling of complete contentment — and that's what it was — and so he hadn't missed it, hadn't realized it could even be a possibility for him.

Now that he'd had it, now that he knew just how amazing he could feel with this woman, how could he give it up?

Maybe this feeling of contentment would fade over time. In fact, he was sure it would. Nothing this good could last. But he wasn't ready to give her up when they were free.

"I can't believe we're escaping tonight," she whispered, staring at the rising sun.

"Why are you here in the dungeons?" he asked, wanting to know the full story behind her odd appearance.

She lay so still for a moment, he thought she might not answer. "I knew something that could lead to a man's death. It was either tell it or end up here."

He picked up one of her curls and wrapped it around his finger, resisting the urge to push. If he did that, he'd owe her a truth about himself in return, a truth of her choosing. And unlike other men, he couldn't lie.

"How did you end up here, Garron?" she asked, turning onto her side and bringing the covers carefully to her chin. He didn't like the barrier between them.

He should have anticipated the question. It was, after all, only fair. "You and I both cannot lie, Caelan. If you want my answer, you'll have to give me more of your story."

She sighed, the sound full of frustration. "I don't mean to be evasive, I'm just so used to giving vague answers, it's hard not to do so now."

"Anyone who cannot lie has to come up with other ways to keep their true feelings to themselves." He cupped her chin because he had to touch her. "It's hard to let people close to us when we can't hide behind falsehoods to smooth our way in life." He knew she would understand.

"During my last few months at the Temple, my ability to communicate with the Goddess went silent, and all the women who had been my friends distanced themselves from me. I realized they'd never been my true friends. We'd never discussed anything significant, never shared our secrets." She unburied her hand from the blanket to catch his. "You're the first person I've ever spoken to about my inability to lie, one of the few people who knows how difficult it is not to be able to speak falsely."

He smiled but knew it was a cynical tip of his lips. "I've heard men compliment women on their dresses when the fabric was so ugly, there was no way they were speaking the truth. That kind of social nicety is cut off from us. So we learn to step around the truth with other truths." Stroking her hand with his thumb, he said gently, "So why are you really here?"

"My best friend fell in love." She slumped onto her back and studied the ceiling. "And she saved her lover's life by sacrificing mine." Her voice was expressionless.

It still didn't make sense. "Her lover had done something wrong, and she said you did it?"

"Brianna was supposed to be given away in a political marriage, but someone told the King she was no long pure."

"Useph is involved with this?" A chill ran over his skin at the mention of the King. He had the reputation of being an unpredictable tyrant. Staying away from those who had angered him would be wise, but Garron knew it was too late to separate himself from Caelan.

"I'm his Speaker." She rolled her head to stare at him. "And he loves Brianna, has since we were children. He'll take her punishment out on her lover, not her. Unfortunately no one knows where Radley is." She paused, then let out a breath. "But me. In the face of Useph's wrath, Brianna let slip that I'm the only one who knows where Radley is, so now I have the choice of either revealing Brianna's lover, which would lead to his death, or rotting here in the dungeons."

Anger at Useph's treatment of his Speaker filled Garron's gut. "And he throws a small, innocent woman into The Abyss?" That behavior smacked of evil madness. Although why would the King not do as he pleased?

Frustration crawled down his spine. Was it too much to ask that the people of this country weren't killed or imprisoned on a whim? That the people were allowed basic freedoms? He'd dedicated his life to upholding the crown. But since Sneed killed his family, he wasn't sure the King was worthy of his allegiance.

"He wasn't always so ruthless."

"Who?"

"The King. When Useph was a child, he was shy and sweet. It was only after his father told him he could never marry Brianna that things changed. Although he's gotten worse since Sneed became his most trusted advisor."

"Sneed," he growled, then stopped himself from saying anything further. Just saying Sneed's name made the old fury return. Garron had given up his plans for revenge, though. His freedom and life were worth more than justice. He'd learned that here in The Abyss. Besides, his escape would leave Sneed seething and looking over his shoulder for the rest of his life, wondering if Garron would ever expose him. Not as good a revenge as death, it was true, but good enough.

"So that's why I'm here, Garron." She tipped her chin up. "Why are you here?"

"I was caught stealing from Sneed's office."

Her mouth dropped open. "I don't believe it. You'd never steal!"

He laughed, the sound bitter even to his own ears. "It's been a day since we met, and you know me better than my closest friends." He jumped to his feet and paced naked across the cavern, unable to believe he was about to confess something he should never tell anyone. "No, Caelan, I wasn't there to steal his riches." He stopped and met her gaze. "I was there to kill him."

"Kill Sneed?" she gasped.

"Yes, and if I don't escape, I'll be one of the six sacrificed to the God of War on Mabon."

Behind them, Danner toppled from the entrance tunnel into the room. "Garron, the guards are coming down to take the woman!"

Chapter Five

It was treason.

Attempting to kill the most favored advisor of the King would be seen as an attempt on the King himself.

A crime worthy of death.

Just as her mother had committed treason against Useph's father.

Old emotions tumbled from hidden crevices, flooding from behind the locked doors of her mind where she'd carefully kept them. Pain seized her, and she wanted to scream, "Not again! I won't live through this again!"

She shut her eyes and rubbed her temple. This wasn't the same. Wasn't the same at all. Her mother's downfall had been falling in love with a man who wasn't her husband and blindly doing anything he wished. There was no way Garron would do something without fully understanding the consequences.

She forced herself to ask more questions. "Why? Why kill Sneed?"

"Because he killed my parents."

"Sneed did? Himself?" Sneed never left the castle unless he was at Useph's side. Or did he? What did she really know about him? She spent her days healing the villagers not watching members of the Court.

"No, he had his man, Farley, do it. My parents ran an inn in Trayborne. They overheard the two of them talking. Sneed had raised the taxes in the border towns without the King's knowledge. After they were murdered, I found a letter my father had written to the King, telling everything. He never had the chance to send it. I'm not even sure he would have. People in border towns are cautious and closed to outsiders." His jaw worked as he ground his teeth.

He seemed so sure, but she just couldn't see Sneed betraying the King. At every turn, Sneed had been

Useph's lackey. "How do you know it was Sneed?"

"Because I tracked down Farley, and he told me Sneed ordered their deaths."

Caelan shivered. No, this was nothing like her mother's crimes.

Caelan's father was the cousin of the king. Her mother's lover had also been the cousin of the king but on the wrong side. Two generations ago, the Monroes had been in line for the throne, but infant Edward Monroe died before he could inherit his father's legacy, and Useph's grandfather, Modred, stepped into the crown. There were those who said that Edward's death had been at Modred's hand.

Caelan didn't know if Modred killed the child. Babies died, especially when a proper healer wasn't near. What she did know was that her mother had not only been caught loving the wrong man but had aided him in his plot to take the throne.

And she'd died for it.

Caelan had been living in the Temple of the Goddess when it happened. Her stay there had kept her out of sight, sheltering her from the fall-out of her mother's actions. When she returned to the castle, her father had insured her position as the castle Speaker, protecting her until his death last year. By then, her mother's transgressions had faded from everyone's minds, replaced by other intrigues.

Caelan had made sure her own behavior never came into question. She'd built her life on the precept of being useful and in the background. She swore she'd never do anything to call attention to herself because she knew that while her mother's actions were buried, they were still there, ready to be used against her at a moment's notice.

"But why kill Sneed? Why not send the letter or tell the King yourself?"

"Tell King Useph." His laugh was a harsh, cutting sound. "How, Caelan? No one gets near him without

Sneed's say-so."

He was right. Even she hadn't been alone with Useph in years. It was hard to even imagine Sneed leaving the castle long enough to meet with Farley, but certainly the less people who knew he stole money from the King, the safer Sneed would be. "I'm sorry, about all of it." She knew the words made little difference. His family was still dead, and if he didn't escape The Abyss, he'd die tomorrow.

Caelan watched dust filtering through the sunlight coming from the small cracks in the cave ceiling. Only days ago, she was healing the sick and living a quiet existence. Now, here she was, deep below the castle, surrounded by cut-throats and thieves.

She knew now in her soul she couldn't live with Radley's death on her hands. But her only escape was to crawl to a freedom tainted by a lifetime of running from the King's men.

"The guards are going to come down! What are we going to do?" Danner's panic brought them back to their current problem. His hands leapt in shakes that had her wondering if there was more wrong with him than just nerves. He looked healthy enough, but hand tremors came from a variety of illnesses.

"We'll hide her." Garron's voice was smooth and sure as he pulled on his breeches and boots.

"They said if she doesn't come to the grate, they'll withhold food until someone gives her up. How long do you think it will be until Rolf tells them where we are?"

Garron shrugged into a tattered shirt. "We need to go to the tunnel and start working in double time."

"But it's daylight. If we break through and someone is near, they'll be able to see us. We'll be caught!"

"That's a risk we'll have to take." He turned to her. "Caelan, you'll be on digging detail with me. Danner, I want you on look out for Rolf. If he seems to be making a move to give her up, tell me, and I'll deal with him."

Caelan took a deep breath, resisting the urge to follow Garron's orders.

This was wrong. If the guards looked for her, they might find Garron's tunnel, and his chance of escape would be over. And tomorrow he'd die. She wouldn't risk that. Useph likely only wanted to ask her if she was ready to tell him where Brianna's lover was hiding. If that was the case, then she'd tell him she wasn't ever acting in a way that would jeopardize a life, and she'd be back here within an hour.

"Garron."

He turned to her, cocking his head enough so the light hit his face fully for the first time. She let her gaze wander over the hard planes of his cheeks, the strong nose, and slash of his mouth. Maybe if she'd met him outside the dungeons for the first time, she'd have seen him as too rough. But now she saw the face of a man who saved her, was in fact going to save her again if she let him. His large body would stand between her and the King.

The idea was so foreign to her, so beyond the possibilities she'd ever imagined for herself, she shivered.

"Take me to the grate." Her voice wobbled but only because she was trying to talk around the lump in her throat.

Because at that moment, she realized how her mother could have done what she did. She finally understood why Brianna risked both their lives for the man she loved.

Before, she couldn't imagine placing her body between someone else and harm. But now she wasn't going to let a man she cared for, a man who had saved her, risk his life to save hers. Not again. Not now that she'd come to care about him. In the short time they'd known each other, she shouldn't feel this way, but she did.

"You aren't going," he said calmly.

She gathered the blanket around her as she stood and closed the distance between them. "He's going to ask me if I'm ready to give up Brianna's lover." She unburied a hand to rest it on his arm. "I'll tell him no and be back here within the hour. There is no reason to risk you and Danner like this."

"I don't like it. The King is rumored to be dangerously erratic. I'm not taking that chance."

He had no idea just how erratic Useph could be, and Caelan didn't tell him. Suddenly it was very, very important that she protect him. If he didn't escape, he'd die, and for reasons that went beyond a repayment to him for saving her life, she didn't want that to happen.

"I'll be fine. He expected me to beg my way out of here by now. He'll throw me back here within an hour."

In the murky darkness, she could feel him studying her, weighing her words.

"Then we can leave tonight like we planned," she added to reassure him.

After they were free, she knew that they would part company, knew that their connection would end once they left the dungeons. But while it would sadden her, leave her feeling as if she'd lost a piece of herself, she would be all right. In that moment, she made up her mind to go to Trayborne, to be the healer they so desperately needed.

"Danner, go see what Rolf's doing," he said without taking his eyes from her.

Without a word, Danner disappeared up the tunnel.

"I'm going to the grate. Please don't fight me," she whispered.

He blew out a breath. "I don't like it."

"Sometimes the best thing to do is also the hardest. You know this is what must be done to keep us all safe."

For a moment, she thought he'd dig in and refuse her. Then he ran his hand down her cheek, and her heart flipped over. Just a simple touch, but it meant so very much to her. The smell of his magic swirled around her, in her lungs, inside her body and soul.

She smiled, and it was bittersweet. What if she'd never met him? What if she'd done as Useph wanted?

She'd be safely in her healer rooms right now. Would she have been better off? No. She was done being someone who faded into the background, who protected herself at almost any cost.

She was strong, had so much to offer, so much life to live. It wasn't until that moment, standing in the dim light of The Abyss that she realized fully how much of her life she'd missed by being so careful.

Maybe when she went to the king, she'd find that Useph had forgiven her or that Radley had been captured. And then she wouldn't be coming back here. This could be the last time she ever saw Garron.

The thought had her meeting his gaze and dropping the blanket slowly from her shoulders.

He stepped back and watched, letting the dim light touch her body. "So beautiful, Caelan. Like a goddess in a ray of sunlight."

"I'm so very glad I met you, Garron. I'm so glad it was you."

"Not as glad as I am, love." Then he stepped close and dropped his mouth to hers in a slow glide, the kiss sweet and light, as if he worshiped her.

His warm, huge hands slid along her back, tangling in her hair as they caressed her. She tugged off his shirt, enjoying the fact he ducked so she could reach him.

Then she kissed his chest, marveling at the muscles beneath her mouth. His body was hot, the warmth radiating into her cool skin even though they stood inches apart.

She trailed her hands down his arms, over the hard muscle of his biceps, smoothing the dusting of hair beneath her touch. Her fingers didn't meet as she circled his wrists. His bulk only made her marvel more that she had the power to own him in this moment. And she did own him. He was more hers than anything had ever been in her life.

His lips found hers, and the kiss ate at her mouth in

slow reverence, picking up speed as the magic inside them swirled and mingled, sealing them in a circle of need.

Then he picked her up, lifting her so high, she gripped his chest with her legs for balance. He easily held her there, while he ran his mouth along her stomach, teasing shivers from her body.

She moaned to release some of the emotion that longed to break free.

Then he lowered her to his pallet, shedding the clothes he'd only just put on in the blink of an eye.

"I promised to bring you over and over, love. If you're going to be gone from me for even an hour, then I can't let you go without knowing you'll spend the whole time with my name humming through you." Like a lazy cat, he stretched out beside her.

She bowed into the hand he feathered along her body, fighting a laugh of pure joy that wanted to bubble from her.

His smile echoed hers. "That's how it feels to me, too, as if I'm about to explode with desire and need and emotions that feel so good, I'm on overload." He caught her nipple between his lips and suckled.

She gasped at the sting that shot through her.

"I want you to think of me every second of every moment you're away from my side."

With effort, she tried to gather her mind and think. She was done letting things happen without her participation. From now on, she was seizing the opportunity to make her own destiny.

Which meant she needed to play a more active role in this seduction. She wasn't going to be the only one aching.

Turning to her side, she pushed him to his back and stroked his huge body in a slow caress. His hand fisted in her hair, bringing her head down for a kiss that went on and on. She wanted to relax into it, let him sweep her away, but she fought for control.

She ate at his lips, not caring if they both ended up

bruised. He could handle it, and she wanted to speed things up, to boil the desire between them to a scorching, dark heat.

Then he rolled her under him, taking control, twisting at the right moment so he ended up resting between her legs.

She bit him on the shoulder in retaliation, her teeth sinking into his skin enough to mark him.

"Little cat," he murmured, tilting her head back to meet her gaze. "I can take anything you dish to me."

"I know," she whispered, realizing that it was true. Unlike everyone she'd ever known, he wouldn't retaliate if she made a mistake, wouldn't whisper about her mother's sins, saying she'd come from bad stock. He would use his body for her protection or her need. Here in the middle of this dungeon, she'd finally met someone who saw her as a desirable woman.

He pulled his body far enough away to part the lips of her sex, lowering himself so his cock rested along the seam. "I want you to ache for me, Caelan. I want you to come when I enter you, you're so aroused." Then he pressed himself tight against her clitoris, the hard length of him pinning her, sending a bolt of desire through her body so intense it wrenched a moan from her very soul.

His mouth devoured hers, one hand supporting his weight, the other feathering along the side of her breast.

Her mind whirled in response, her magic building inside her to a massive height. Somewhere, a voice of reason warned her that a large outlay of power would deplete her, that she should save it just in case. But where she was going, she knew the person who was at greatest risk to be hurt was her, and she couldn't heal herself.

Magic built like an intense pressure inside her, aching to break free.

Rotating her hips, she tried to slip him down, tried to slide him inside to stop the mad pressure that was building. He caught her hips and held her perfectly still while he ran the head of his cock over her clitoris. Again and again.

"Garron," she whispered on a gasp, wanting to tell him he had to stop, even though part of her didn't want him to stop at all.

"Ask for what you want, Caelan." He increased the pressure, sliding easily in the desire that pooled for him.

The lips of her sex felt heavy and full, cradling his erection, the sensitive nerves there increasing the sensation.

"I need—" She took a breath, the magic inside her burning to a screaming pitch.

And then it was too late. Like a waterfall, magic poured out of her, giving her the strength to drag his head down and press her lips to his. She had to push the power into him, had to gift him a piece of herself.

The moment her lips touched his, his cock slid home, the sensation of being filled while releasing the pressure of her magic so wonderful, her orgasm rushed through her body in a raw, shaking release that seemed unending.

He ripped his mouth from hers. "Dammit," he growled, thrusting deep, fighting the contractions of her sex, the movement of his cock continuing the tremors of release riding through her.

He rammed deep, his shout filled with joy and triumph as it echoed through their cavern and beyond, his magic amplifying it into a hair-raising battle cry that she felt in her core.

Then he lowered his head and kissed her, pushing a mix of her magic and his back inside her body. It burned her throat and felt like no power she'd ever experienced.

They'd mixed magic this time, not merely borrowed it. There was a reason the Goddess cautioned people against mingling their power. Legends warned that sometimes magic that was perverted this way would never change back to its original form.

"What have we done?" she whispered.

* * *

He helped her crawl out of the tunnel, holding her hand to steady her. The action was almost courtly, as if he supported her in a deep curtsy to the king, only the shredded mess of her skirt would never pass muster in the throne room. The fabric of what had once been her best healer gown hung in gauzy, lawn-colored tatters, but for some reason, with his hand holding hers, none of that mattered.

When they neared the grate, there was a shift around them, a presence of many bodies filling the cavern. She realized they walked through a gauntlet of prisoners who'd lined up to watch them pass. Silence filled the hollow space, but underneath was a ring of anger, the feeling sliding up her spine to make her stomach twist.

Garron squeezed her hand in reassurance, drawing her behind him slightly so if anyone moved, he'd be the one to take the brunt of their attack.

Caelan wondered why people came to see her departure. Did they hate her so much for having the chance to be hauled out of The Abyss that they'd come to growl and sneer at her as she left?

As if by magic, Rolf appeared before them. "Where you taking her?"

Tucking her more fully behind him, Garron seemed to grow bigger, his body going from a relaxed panther stride to the balls of his feet. The air shimmered with his alertness and warning, the tension in his shoulders causing the muscles along his arms to bulk up and ripple.

The danger dropped away, and Caelan felt a flash of pure desire shoot through her. He was everything she never knew she wanted. Who could have suspected that a man who would defend her with his very life could turn her on in a way she'd never felt before?

"Get out of my way, Rolf." The growled warning brought Caelan out of her daze.

She finally had someone to protect her, and the old

Caelan would have gladly hidden behind him, but the new one wasn't going to risk Garron's life when she had the power to protect in return. Taking a deep breath, she stepped between the two men. "I'm going to the grate, Rolf."

He spared her a contemptuous glance before returning his gaze to Garron. "You give her to them, they'll just kill her."

For a moment, Caelan's mind couldn't comprehend what he was saying. Then it clicked. "Wait, you don't want me to go?"

Rolf snorted. "I don't care if you go or stay. But we don't give those bastards anything. If they come down here, we make them pay for it." He turned back to Garron. "We can barter food for her. Extra bread rations at least."

"Get out of my way, Rolf." Garron's voice was soft, reasonable, unemotional. And it made his words shiver through the air like the sharpest of warnings.

"You've always thought you were better than us, haven't you?" Rolf shifted his body sideways, his right hand sliding along the side of his thigh.

Caelan wasn't going to let them fight, wasn't going to risk Garron's life over something that made sense to her. "Garron," she said, keeping her voice as level as his had been. "If bartering me brings them something, why not let them?"

He held up a hand palm out to Rolf, then pulled her close to his chest to whisper in her ear. "I don't think it would worsen your circumstances to be used as an exchange. The guards will expect to pay for you. It's the price of saving them the trip down here."

She shook her head. "If you thought this, why did you act as if you were going to fight Rolf?"

"Because, love, the decision was yours to make, not mine. And Rolf doesn't get near you without a fist in his face."

"Thank you," she said, feeling powerful and right,

loving him for letting her choose her own fate. She turned to Rolf. "Make your deal."

***

Garron didn't like it. The closer they moved to the grate, the more the bad feeling he'd been fighting since he agreed to this madness crawled up his spine. She'd said she'd be straight back in the dungeon tonight, but what if something happened to her, and she didn't return until the morning? If he left on schedule, she'd be down here without him.

But they were a good night's work away from breaking out, and he had no way to protect her from a battalion of soldiers. He had to trust that she was right in this.

Pulling her into his arms, he caught her chin in his hand. "I'm not sure I like this."

A cheer swirled through the air as the bargained bread was thrown into the cavern.

"There aren't any other choices here that make sense, Garron. I go, or they come down and take me." She slid her fingers around his wrist, then turned the palm up so she could kiss the center. "I'll be back. I'm not telling them what they want. He'll sentence me here for another day."

"Good. I'll be waiting by the grate until you return." He said the words, but something nagged at him. It was most likely the fact that she would soon be out of his sight. He didn't like it.

"Kiss me," she whispered.

"Gladly." He lowered his head, enjoying it when her arms wrapped around his neck. Their lips met and immediately parted, tongues seeking to deepen the intimacy of the act. Her magic and his mixed. The world around them faded as he threaded his hands through her hair.

She rose on her tiptoes to reach him better, and if they'd been alone, he would have pulled her off her feet, would have encouraged her to wrap her legs around his waist.

He heard Rolf move behind him before he spoke. "They've lowered the rope for her."

Garron took his time, finishing the kiss, then rested his forehead against hers. "Be back here by tonight," he whispered.

"I'll try." She pulled away and stared at something over his shoulder for a moment. Then she looked back at him. "But if I don't return, don't wait for me. Go while you still can. Tomorrow is Mabon. You have to escape while you still can." She paused, then caught his sleeve. "There is always a chance that King Useph will let me out of my punishment."

He nodded, even though he knew that was an impossibility. Useph had never done anything for his subjects. He was a tyrant and self-focused bastard who cared about his subjects less than he cared for his dogs. "Just be safe."

"I will."

Then she was gone, and he was left staring at the closed grate, that bad feeling swarming in his gut.

Chapter Six

With every step of the long walk to the throne room, her understanding of why her mother and best friend had both sacrificed for love grew. Brianna risked herself for Radley because if he died, a piece of her would, too. Her mother risked her life to be with her lover because her existence must have been an empty shell without him in it.

Now that Caelan had been with Garron, the thought of the rest of her life without him left her heart aching. Her connection with Garron had built through the trials of the dungeon, through the bond they'd built by sharing their bodies and their magic. Life without him stretched before her, dull and gray, and she realized she might have somehow fallen in love with him.

How had her mother faced day after day without the man she'd thought she loved? To live in the same castle with Garron and not touch of him would be a torture. Her mother must have spent every day in agony.

Another realization burned inside her. How dare Useph treat both her and Garron as if their lives meant nothing? She was his Speaker. Garron had been his Protector. They were loyal subjects working tirelessly for their king. A ruler who didn't understand that he needed his subjects as much as they needed him didn't deserve his people's fidelity.

The thought was so foreign to her she stopped in the barren stone hallway, her mind turning the idea over and over. A leader just didn't lead because he wanted to. A leader led because his troops respected him enough to follow. Things had deteriorated because Useph was a bad leader. More and more people weren't following his directives. If Sneed was stealing from him and killing people to cover it up, then Useph's hold on his country was more precarious than she'd realized.

The guard beside her started to reach for her arm, but

then hesitated with a grimace, staring at the dirt on her skin. "Speaker, the King awaits," he prompted.

"Yes, he does," she murmured, controlling the building anger inside her.

She swept into the throne room, her mind setting itself for whatever might come. She wasn't going to tell Useph what he wanted. She'd made that decision. Useph could throw her back into the dungeon, and tonight she'd escape with Garron. She'd go to Trayborne and become their healer. They needed her, and she burned to help them and to be appreciated for who she was inside.

The sight that greeted her had her stumbling to a halt.

Instead of the usual throne chair on the red dais, a large bed took up the space. It was surrounded by Useph's advisors, Sneed at the position of honor on his right hand side. On Useph's left, Brianna sat on the red satin sheets dressed in white, her head bowed, her shoulders shaking as if she wept.

"Your Speaker, Sire," the guard at her side announced.

Of the people surrounding Useph, it was hard to tell one person from another. Their clothing blended together, and their faces were a mixture of concern and worry. But underneath the surface, excitement shimmered, peeking out in the slightly too-wide eyes of the watchers as they leaned forward for a better view of the possible death of the King.

Useph hadn't hauled her from the dungeon to receive a confession.

He'd brought her here because she was one of the best Speakers in his nation, and he needed her skills.

And with that realization, a strange idea formed in her mind. Useph had fallen ill, or he wouldn't have sent for her. The fact he needed her gave her power — the power to ask for something in return.

And she knew what she'd ask for. Garron's freedom. Then he wouldn't have to escape, wouldn't have to spend his life running. He'd saved her life, given her an experience which had allowed her to spread her wings and discover who she really was inside, and now she could pay back her debt to him.

Hope twisted her belly, but she moved towards her king with a measured tread, stopping four feet away to curtsy in respect.

Sneed recoiled from her. "My Goddess, she smells."

"It's the smell of your dungeons, Sire." She said the words as starkly as she could, careful to wipe the sarcasm from them. For the first time, Useph really needed her, and she wasn't going to let this opportunity slip away because she couldn't control her temper.

"How dare you enter this room without bathing! You must wash yourself and change clothes." Sneed covered his mouth with his hand as if her stench was too much for him.

"I was brought straight here without a chance to change." She turned to Useph. "You are ill, my King?"

Useph opened his mouth, but only coughing emerged. Quickly, Sneed pressed a flawless white square of linen into his hand. The hacking came from deep within him, as if his lungs were drowning. When the King straightened, blood covered the handkerchief in his grip.

Someone in the faceless crowd gasped, the sound a mix of horror and titillation.

Useph wiped his mouth with a shaking hand, but his eyes were filled with calculation, just as they always were.

Her healer's gaze took in his condition. He was weak, but not so weak that he'd lost movement nor was his mind slipping.

Then she saw the shadow around his lips. The shade of blue was violent cerulean, a message from the Goddess herself that only a handful of Speakers could envision.

"What's happened to me?" Useph's voice came out as a harsh rasp.

"You've been poisoned," she said, keeping her tone

level and calm.

The throng of onlookers gasped as one, but Useph didn't seem surprised. "How did poison slip past my tasters?" he asked, his voice mild, but under the surface a storm was brewing.

"I don't know." She had power here, she reminded herself, fighting the desire to fade into the background in the face of Useph's growing anger. Her abilities were valuable, valuable enough to use to save one man's life by saving a King's.

"Heal me," Useph ordered.

Caelan controlled her sudden spurt of anger with effort. Here he was, about to die without her help, and yet Useph still did not appreciate her. "No."

The room stilled on the word.

From where she sat in a defeated huddle, Brianna raised her head. Her friend's face was a mass of black, blue, and green, the colors fading and molting during the time Caelan had been gone. But the look in her eyes was no longer angelic and loving. Hate and fury seethed in her gaze, the twist of her lips tightening her mouth into a prune.

Rather than look at her, Caelan stared at Useph's calculating face, pushing away the chill at the change in her friend over mere days. She needed all her wits about her if she would win Garron's freedom. One problem at a time.

"So you finally wish to bargain." Useph's tone of voice said he'd expected her to ask him for something in return. "I thought of all people, your skills came for free."

She took a deep breath and focused her new found strength. "Not anymore, Cousin."

The King waved a shaking hand. "I grant you your freedom. Brianna has agreed to be my paramour, and we have resolved the matter between us, so I no longer need your knowledge."

Horror crept up Caelan's spine. He was going to take

Brianna, his cousin, as a lover. Their relation alone gave her pause, but everyone knew when it came to bed sport, King Useph could be a cruel master.

Caelan swallowed around the bile creeping up her throat. As handsome as Useph was, she'd healed the ripped and torn bodies of his bedmates.

Her breath went shallow, but she had to concentrate, had to say the words that would lead to Garron's freedom, allowing him to live without spending his life looking over his shoulder. That would be her parting gift to him, a thank you for everything he'd done for her. "I do not ask for my own pardon."

"Oh, and whose are you asking for?" Useph coughed, his shoulders shaking with the spasms in his lungs.

Usually Caelan would ache for someone in such obvious need, but now she felt nothing. She couldn't afford to go soft. This was about doing what was right.

"In return for healing you, you will agree to pardon Garron the Protector."

"What?" Sneed gasped.

"Who is that?" Useph snapped.

"The border rat I caught stealing in my office. He would have attacked me if the guards hadn't come."

"You're alive, Sneed. I am your King, and I am dying." Useph's voice came out clipped, as if after all these years he was finally growing tired of his advisor. "I'm not sure you have it in you not to heal me, Caelan. I don't think you can stand there and watch me suffer."

Caelan felt Garron's magic running thick and strong in her veins. She called on it to help her show no mercy. "Watch me watch you die." She met his gaze, never more sure of anything in her life. "When you lowered me into The Abyss, I changed, King Useph. I can stand here and watch you suffer. Trust me, I can. Garron saved my life. I would have died without his protection, and now you will die if you don't grant him a pardon."

Useph's shrewd eyes narrowed and searched her face.

"I believe you might actually do it." Tapping his fingers on the satiny coverlets, he hummed softly. "So his life for mine?" Useph studied her, the blue ring around his lips deepening, signaling his time was running out.

"He is one of the six to die at Mabon! You cannot pardon him!" Sneed's protest held a note of panic in it.

It was hard for Caelan to keep from smiling. Sneed deserved to worry after what he'd done to Garron's parents, but she wasn't here to right old wrongs. She was here to save the life of the man she loved. Although a thought struck her. If Sneed would steal from Useph, would he poison him also? No, she decided. Sneed needed Useph to feed on like a mosquito needed blood to survive.

"You were going to sacrifice him? For a failed attempt at thievery? Really, Sneed. The Abyss is filled with people whose crimes make them better choices to be sacrificed." The King waved his hand, dismissing Sneed's concerns. "We will make our deal, Cousin. I will pardon Garron once you save my life." He settled back against luxurious pillows, his face turning smug. "I'd always thought you'd be the only person in the castle who wouldn't succumb to selling your gift from the Goddess, but I'm glad to see I'm wrong. It bothered me that you couldn't be bought."

"I find that I can ill afford to be so pure, my liege."

She'd done it! She'd bargained and won. Excitement and confidence raced through Caelan's veins.

She'd risked everything for a man. Just like Brianna. Just like her mother. And for the first time, she understood. She wished her mother was alive so she could tell her. An odd sadness washed over Caelan, pain from years of anger and blame escaping from her very pores, leaving her feeling hollow and lost inside.

* * *

The dungeon darkened as the sun set. Garron stood below the grate, a growing feeling of dread spreading from his gut through his body, down into his fingertips and toes. Something had happened, and Caelan wasn't coming back. How he knew, he wasn't sure, but he did.

"We need to start digging," Danner whispered, his urgency turning his words into a hiss.

"In a moment." Time was running out. Tonight was the night. He had to go.

Gazing upward yet again, he debated his options. As sure as he was that she wasn't coming back, he couldn't seem to bring himself to leave. If he was wrong, she might be attacked and hurt before he could reach her.

But he had one last night before Mabon, and it was either leave now or die tomorrow. What if he left tonight and she was returned after he was gone? Goddess above! The thought of his freedom while she was swallowed whole in The Abyss by some half mad prisoner made his insides wrench.

Rolf appeared beside him, crossing his arms exactly as Garron had his and staring up at the grate with a slight sneer twisting his meaty lips.

For a moment, they stood like that, then Rolf broke the silence. "Think she's coming back?"

"No," Garron said, keeping the emotion from his voice.

"Then why are you standing here?"

"I'm not sure."

Rolf nodded as if that made sense. "I think you and I can come to an understanding, Protector. You allowed us to bargain your woman, and one good turn deserves another." Rolf grinned, his lips an ironic twist. "I think we don't need to be at war, and as a gesture of my good faith, if your woman is lowered down, I'll bring her to you unharmed."

"And what do you get from me for this service?"

"Peace. You stay out of my business, Garron, and I'll stay out of yours." Rolf leaned closer, lowering his voice. "So you don't have to waste precious digging hours waiting for her to return." A knowing grin twisted his lips.

So Rolf knew he was tunneling out. Garron debated what to do about it. Acting as if Rolf's information was wrong would be unwise. Rolf's assured stance said clearly that he knew beyond any doubt what Garron was up to. "If you know what I'm doing, why haven't you reported me?"

"Because it's going to be fun to watch them scramble when Mabon comes, and they're missing two of their precious six sacrifices. Both you and Danner are supposed to be killed tomorrow." Rolf snickered. "Won't the God of War be pissed when He isn't honored properly?" Rubbing his hands together in glee, Rolf looked like a child in a room full of sweets. "Maybe King Useph will go into one of his rages and have them sacrifice Sneed instead."

"A nice thought," Garron agreed, but he wished he could see Rolf's face better. This sudden change of heart didn't sit well with him. Still, there were few choices. He either tunneled or died. If Rolf turned him in to the guards, then he was no worse off than he'd be tomorrow if he stopped his plans to escape. "Why don't you come with us?"

"My kingdom is here, Protector. And here I'll stay. Having you leave will ensure I don't have to kill you. Or that you finally become lucky and end up killing me."

Garron knew Rolf was born to rule this dungeon. Top side, he'd be a mean little man people avoided, but here prisoners worshipped him.

Garron took one last glance at the grate, saying a silent goodbye to a woman he'd come to feel more for than he'd thought possible in a few short days. "Bring her to me, Rolf, if she comes."

"She's not coming."

"No," Garron agreed, sadness at the thought twisting inside him. "But just in case. And I'll escape so that you can have your laugh."

"We have a bargain then."

* * *

Useph's breathing went shallow. Sweat and poison covered his face.

Caelan had bathed quickly, changing into the robes that someone had brought her. Now she knelt in prayer to the Goddess, asking for healing power.

Hours had gone by while she fought the fast acting poison, which seemed able to regenerate itself more quickly than she could expel it. She'd gotten here just in time. She hoped. As she prayed, she wondered for the first time if maybe she wouldn't be able to save the King.

"Why haven't you healed him?" Sneed snarled yet again. Over the last hours, Caelan had watched him become more and more concerned that Useph might actually die. Panic had set in. Sneed might be stealing money from the crown, but he needed Useph to maintain his place in life.

"The poison is different from anything I've ever seen before. It's as if the moment I take a piece of it out of him, another piece duplicates itself."

That was true. What she didn't say was that her connection with the Goddess didn't feel right to her. Worry made it hard to focus, the strange hum inside her a constant distraction. She'd exchanged power with Garron only a few hours ago, so perhaps it was his energy she felt twisting inside her. But it didn't feel like the warm aggressive hand of his magic. It felt softer, more rich — more like the feeling of the first sunbeam of spring hitting her face than the thrust of Battle Shout.

She raised her hand over the King's chest. Speaking was a slow and draining art. Even small cuts could take many hours to heal if the connection with the Goddess wasn't strong. With complete focus, she blocked everyone and everything out of her mind. Holding her hand over his heart, she tried to draw the noxious green fluid from him.

"Goddess, help me take this poison from King

Useph's body," she said for the hundredth time. And just as it had every time she'd asked, a small piece of herself was lost, left in exchange for the Goddess's help. It was a depleting process that left her feeling as if she'd been wrung like a wet rag, twisted, squeezed and battered.

Another Speaker finally arrived from a nearby town, answering Caelan's request for help. Shandra's face glowed with the excitement of standing close to the King for the first time. She staggered through her curtsy, young and green, full of potential that might never arrive.

Just looking at her made Caelan ache inside as she beckoned the girl to her side. She'd been Shandra once and had ended up turning into only a healer, albeit the Speaker to the King, instead of one of the all-seeing, all-knowing Council Mothers who'd devoted their lives to communion with the Goddess.

Glancing back at the King on the edge of death, she realized there was no shame in that. Speakers saved lives. Speakers had their own power.

Shandra wrinkled her nose. "Poison, then."

"Yes," Caelan agreed. She could no longer smell it. It had permeated the air long so that her nose had blocked the stench out, but if she concentrated, she could taste a bitter tang on the back of her tongue. "I'll need you to bathe the poison away as I draw it."

After the short break, Caelan felt her exhaustion tenfold. Shandra would need to spell her so she could commune with the Goddess and gather her energy to heal again. Whatever the King had been poisoned with wasn't reacting to the usual words.

"Can you Speak to him while I refocus?"

Shandra nodded, shifting to take over, her hand sliding beneath Caelan's.

As she climbed to her feet, aches she hadn't even notice screamed at her. She had started the healing already tired, hungry, and dehydrated from her time in The Abyss. Now, with her spiritual energy depleted, she felt a hundred years old.

"Where are you going?" Sneed growled, catching her arm, his fingers biting into her skin.

"I must refocus by praying to the Goddess. The poison is fast-acting and difficult to expel. I'm going to the King's Altar Room."

"You're not leaving," he snarled. "You will stay until he is healed."

"Use your mind, Sneed. She isn't going to leave without healing me. She'll only get what she wants if she cures me. Let her go." Useph's weak voice held complete conviction, and Caelan realized that because she'd asked for something in return, she'd finally become someone Useph understood.

Sneed dropped her arm, and she slid quickly into the Altar Room. This was the King's personal place to commune with the Goddess.

The space was washed in mosaics, the walls a panoramic view of the nearby Goddess Temple where Caelan had lived for two years.

For a moment, she stopped and stared at the familiar view. She hadn't thought of her time there in so long, choosing to block out that time in her life completely.

When she'd first arrived, she'd been filled up with the Goddess's love and spirit, able to envision the past and future, as well as see when people spoke falsely. A life of study, meditation, and communion with the Goddess had stretched before her. Caelan had been so proud, so sure she was destined for the greatness of the Council.

Staring at the mosaic of the Meditation Garden, she remembered her last time there. She'd sat beside the small waterfall, rage the likes of which she'd never known coursing through her body. Memories flooded back, her thoughts from that day swirling in her mind.

How dare her mother dishonor their family? How could she have ruined them all with behavior so crass, so base, and unworthy? Had her mother been so caught up in this man she'd claimed she loved that no one mattered more to her, not even her only child?

Her mother had been put to death for aiding her lover in his plot to kill the King. It was absolute and utter insanity, and if her mother hadn't had her head separated from her neck the day before, Caelan would have told her mother exactly what she thought of her.

But now she knew why her mother had acted as she had, even if she didn't agree with all her decisions, and she mourned her death for the first time.

Caelan stared at the bench she'd sat on and realized she hadn't just blamed her mother for what had happened. She'd blamed the Goddess. Secretly, she'd wondered how the Goddess, who was all knowing and all seeing, could let this happen.

A shiver raced along her skin as Caelan finally saw what she'd done. She'd blamed the Goddess for her mother's sins, and it had cut her off from the loving power of her deity. How could Caelan feel the Goddess's love when she was so busy blaming the Goddess for her mother's wrongs? How could she feel the Goddess's power when she had been so filled with accusations, righteousness, and rage?

Trying to still the trembling in her hands, Caelan lit seven candles, saying a prayer over each one. Then she knelt on the steps in front of the statue of the Goddess and bowed her head. "I have been blinded by my own anger and hate. I have pushed You away. I have blamed You for things that were not Your fault." Tears built behind her eyes, and she blinked them away to focus on the loving gaze of her deity. "I see it now when I couldn't see it before, and I ask Your forgiveness."

She knew why she'd been able to have this epiphany. Through her relationship with Garron, she'd finally understood how a woman could love a man enough to sacrifice herself, sacrifice anything to save the man she loved. She still didn't agree with what her mother had done. It was selfish and wrong on so many levels. But Caelan finally at least understood how it could happen.

And once she understood her mother, she was able to see that she'd blamed the Goddess for the trauma in her life, even though a child could have told her that the Goddess let people make their own mistakes.

Tipping up her face and closing her eyes, Caelan felt the Goddess's love pour down onto her.

Joy and power spilled from her eyes in silent tears, celebrating the end of ten years in a spiritual desert.

And in that moment, Caelan finally understood that the Goddess had been with her this whole time. She had not been silent. She had only been waiting for Caelan to listen to her once more.

Chapter Seven

Garron passed the last rock to Danner, seeing the first ray of daylight cresting the horizon from his newly finished escape tunnel. The rush of excitement he'd expected didn't arrive.

Sitting in the tunnel, he took a deep breath of the fresh morning air, the crisp sting of new spring filling his lungs. Worry ate at him, fear growing about where Caelan was and what could be happening to her.

"We did it!" Danner said, his nervous voice quavering on the words. "We're out."

Garron closed his eyes, and there, behind his lids, a picture of Caelan came to him. She knelt on cold marble, tears streaming down her face, the sleeves of her white robe pooled around the elbows of her outstretched hands.

Danner shoved his shoulder. "What are you waiting for man? We're here. Let's go!"

He couldn't do it. At least not without checking one last time that she hadn't been returned to The Abyss. "I'm going back to make sure Caelan isn't here." He started to slide backwards, but Danner's body blocked him.

"Are you insane? Garron, if you return, something might happen that keeps us from leaving. We must go now!" Danner's voice threaded with panic.

"You can go. I'm not stopping you," he said, understanding that his action made no sense. He just couldn't help himself. "Just back up so I can pass you and then you can leave. I need to make sure she's not here." He knew she wasn't, but he couldn't afford to trust his gut.

"No. I'm not going any place but out!" Danner's voice raised an octave. "Move so I can escape!"

Garron sighed, and pulled himself through the entrance. Danner had finally gone around the bend, his nerves getting the better of him. Climbing to his feet, he made a sweeping motion with his hand. "Go, so I can check for her."

Sliding through the hole, Danner looked beyond him. "Here," he yelled, his voice cracking on the words.

Men jumped from the woods, their spearheads glinting in the fragile sunrise. And in the blink of an eye, Garron stood surrounded, the action so fast, he couldn't think, his mind still on Caelan and the fact she might possibly be in The Abyss, that she might need him.

His fighting instincts rushed through his veins too late. He counted twenty King's soldiers, all dressed in full battle regalia. Fleeing into the cave was his only option, but when he spun, Danner blocked him.

Danner had betrayed him. Danner, not Rolf. Why hadn't he even suspected? "Is this how you repay me for helping you?" Garron asked, his voice more tired than angry.

"They caught me pilfering the tools. They'd laid them out to trap us." Danner raised a shaking hand. "Garron, you have to believe me. I didn't approach them to betray you."

Rough hands grabbed Garron's arms, twisting them behind his back.

"Yeah, you're a real Saint, Danner," one of the guards sneered. "He traded your life for his. Sneed's long suspected someone would try to tunnel out."

"I have to live, Garron. I have to live." Danner held up a hand in a plea.

"Back in the hole, Danner."

"I'm sorry, Garron. So sorry," Danner whimpered.

"If you're truly sorry, then promise me you'll protect Caelan if she ever comes back to The Abyss." Garron put the full force of his Battle Shout not into saving himself but into reinforcing his order.

"Y-yes," Danner stammered. "I swear I will."

Garron nodded. It was the best he could do. Two guards yanked him away, taking him not to freedom and not to The Abyss, but to death. He'd be one of the six sacrifices today to the God of War.

* * *

The King was healed.

In the windowless room, it was impossible to know the time, but Caelan suspected morning was approaching quickly or perhaps it already arrived. Garron would be close to tunneling out now, or maybe he'd already slid from the ground, lifting himself to freedom.

She hadn't considered that healing Useph would take every ounce of her skill and so many hours that time stopped having meaning. Her bargain with Useph no longer mattered as it once had, since by now Garron would be gone. But she'd see it through.

As Sneed helped Useph to his feet to enter his royal bath, she took a deep breath. Now was the time to remind the King of his promise, now was the time to be strong, even when she could barely stand on her own two feet, she was so exhausted.

"My King," she said, dropping to her knees before him.

"Caelan," he said, arrogance once again strong in his voice.

"I ask you respectfully about your promise." She didn't look up, too scared he'd go back on his word. What would stop him? *Garron's escaped. He may have been free for hours.* So would this really matter? Still, it was something she wanted to do for him, something she had to do to repay him.

"Sneed, take care of it," Useph said, his voice dryly amused.

"But Sire, he's part of the Mabon sacrifice."

Useph's eyes narrowed, and the room seemed to contract. "Not any longer." Wrath swirled around him at Sneed's protest.

Sneed dropped to one knee. "Yes, Sire. I will take care of it."

"And find out who poisoned me. I want their head on

227

a pike." The King straightened to his full height and walked from the room unaided.

Sneed's gaze met hers. Rage and fury simmered in every jerk he made as he climbed to his feet. "You little bitch. You had to try to save the one man who must die." He paced a tight circle. Then he turned, striding from the room in a swish of his ceremonial robes.

Garron should be already free. Sneed just didn't know it yet. *My sacrifice came too late.*

In a daze, Caelan walked down the long corridor from the throne room, trying to figure out where to go. It didn't seem right to return to her old life. She wasn't the same person any longer.

Ten years ago, why had she even returned to the castle? Why, when she'd become a Speaker, had the Council of the Goddess Temple sent her here? She was an excellent healer, but they could have sent someone else, someone with a less painful history.

Stepping onto the battlements into the fresh, bright late morning sunlight, she realized why they'd sent her here. The Council in their wisdom had known staying in the castle would force her to eventually face her past demons.

And she had.

"It's so late," she whispered into the crisp spring wind. "He's gone." She wished she could see him in her mind, as she'd once seen visions as a child. But even if that power had returned to her, exhaustion made that impossible.

Looking down at the rolling green hills of Useph's kingdom, Caelan decided to leave the castle, with the Council's blessing or without. She'd go to Trayborne and be their healer. Nothing had ever sounded so right to her.

"You saved him," Brianna said from the shadows behind her.

Caelan faced her friend. "Yes. Did you think I wouldn't?"

"One can only hope." The words were bitter, grating against the beautiful day. Bree's face, molted into a million colors of pain, held the twist of desperation and maybe a touch of madness.

And then Caelan knew. "You poisoned him," she whispered.

"Yes." No regrets. No sadness. Her loving, gentle friend was gone.

"With what?"

"Mulgwort."

It fell into place then. The first time Brianna had told her about Radley, her face had been filled with joy and a happiness so deep, it shown from her face like a beacon. "I never thought I'd love anyone like I love him," Bree had said, hugging herself as if she would split apart with all the love inside her.

Caelan had tried to hide the worry and dread that filled her. "Bree, just be careful," she'd cautioned. "You're playing with fire here. If Useph finds out—"

Fear had flashed over Brianna's face, and her eyes had darted around the room, landing on a lockbox Caelan kept in the corner of her workroom. "What do you keep in this thing anyway, Caelly?"

Caelan had sighed but had given in to the change of subject. "Mulgwort." The Council had given it to her for a case of wasting sickness. "It's deadly, so I keep it locked away."

"Why would you have this if it's so dangerous?"

"The people who are given Mulgwort are dying anyway, Bree. In tiny doses, the poison might kill off any growths a person with wasting sickness has inside their body. But even a thimble full of it would kill them."

Caelan blinked, returning back to the battlements and the present. "Do you know what you almost did, Bree? You almost killed our King."

"He raped me." The words were stark, no more tears left for her friend to cry. "I wanted him dead. Then I

229

planned to kill myself."

"You don't have to stay here," Caelan whispered, trying desperately to save her. If Brianna knew there were options, she might be saved. "Come with me to Trayborne. Or go to the New Worlds and find Radley. But don't stay here."

Brianna laughed, a sharp bark of pain. "You think Radley would want me now?"

Caelan remembered his face, the love he'd felt shinning from his eyes. "Yes," she whispered. "I do. But even more importantly, do you want to spend your whole life trapped with Useph, wondering, aching for Radley?" She crossed to her friend, gripping her arm even though Brianna flinched when she touched her. "Even if you never see him again, you have proven yourself strong enough to be free from here."

"I betrayed you," Brianna whispered, the hard shield falling from her eyes, letting the pain shine plainly there.

"I forgive you," Caelan said, embracing her friend in a tight hug. "Run. Run, Bree. Don't stay here to die. Now is the time for us to grab our destinies with both our hands and spread our wings to become something. It's now or never. Take a chance. Failing is better than staying here to become Useph's victim."

She felt Brianna nod and tightened her grip when tremors of fear wracked her friend. "I know you're scared. I'm scared, too. But we can make a life for ourselves away from here. I swear to you."

Brianna nodded, then began to cry.

* * *

Garron's head snapped back under the driving force of Sneed's fist.

"How did a nothing like you even meet her?" Sneed paced the length of the cell, his rage suffocating in the small space.

Garron suspected the King's advisor had lost his mind. "Who?" he asked, then regretted it when he started the blood flowing from his bottom lip again.

He'd been decently treated after he'd been caught escaping this morning. It had only been moments ago that Sneed had him tied to the chair. Now it appeared he would not be sacrificed to the God of War without being tortured first.

"Speaker Caelan," Sneed spat. "That nothing of a girl. She'll ruin all my plans."

Caelan's name ran like a dagger through Garron's body. Instinct had him fisting his hands and struggling against his bonds. He forced himself to calm immediately. If Caelan was in trouble, revealing his feelings for her would only give Sneed more power over them both.

Sneed laughed, a short spurt of disgust. "She bargained for you with the King." He crossed the room in three strides to stare at Garron as if he was a bug caught in a net. "She's scared of her own shadow, but she negotiated for your freedom." Sneed's feral eyes narrowed. "Why?"

Garron fought to keep his face blank as his heart sang. She'd tried to bargain for his freedom. He'd never had anyone protect him before. Always he'd been the one sacrificing for others. But Caelan had tried to save him. Finding his voice and damping the joy from it, he said, "I have no idea."

"There her best friend was, a slave to the King, and she didn't save her. She chose you." Sneed gripped Garron's hair, yanking it back. "I want to know why. What does she know?"

"Nothing." Garron narrowed his eyes, trying to sound scoffing when his neck was exposed to a mad man. "You threw her into The Abyss, Sneed. I found her and saved her from being torn to shreds. Of course she would feel in my debt."

"How noble of you, Garron." Sneed's voice was filled with a heady brew of rage and volatility.

Garron had to do something to distract him from

Caelan, to turn the focus back onto himself. "Not noble, Sneed. She paid for my protection with her body." It had been so much more than that. She'd filled his very soul, and he knew without her in his life, a piece of him would be missing forever. But if he had to cheapen what they had to protect her, then cheapen it he would.

As he'd anticipated, Sneed stepped back, tapping his lips with one finger, as if he couldn't decide if he believed Garron or not. "Why would she save you if you used her? That makes no sense."

"She would have died."

Sneed flapped a hand. "Yes, yes, but women hold grudges forever when you force them."

"I'm telling you what happened. She was nothing to me. Just a woman I bedded. I wasn't even planning to bring her with me when I escaped."

"Yes, yes, the escape." Sneed tsked. "Really, Garron, do you think you can escape me?"

"I was hoping to, yes." Garron didn't release the breath he'd been holding as Sneed turned his attention from Caelan.

Sneed laughed. "For a border rat, you have been a worthy adversary. Which saddens me that you must die. You're the only one left who knows what I did in Trayborne, and I know you'd kill me for it if you could. I won't spend my life looking over my shoulder." He pulled a black scarf from his pocket.

Garron fought his natural instinct to fight his way free. Battle Shout was a useless power when he was tied. Even if he forced Sneed to flee, he still would be chained here. "It isn't as if I can prove it was you in Trayborne."

"It wasn't me. It was that idiot Farley I put in charge of collecting the extra taxes. He killed your parents without consulting me, claiming I'd said to make sure no one knew what he'd done." Sneed shook his head. "I always wondered how you found out my connection. I'd thought I'd insulated myself well enough."

"Farley told me without my having to lay a hand on him. I agreed that the man who ordered my parents' death would be a better person to kill than him." The fact was, as many people as Garron had killed on the battlefield, killing Farley in cold blood hadn't been something he could stomach. Killing Sneed was a totally different matter. He'd been ready to do it. Now he just wanted his freedom. And Caelan.

"Farley is a bigger idiot than I'd thought. I'll have to take care of him after I take care of you."

"I believe he's left the country."

"I'll find him. I can always find my prey." Sneed tied the scarf across Garron's mouth, causing the coarse fabric to bite into his cheeks. "Luckily for me, the sacrifices to the God of War are led in with hoods on their faces. Yours will just have an extra piece to it." He gave the scarf an extra yank. "No one will ever know it's you up there."

As the black hood lowered over his head, Garron's last sight was of the man who'd killed his parents.

* * *

Within the hour, Caelan had traversed the long palisade between the castle and the Temple of the Goddess. It had been years since she'd made this trip, but she was finally ready.

As she entered the Council's inner sanctum, her exhaustion dropped away under the weight of fear she always felt when she came here. It had been ten years since she'd last stepped foot in this room and received her assignment to become the castle Speaker.

The round citadel hadn't changed. It was as if time had stopped here while the rest of the world moved on. From the ceiling, light spilled down onto the cold, blue marble floor. Statutes ringed the room, the Goddess displayed in her seven forms. The loving mother, the healer, the seer, the warrior, the benevolent Goddess, the bringer of justice, the savior — she was all these things.

Caelan walked to the center of the room, up the three

round stairs to the empty dais to stand in the perfect circle of light there.

Warmth from the sun spilled onto her up-tipped face, and magic purred through her body. Loving power from a Goddess who had never left her. Without thinking, Caelan raised her hands palms upward to feel the light. "Thank You for waiting for me to understand," she whispered.

"So," an old woman said behind her. "Your power has returned, Caelan."

Caelan turned in slow motion, reluctant to give up the loving communion. "Council Mother, I come to ask for a new assignment."

"Yes," the Mother of Healing said, her old eyes large in her face, one a normal blue, the other an odd, opaque gray. In Council style, her hair had been shaved, the hood of her robe sitting far back on her head, leaving only the stark, sharp features of an old woman who had spent her life in worship.

"I want to leave the castle." Caelan's voice trembled, all her old fears hovering in the corners of her mind. She pushed them aside. "I will be leaving the castle."

"Interesting." The Council Mother studied her for a long moment.

Caelan held perfectly still.

"And where will you go?"

Pulling herself up as tall as she could, Caelan took a deep breath. She'd leave with or without the Council's support, but she would dearly love to have them approve her decision. "I've heard Trayborne, a small village on the border, is in desperate need of a healer."

"I have heard this also." The Mother turned on her heel. "Come," she said. "We have places we must be. We'll speak on the way."

Only they didn't speak. With a speed belying her age, the Council Mother strode through the temple, her cape flowing out like wings behind her.

Footsteps sounded, and when they rounded the

corner to the foyer, they were joined by four other Council Mothers, their faces eerily alike as if they were clones of one another.

Fear climbed in Caelan's belly. There was something about the way they strode down the marble stairs that said the side of the Goddess they were about to display was more warrior than benevolent kindness.

The five Mothers formed around her in an odd circle. The pace was grueling as they strode down the long palisade that carried the name The Walk of Kings. It connected the Temple of the Goddess with the castle. She'd once been told that the Temple and the King had worked hand in hand to run the country, but that had been many generations ago. The Temple had little to do now with kingdom politics.

As they neared the castle, they entered the sea of Mabon revelers who had come to see the annual sacrifices to the God of War. The commoners, most with faces flushed from too much drink even this early in the day, parted before the Mothers, stumbling away in instinctive flight. The Goddess of All Things had, in legends, always hated the God of War. They were bitter enemies, and seeing five Council Mothers on the God of War's sacred day must have been a shock.

They continued without pause, and suddenly, Caelan knew where they were going. Fifty feet before them, Useph sat on a high platform surrounded by his most trusted advisors. The bright reds of their celebration robes splashed against the browns of the common men surrounding them. Directly across from Useph was another platform, filled with six hooded men tied to six large stakes.

Caelan's breath hitched in her throat. She'd never come to this celebration, was, in fact, forbidden from attending as a follower of the Goddess of All Things.

A hand steadied her when she stumbled, before she stumbled, actually, as if the Council Mother had known she would trip.

Commoners retreated, pushing back to form a circle in the center of the two platforms. A hush settled as people anticipated an added show for their amusement.

Caelan wanted to crawl into a hole and hide there. She might have reclaimed the Goddess's touch, but at that moment, she realized she wanted to live a quiet life, full of helping people and changing the world for the better through small victories. This kind of intrigue would never be for her.

Useph rose, his calculating eyes briefly landing on Caelan, before taking in the Council Mothers before him. "It is Mabon, Goddess worshipers. To what do we owe this most unusual visit?"

"Do you make a liar of yourself, King Useph?" the Council Mother at her right asked, her old voice creaking through the words as if she rarely spoke.

Useph's mouth spasmed on words he obviously stopped from voicing. He had to be careful, Caelan realized. Starting a war with the Temple would bring him nothing but more problems. The Council still had power. "I am no liar, Council Mother."

"I hope not," the Mother said.

It was then that Caelan felt it, the shiver of magic at her back. Shouter magic. Garron's magic.

She pivoted in slow motion.

"I don't have time for this nonsense." Useph threw himself into his throne chair with a huff. "Proceed with the ceremony!"

Caelan recognized Garron immediately, the huge body standing ramrod straight, the large expanse of his chest that she'd memorized under her fingers.

Six men lined up before the sacrifices, arrows already notched in their bows.

"No," she whispered. Then louder, "Useph, you promised to pardon him!"

Sneed stepped forward, stumbling in his haste.

"Under the law of this land and the God of War, we sacrifice these men, to bring us glory in battle for the coming year!"

It happened as if it was a dream, her body moving of its own accord, sprinting up the steps, racing toward Garron's bound body.

"Stop!" she cried, the force of Garron's power that was still inside her filling the air.

The arrows flew through the air so slowly, she wondered if magic held them at bay.

She reached him as the arrow arrived in slow motion, batting it away with her hand like she might shoo away an annoying fly. The arrow tip grazed her palm, barely cutting the surface.

With shaking fingers, she ripped the hood from Garron's face, pulling the gag from his mouth.

"Caelan," he whispered, her name like an anthem from his lips.

"You promised to pardon this man, did you not?" one of the Council Mother's said into the silence behind her.

Caelan tried to undo the ropes at his wrists, but her fingers were numb. She looked on helplessly as her right hand fumbled, unable to grasp his bonds.

"I have no idea. Did I?"

"You did!" Caelan yelled to him, feeling strange. "You promised me."

"Sneed, you will provide an explanation." Useph turned to his advisor.

"There must be a mistake, Your Highness. I'll look into it immediately."

"There is no mistake." Garron's voice rang through the clearing. "He needed me dead. I knew about him stealing tax money from you, King Useph. He had to make sure his secret died with me."

Caelan stared at her hand, her palm and fingers puffing up in front of her eyes, although she couldn't be sure, since things were blurred, fading in and out.

"He's using his power of Battle Shout to cloud your judgment, King Useph. Do not listen to him!"

"He cannot lie, or he loses his abilities. Just as a Speaker will lose her ability to heal," one of the Mothers said from far away.

Caelan's sight narrowed to just her palm, and suddenly, her legs could no longer support her. *I've been poisoned*, she thought, as the ground reached up to meet her falling body.

Chapter Eight

Garron watched Caelan fall, his hands still tied so he couldn't reach for her. Helpless. He was so helpless. It made him want to hurt someone, preferably Sneed.

The witches from the Goddess Temple ran to his woman. He didn't want their hands on her. "Untie me," he ordered the one with the odd light gray eye that seemed to stare right through him. "Untie me," he said again, this time infusing the words with power.

"Ahh," the old witch said, the word like a purr of satisfaction. "A man blessed with Battle Shout."

The other four witches looked at him with suspicion.

"You dare to defy my direct order? You'll die for this," Useph yelled, but Garron could barely hear him over the ringing in his ears. He had to reach Caelan, had to touch her.

The one with the gray eye stood up and pulled a ceremonial dagger from her sash, then disappeared behind him. Garron tensed as she cut him free, not entirely certain she could see well enough to wield the knife.

"The arrow had poison on it," a Mother said, her voice expressionless.

Garron dropped to his knees. "Caelan, love," he whispered, running his thumb over the blue ring forming around her lips. "Don't die."

He'd tasted her healing power, still held some of the soft glow of it inside him. Could he use her own power to heal her?

Leaning over, he rested his lips against hers, then blew her magic, mixed tightly with his, into her mouth.

"He attempts to heal her." He could feel the Council Mothers' disapproval.

"Unusual," said the gray-eyed witch.

Caelan's eyes blinked open.

"Tell me the words to Speak, Caelan, so I can heal

239

you," he whispered to her.

"You don't need words, Shouter. You only need the love of the Goddess."

"If you have the power, help her," he growled.

"We are not here to change the natural order of things. She chose to give her life for yours. Who are we to change that?"

"So you won't save her?" A snarl formed on his lips, but he fought it when Caelan's eyes blinked open once more. "Tell me the words to heal you, love. I have your power inside me."

A chill shivered over her, but her gaze was unclouded. "You say," she whispered, then stopped to swallow. The breath she took rattled through her lungs, as if it was hard for her to breathe.

He waited, but nothing more came from her lips. Clasping her hand to stop the tremble, he stared into the sky. "Goddess, if you hear me, I offer the trade of my power to heal her."

The witches gasped as one. To lose his power would mean to lose a piece of himself. But if he couldn't have Caelan in his life, then his magic was nothing.

"Do you know what you are asking?" the gray-eyed one asked.

"Goddess, I offer you my power for the ability to heal Caelan from this poison."

"Say it again, and it may come true," the witch murmured, her eyes narrowed into considering slits.

"Goddess, I offer my power for the ability to heal Caelan, my one true love."

"He invoked love magic," someone whispered, but Garron was too busy staring skyward.

He knew the Goddess wasn't really in the sky. She was all around him, but he needed to visualize the Goddess's loving gaze in his mind.

Like a cool wind, something whipped through him, and he felt a piece of his soul rip away. Pain ran fast on its heels, as if someone had peeled a layer of his skin from his body. He dropped onto Caelan's chest, balling around her like the lifeline she was.

Then a light poured through him, filling him up, replacing his magic with something else, something more powerful and right.

When he straightened, he knew he didn't have to speak words to heal her. Placing his mouth upon hers, he breathed in healing life, forcing the poison from her very pores.

On and on he jammed the magic into her body with his breath, filling her lungs, filling her every cell.

When her eyes blinked open, he knew the Goddess had prevailed.

Panic broke out behind him as a group of guards raced into the celebration. "King Useph! All the prisoners in The Abyss have escaped!"

Garron smoothed back the hair from Caelan's face, unable to stop the smile spreading on his lips. Rolf had wanted him to break out of the dungeons to cover his own escape. Sneed would face his own death for his betrayal of the King. Caelan would live. Amusement and joy swirled in his chest. He kissed Caelan slowly to celebrate.

"I love you," he whispered. "More than life itself."

"And I love you, Garron. More than life itself."

* * *

Caelan had awoken in the Temple of the Goddess two days ago, her strength rapidly returning after her near brush with death. She'd seen Garron but only with one of the Council Mothers in the room.

The life in the Temple was based on celibacy to attain a closer relationship to the Goddess, and a man in the Temple had been enough of an anomaly. The lack of contact, though, had her second guessing his words of love to her. After all, she'd saved his life. That would inspire anyone to say they loved her. Doubt sat in her stomach like a tight knot.

This morning, she'd been summoned to the Council Chamber, a long marble hall full of cold spots that brought a chill when Caelan walked through them, as if ghosts were chained to the floor at intervals. The hair on her arms always rose when she entered, made worse by the fact that the Council Mothers never called people to them for anything but the direst of events.

When she entered the chamber, the spring sun appeared cold on the blue marble floor, the windows leaving arched splashes of light leading to the end of the room where the Council Mothers waited behind a long, bare black marble table. There were seven of them, one for each face of the Goddess, their features blending together with their shaved heads and gray hoods resting away from their faces.

Garron stood before them, half turned to watch her.

As she passed into the sunlight, then out again, Caelan tried to anticipate why she'd been summoned. Her healing powers remained intact, but the Goddess had returned some of her old abilities. She just wasn't sure what they were yet.

She could feel the heady glow of power, the sensation similar to what she'd had when she was thirteen, but nowhere near as strong, she knew. That was fine with her. She wanted peace and simple healing, not a life in silent contemplation and worship.

Passing from the last arch of sunlight, she stopped before the Mothers, bowing to them with respect. The only difference between now and the other times she'd stood before them was that, while she respected their guidance, she knew exactly what she planned to do with the rest of her life. And who she'd like to do it with.

"Your powers," said the Mother of Healing. "They are still intact?"

"I believe so, yes." Caelan paused, then admitted, "Although I feel they have changed in some way. I do not know exactly how yet."

Another Mother smacked her hand on the table, the sound so surprising, Caelan jumped. "Of course they've changed. What do you expect to happen when you've traded magic with a man? Have you no sense, Caelan?"

"I'm sure I do have some sense, Council Mother." Caelan found she wasn't upset, instead fighting a smile. Her relationship with Garron brought her only happiness inside.

"We can't do anything about their exchange now. It's done," the Mother of Healing said, her tone dry. "But perhaps you should ask yourself what the impacts were to Garron before you become too smug."

Caelan's gaze found his. "Garron?"

"Tell her now," one of the Mother's ordered.

He smiled, a slow tip of one side of his lips, but his eyes were warm deep blue. "I gave up my ability to Battle Shout in order to heal you."

"Oh no!" Dread climbed up her spine. To lose his powers—she knew all too well how that felt. The experience was like having a piece of one's soul torn away. Tears of grief for him gathered, and she blinked to hold them back.

In two strides, he crossed to her, cupping her chin in his palm.

"This is not the place for that," a Mother barked, but Caelan had no idea who said it. Garron filled her world, so tall and big and wonderful, touching her for the first time in two long days.

"Don't cry, love." He kissed her forehead, the action gentle, although his lips stayed on her skin a few moments too long, as if he couldn't bring himself to stop touching her. "I've lost my ability to Shout but gained one of your old talents it seems."

Gained her magic? Legends claimed that it could happen, but she hadn't believed it was really possible.

"He's gained the ability to see lies, Caelan," the Mother of Healing informed her.

"It's a talent I can use as a Protector, love. I'm not upset at the change. It was worth the sacrifice to save you."

Caelan stared at him, her stomach filling with hope that they would stay together.

"Do you still plan to leave your position as castle healer?" the Mother of Healing asked.

Garron stepped away so Caelan could see her, but his hand tracked down her arm and curled around her fingers. Inside, her body jumped, instantly wanting him, even with so small a caress.

"Yes," she said, her voice shaky but not from her choice.

Garron's gaze slid to hers, and he winked.

He knew, she realized. Knew that she wanted him.

"What will you do?"

"I'm going to Trayborne," she said, ignoring the man rubbing his thumb over her hand in a slow tease. "They need a healer there."

"Yes, they do. Are you prepared to give up the glories of the castle for a hard life in a border town?"

"Yes." She was. She knew in her very soul that Trayborne was where she belonged, with or without Garron.

"Interesting that you both plan to go there," the Mother of Healing said, her eyes sparkling. Caelan had the odd thought that she was amused, but Council Mothers didn't have that emotion.

"You're going there, too?" Caelan met Garron's gaze and once again became lost in the deep blue of his eyes. This was the first time she'd been so close to them in the light.

"We'll go together," he whispered, and the words ran down her spine like a caress. "They need a Protector, as well as a healer, love."

The Mother of Healing cleared her throat. "You will be assigned to heal in Trayborne then, Caelan. Now both of you will leave us. This behavior is inappropriate for this sacred hall."

They didn't have to be told twice. Her mind was in such a whirl, Caelan didn't notice the rooms as they passed through them, didn't notice anything but the joy in her heart.

She was going to Trayborne with Garron at her side!

He pulled her along at almost a run, steadying her as she stumbled. "We have to get out of here," he said, his voice so urgent and full of desire, her stomach turned over. "Now."

* * *

Garron had to have her. Now, now, now. His patience was at an end. But first, he had to get out of the Temple. The witches' citadel gave him the creeps. It felt like he was surrounded by dead people begging to be freed. He had no idea why others felt the blue marble fortress was a peaceful, restful place.

They were running now, although he was forcing himself to slow down to match her shorter stride. "This is silly," he said to himself and swept her into his arms without pausing, eliciting a yip of surprise.

She didn't protest, though, curling her arms around his neck as he burst through a side door, not even caring where it led, just as long as it was out.

"We're not ever going back there," he told her, sure of that one thing above all others.

"No," she agreed.

He took her through the garden, needing to get away from the Temple lands. A small gate appeared in the wall and opened easily as he burst through it, releasing them as if by magic.

They ended up in a field of wheat, the ripening heads blowing in a soft breeze, enjoying the sun beating down on them.

He dropped to the ground, rolling so his body took the impact of their fall.

Her face, a beautiful mix of small features and pretty leaf green eyes, glowed as she stared at him. He smoothed back her hair with a shaking hand. "You're too beautiful for me," he said, speaking the truth. "But it's too late for you to escape."

"I don't want to escape," she whispered, her smile full of such obvious happiness, he had to kiss her.

The action relieved a giant pressure inside him, but rapidly built another. "Trayborne," he whispered into her lips when he came up for air.

"Yes." She was certain.

He kissed her again because he wanted to, and he could.

Then as one they struggled with their clothes, the drive to be naked against each other sharp and strong.

He rolled her onto his body and spread their clothes out as a makeshift bed. Then he placed her on them, following her down so he could have the maximum amount of her body touching his.

"I need this. I need you, Caelan. I love you." There was no embarrassment in the statement, only truth. He'd said those words to her already, but they had to be said again, or they'd burn him up inside.

"I need this, too, my love," she whispered.

He captured her lips, then ran his tongue down her neck in a slow sweep.

Her hands caressed his chest, his arms, his hips in an erotic massage that made him purr inside. "Just your hands on my skin brings me so much pleasure."

"I could touch you for hours." And something in her voice made him know she planned to touch him for hours right then.

"Not now." He captured her nipple in his mouth, suckling with just enough pressure to elicit a hiss and her hands in his hair. "Now I'm having you as fast as I can, while still bringing you pleasure."

She laughed, a throaty purr that he felt along the skin

of her breast as he ran his tongue there.

"Two days those witches kept me from you, and I played along, because I'm willing to do anything to have you." He cupped her sex, pushing with his palm to pin her clitoris. She arched in response. "But now I need you, Caelan. I need my cock inside you. I need to feel you holding me tight as we both find release."

"Oh," she said, her body writhing in a sensual stretch that told him he wasn't the only one on the edge of madness.

Parting her sex, he found her wet and ready but couldn't stop himself from ducking down for quick taste. He swept his tongue across her clitoris, tasting her desire. Then he pulled the bud into his mouth. Once, then twice, loving the look of pure desire and need which transformed her face.

"Garron, please."

"Please what," he whispered, wanting the words. He worked first one, then a second finger into her core, readying her to take him.

She opened eyes that had turned dark green with desire. "Please put yourself inside me."

"It will be my pleasure."

He gathered her hips into his hands, steadying her. Her fingers cradled his cock and guided him home. It was like heaven, like the most brilliant of fulfillments, made even more complete when she whispered, "I love you."

"I love you." He kissed her as his cock pushed deep. "I will always be with you, for as long as you'll have me in your life." His new found magic spun inside his body. The witches had warned him not to share power with her anymore, that it was too dangerous, but without a thought, he spilled his magic over her.

"Oh, Goddess, Garron it feels so good," she said, tears escaping from her tightly closed eyes.

Then she gazed at him, and her magic ran along his skin. He captured her lips so it could pour inside him.

That was enough to tip them over the edge.

The orgasm streamed over them both, filled with magic and love.

"You are everything to me," he gasped, knowing that it was true and that he would fight to his death to keep this one woman in his arms for all time.

AWAKENING

Vivi Anna

Prologue

The long, filmy, red curtains billowed out from the open windows, fluttering around her naked form like silken wings. Stepping through them, she approached the four-poster bed, draped in white satin sheets, in the center of the empty expansive room.

With each step, her heart hammered painfully in her chest. Sweat trickled down her back, and soft flutters of desire began to flicker between her legs.

The dream was the same every time.

The thought of seeing him naked on the bed brought swells of delight surging through her body. Already she was wet with an intense craving that left her breathless.

As she neared the bed, she could see the outline of him lying on the satin covers through the translucent white curtains hanging down from the canopy. With a trembling hand, she lifted the drape from the bed and knelt onto the mattress.

He was waiting for her, like he did every night. Stretched out across the bed, his head supported by his hand, he looked like a golden angel. His long blond hair was arranged artfully over his shoulders and fanned out around him like spun gold. He had flawless skin the color of alabaster, and it only accentuated the ripples of muscle in his arms, chest, stomach, and legs. Everything about him screamed perfection.

But it was his eyes that had always drawn her. Pale as moonlight and just as mysterious, they pulled at her insides. When he looked at her, she was like raw clay in his hands with which he could do anything he wanted.

"I have been waiting for you, my love."

His crisp lilting voice sang in her head, reminding her of a bubbling brook, much like the one in the garden of her childhood home. Smiling, she slid onto the bed, nestled her body next to his. His heat penetrated her skin and warmed her blood. When he touched her, she knew nothing but his flavor, his intensity. Here, in his arms, passion was the only thing that existed.

"And I am here." Lifting her head, she pressed her lips to his.

Raising his hand, he buried it into the tangle of her long auburn hair and pulled her closer, deepening the kiss. She sighed as his tongue touched hers in a long, liquid dance. Ripples of pleasure coursed over her, gathering into a tight sizzling ball right at her center. Thinking no longer seemed possible as pulse after throbbing pulse surged up from between her quivering legs.

His palm cupped her cheek. With one last press of his lips, he pulled back and gazed into her eyes.

"It is time, Branlyn."

"Hmm?" She sighed, cuddling into his warmth.

"You have run for long enough."

Closing her eyes against the memories of another time, she shook her head. "It is never long enough."

He wrapped his arms around her and pulled her close. "I know it is painful, but you must return."

"I can't."

"You can, and you must." He snuggled into her neck and kissed her gently. "It is time you went home."

Sighing, Branlyn felt the tears welling in her eyes. She knew this moment would come. The first night he visited her in her dreams, he said that one day would come when he would ask her for something. If she had known he would ask this of her, she might have pushed him out of her mind the first time he materialized.

"Will you be there?" she asked, her voice wavering.

"Of course, my love. I have never left."

Chapter One

"Are you sure you're ready, Branlyn?"

Branlyn Carmichael turned from the twentieth story window and looked at her lawyer and surrogate uncle, Thomas Brady. He was leaning forward in his chair, his hands clenched nervously on top of the old mahogany desk.

"No, but it's time. Fifteen years is a long time to be running. I'm tired, Thomas. I need to go home."

Smiling, he closed the thick manila file folder and stood. Rounding the desk, he took her hand and pressed his mouth to the back. "I am delighted you are here."

"Thank you." As she said the words, her stomach rolled over. Was she really ready to do this? During the flight from Toronto, she had three drinks and some percodone so she didn't have to think. Now that she was standing in her lawyer's office in downtown Vancouver, too many memories had rushed into her mind. She was dizzy from them.

Three days ago, when she had woken from a dream in her bed in a small flat in Paris, she had a desperate urge to come home. Need clawed at her mind, forcing her to think of nothing else. But now that she was only a ferry ride and a three-hour drive up the coast away, she was petrified to move.

Thomas must have seen the fear in her eyes because he helped her to a chair and sat her down, still cradling her hand in his.

"Do you want me to go with you? I could have Maureen clear my schedule in a matter of hours."

Smiling, Branlyn shook her head. "I appreciate the offer, Thomas, but this is one thing I need to do on my own. I owe my dad at least that much."

Nodding, he patted her hand and then stood. He went back around his desk and raised the watercolor painting hanging on the wall. Behind the artwork was a safe. Quickly, he unlocked it and brought out a small metal box, setting it on the desk.

Swallowing down the bile slowly rising in her throat, Branlyn watched as Thomas opened the box. She knew what was inside. Thomas lifted out a set of keys. They jangled in his hand.

"When you called to say you were coming back, I had Maureen get your dad's BMW out of the storage." He turned and offered her the keys. "It's all washed, gassed up, and ready to go."

Gingerly, she reached out and accepted the keys. She held them in her hand, feeling the solid weight of them in her palm. The keychain was still the same. *Hot Rod Dad*, it read in fire-red letters emblazoned across a photo of an old jalopy. It was a gift to her dad for his forty-fifth birthday. The last gift he ever received.

A single tear rolled down her cheek as she fingered the engraved metal.

"I thought you sold it at the auction."

"The other cars went, but I couldn't let this one go. I knew how much Harrison loved this car. It didn't seem right."

"Thank you." She squeezed the metal tight in her hand.

Nodding, he took out another set of keys and a folded set of documents.

Her heart raced like a speedboat in her chest, and her throat tightened with dread as she eyed the dangling silver metal. She leaned back in her chair, shrinking from Thomas's outstretched hand.

Take them. It's all right. They can do you no harm.

His lilting voice sounded in her mind, relaxing her instantly. Taking a deep breath, Branlyn sat forward and reached out toward Thomas. Carefully, he set the keys in her outstretched hand.

"You are officially the owner of Carmichael Manor. Electricity, heat, and water are all functional. So you don't have to worry about that. I hope you can finally find a sense of peace there."

"Me, too, Thomas. Thank you." She glanced down into her hand and took in the familiar shape of the keys to her childhood home. A place where she had been blissfully happy for fourteen years and then her whole world had been destroyed. Her father and stepmother had been brutally murdered before her eyes, sending her spiraling into a never-ending nightmare.

After the funerals, Branlyn had been shipped off to England where she lived for awhile with her paternal grandmother. In and out of counseling, she had been a handful for the elderly woman whom she had only met once before. The woman had never been motherly.

When she turned eighteen, Branlyn took a sizeable portion of her inherited estate and hit the road. Traveling from country to country, she never stayed in one place too long. At all costs, she avoided settling somewhere and growing roots. She also flitted from relationship to relationship. The only constant in her life was the nightmares of that terror-filled night. Until *he* came into her dreams.

It was only when *he*, the golden man with no name, was with her that she could forget. His presence lightened her heart and occupied her mind with thoughts of desire. He turned her frightened mewls of terror into moans and gasps of pleasure.

She had fallen in love with that dream. Too bad, he wasn't real.

One of the keys on the ring caught her attention. It was odd and out of place. With its long skeletal shape, it looked like an old brass key, possibly something from Victorian times.

"What's this?" She held it up toward Thomas.

Narrowing his eyes, he stepped closer. "You don't recognize it?"

"No. I've never see it before."

"It was on your step-mother's ring, I believe."

Branlyn rubbed her thumb over the metal and shivered. Something about it caused her stomach to tighten into a knotted ball.

"It looks old. Possibly Tamora had a chest or trunk?" Thomas offered.

Branlyn nodded absently as she continued to stare into her hand. Why such a simple thing should give her the creeps she couldn't fathom. It was just a key, was it not? Nothing as sinister as her heart pounding painfully registered. It was most likely as Thomas suggested. A key to an old chest or trunk. An heirloom perhaps that Tamora brought with her when she and Harrison had wed. Branlyn had been only seven when they married. It was not as if she could remember what the woman had brought to their home.

Still, shivers raced up and down her spine. A feeling of dark malice had crept into her skin, and she could not shake it.

* * *

Turning down Thomas's invitation to stay another night in town, Branlyn jumped into her father's BMW and drove to the ferry station to catch the three fifteen boat to Nanaimo on Vancouver Island. Branlyn knew if she delayed another moment, she would never again muster the courage to face her past.

The two-hour long trip seemed like an eternity as Branlyn stood on the main deck and watched the water. Now that she had made the decision to come home, she wanted to be there. The journey was nearly killing her inside. It had been a fifteen-year long road trip, and now that her final destination was within her grasp, she wanted to grab hold immediately. For she feared if she didn't, she would never make the effort again.

There was something this time that was driving her back. Tempting her home. The not knowing was like a pinprick in her mind.

The announcement that the ferry was nearing the Nanaimo port sounded over the speakers asking people to return to their vehicles. Branlyn stayed where she was, leaning over the railing, watching the way the boat cut through the water. Her heart felt the same as they neared the port. With every mile closer to her home, she could feel the pain of the past slicing into her.

As the dock came into view, she could hardly breathe. Her lungs burned with every quick intake of air, and her heart pounded against her ribs as if to break free and escape from the pain of her memories. She was only three hours away from her home. Three hours away from facing something she had been running from for so long. Was she really prepared for this? Was her mind stable enough to cope with the rush of distressful memories she was sure to encounter?

As the ferry prepared to moor, Branlyn straightened and took in a deep breath of salty ocean air. She would be all right. It was only a house. A house she had once loved dearly. Two rambling stories on an acre lot atop a cliff looking over a small-secluded strip of white sandy beach. How many times had she stood on her bedroom balcony and gazed out over the ocean, thinking how lucky she was to live in such a glorious place? Every day.

You will again.

His voice touched her mind like a lover's soft caress. She reached for that thought and held onto to it tightly. His presence, even fleeting and surreal, gave her the strength to turn and descend the stairs to her waiting car. That was the hard part—the rest she hoped would just come like the tides she so often watched out her bedroom window.

* * *

By the time Branlyn eased the BMW into the spatial estate's driveway, the sun was starting to set, and long shadows were cast over the immaculately kept front lawn. Turning off the ignition, she stared at her childhood home through the windshield, unsure if she could actually open her door and walk to the front stoop.

The house hadn't changed since she left. In fact, it looked exactly like it did the day she was forced to pack her suitcases and was shipped off to England.

From Thomas, she had learned that a local landscape company, paid by her family's estate money, kept up maintenance on the house and the grounds in hopes that Branlyn would one day return.

Now, here she was.

Grabbing her purse, she opened the car door and slid out. She walked around the car and made her way slowly up the front stone steps to the big white door. Hands shaking, she managed to put the key in and turn it. The audible click of the lock nearly made her jump out of her skin.

Taking a deep breath, Branlyn turned the doorknob and pushed opened the door.

A rush of memories surged over her on the stagnant air, and her knees buckled. Grabbing the doorframe, she kept herself on her feet but knew if she didn't sit down soon she would collapse.

Sinking to the threshold of the door, Branlyn put her head between her knees to take in some deep cleansing breaths. It was too hard to face. She wasn't strong enough. She should have never come back. The past should've remained behind the locked door of her childhood home.

You have the strength to do this, Branlyn. Look inside, and you will find it.

His voice sounded in her head, instantly calming her. Lifting her head, she took in a final cleansing breath and pushed to her feet. She turned and stepped past the doorframe and into the front foyer, shutting the door behind her.

Glancing around the high-ceilinged entrance way and through the arched way into the living room, Branlyn noticed that everything was still in place. None of the furnishings had been moved, just draped with white cloths to keep the dust and dirt from settling onto them.

She shuffled farther into the house and stood at the base of the curving staircase looking up toward the second floor where the bedrooms were housed. Clutching her purse tightly to her chest, she mounted the steps, taking each one with slow deliberate movements. She counted each one as she had when she had been a child. When she reached thirty, she was on the second floor landing.

To the right was her dad's office, her stepmother's sewing room, and a small half bathroom. On the left was her old bedroom, her dad and step-mom's room and another bathroom, the one she had used growing up. Taking a deep breath, she turned left.

The walk down the wide hall seemed to last an eternity. Her legs vibrated with each step. When she came to the first door on her right, she opened it and walked through.

Her walls were still pink, a soft hue like in a sunrise. All her girlie posters of movie stars and music idols were tacked up with hot pink thumb tacks. Pulling off the cloth covering her dresser, she smiled when she saw all her trinkets and knick-knacks she'd collected over the fourteen years of her childhood.

With shaking hands, she picked up the music box her mother had given her before she'd died. Branlyn had been only five, but she could still remember the day as if it had recently happened. Slowly, she opened the lid. Soft strains of Chopin floated out from the box's small speaker, and the little swan spun around on a blue crystal representing a pond. Tears streamed down her cheeks as she ran her finger over the tiny little bird. She remembered her mother calling her, her little swan.

Shutting the lid, Branlyn set the box back on her dresser. Turning, she walked out of her room and went down the hall to a set of double doors. Her father's bedroom. With pain swimming around in her heart and tears blurring her vision, she turned the brass knob and pushed open the doors.

A rush of stale air surged over her. Underneath it, she swore she could smell the woodsy cologne her father was so fond of wearing. The scent nearly brought her to her knees.

She had spent many years grieving for her father. For a few months she had retreated so far into herself, her grandmother had sent her to a child psychologist. The good doctor didn't do anything for her except push her farther into obscurity. By the time she was done with therapy, she was an angry withdrawn fifteen-year-old instead of just withdrawn.

All those same feelings came surging through her. Instead of an independent woman of twenty-nine, she felt like a frightened angry fourteen-year-old all over again, having just realized that she'd never see her father again.

Like a zombie, she wandered into the room. She pulled the sheet off her father's king-sized platform bed then collapsed onto it, her sobs so intense she could barely breathe. Curling herself in a ball, she cried. Wept all over again for losing her family and being left to fend for herself. She had been too young to be without someone to depend on, someone to love. She had been too young to be completely and utterly alone.

As she sobbed and wept, she had the distinct feeling of being comforted. As if a phantom had sat down beside her on the bed and put its arm around her. A male arm. She knew in an instant it was her dream lover comforting her. The wild scent of him swirled around her, and she breathed a sigh of relief.

* * *

Hours later, after full dark had settled in, Branlyn rolled off her father's bed and stretched. She had cried until, spent, she had fallen asleep. She supposed she needed it, having not slept more than two hours since leaving Paris almost four days ago.

Her crying jag had exhausted her, but she felt surprisingly refreshed. She felt cleansed. Maybe she needed to purge herself of her pain. To finally have it all come out. Now, maybe she could finally put the pieces of her life back together. In the same place where it had all fallen apart.

Twisting side to side trying to ease the aches starting to creep up on her, Branlyn wandered toward the floor-to-ceiling windows of the balcony and looked out over the manor's expansive garden. Pushing the door open, she stepped out onto the veranda. The fresh salty air swept over her and made her smile. There was nothing like the smell of an ocean breeze. That was one of the things she missed about living on the island.

She lifted her arms up and stretched her back. Then she froze.

There was someone in the garden.

Branlyn could see a dark shape standing by the stone water fountain.

"Who's there?" she called.

The form didn't move.

"I'm calling the police if you don't leave."

Branlyn.

She shivered as the sound of her name floated up to her on the warm salty breeze. She felt a sudden tug at her body, compelling her to go down into the garden.

Turning, she rushed from her father's room, ran down the stairs, and marched into the large kitchen facing the garden. She went to the glass doors at the breakfast nook, threw the lock, and opened them.

Branlyn. I've been waiting for you.

Again feeling something pulling her, as if an invisible rope had been tied around her waist, she walked out onto the porch.

Was it her dream lover calling her? Although she knew it to be impossible, she wanted desperately to see him. To be able to touch him. The seductive summons from the garden seemed familiar. Like the sound of her golden man's lilting voice. Curls of desire started to unfurl between her legs as she stepped down the steps and onto the garden's stone path.

She walked briskly, with purpose, as if whatever was calling to her wanted her to hurry. She could feel the urgency in the summons. And the seduction.

As she neared the fountain, her heart started to hammer in her chest. The little hairs at the nape of her neck rose to attention as a delightful tickle rushed down her back. She gasped as the pleasant sensations moved over her body and brushed at her inner thighs as if to coax them apart.

A sudden urge to rip off her clothes rippled over her. She wondered how the warm breeze would feel blowing over her heated flesh. And hot she was. Sweat dribbled down her chest to pool in her navel. Lifting her hands, she unbuttoned her blouse, her fingers quivering with the effort. Finally, she was able to shrug the cotton off and let it drop to the ground.

Instantly, she felt relief as the ocean air caressed her skin. However, it was not air she wanted to touch her skin. It was other flesh. A man's hands. Her dream lover's hands.

Certain he was waiting for her at the fountain, Branlyn jogged down the stone path eager to finally be in his solid arms. However, when she reached the stone circle, he was not there. No one was there waiting for her. Not that she could see. But she had a sense of being watched.

Turning in a slow circle, she surveyed the surrounding area, searching for the source of uneasiness.

Where was the form that she saw near the fountain? Had he ran off when she threatened to call the police?

"Where are you?" she called, her voice quaking with a mixture of fear and excitement.

I'm here, Branlyn, waiting for you, my love.

She turned toward the seductive whisper. She sucked in a breath as a presence neared her. A dark yet sensual presence. Her nipples tightened into hard peaks, and things between her legs began to quicken and pulse. Please touch me, she wanted to beg. She'd been waiting too long for release, for surrender.

Closing her eyes, she pushed out her breasts and took in a deep breath waiting for his touch. She could feel him so close. Nearing her with every shaky intake of air. Titling her head up, she parted her lips on a sigh, eager for his mouth.

Oh my darling, I have waiting so long…

No! She's not for you! You cannot have her!

Branlyn snapped out of her stupor and opened her eyes as a second voice reverberated around her. She spun around searching for the source. She spied nothing but plants, flowers, and the stone fountain.

"Who are you? What do you want with me?" Fear swelled over her. She had the sudden thought that she was in danger.

I want you, my love. You were born to be mine. Your father could not stop it.

Branlyn went still as her heart raced faster. Bile rose in her throat, and she had to swallow it down. "What do you know of my father?" she whispered.

Everything.

Before she could respond, a black shape rushed out of the shadows. Red glowing eyes, like flames, floating toward her.

She screamed.

But before the dark form could reach her, a bright light exploded all around. Squeezing her eyes shut from the intense glare, Branlyn had the distinctive feeling of being lifted into the air, and a powerful angry voice rang in her mind.

Thane!

Chapter Two

Sunbeams played across Branlyn's face as her eyes fluttered open. Blinking a few times, she took her time trying to decipher exactly where she was. The pink walls quickly gave it away.

She was in her old room, tucked safely into her bed. Rolling onto her back, she rubbed at her face and wondered what time it was. By the way the sun streamed in through the gauzy pink curtains, she thought it was still morning.

Stretching, she tossed back the down-filled duvet and sat up. A shiver ran through her. It was then she realized she was naked and that she had no clue how she had wound up that way in her old bed. The last thing she remembered was being in the garden at night. Why she had been there she couldn't quite recall, either.

She glanced around her room for her clothes and noticed them neatly folded and stacked on the easy chair in the corner by the big window. A sense of uneasiness washed over her. It was very unlike her to fold her clothes. More often than not, when she changed for bed, she tossed the old ones on the floor until the next morning when she would take care of them. And when did she ever sleep in the nude? Never.

She supposed she didn't have a choice as she left all her luggage in the trunk of the car. She must've been more exhausted than she thought and operating on autopilot. That would certainly account for the lack of memory of getting from the garden to her room.

Yawning and rubbing her eyes again, Branlyn stood and dressed in yesterday's clothes. The first thing she'd do was go down to the car, get her luggage, and change into something else. Clothes made for work because that's what she intended to do today. Patter around the house, remove all the coverings, and start to dig into her past. Ready or not, that's what she was here for.

After bringing in her two suitcases, Branlyn padded into the kitchen to make a list of what she needed to buy at the grocery store. Her stomach grumbled, reminding her she hadn't eaten in over eighteen hours.

She opened up the pantry door and nearly stumbled backwards. It was completely full. Rows of cans and boxes lined the six shelves. On the top shelf were seven cereal boxes—all her favorites. Well, they had been her favorites when she was a teenager. Her stomach rumbled again. Reaching up, she snatched the box of *Shreddies*. She loved eating them without milk anyway.

After opening the box, she dipped her hand in and came away with a handful of the wheat squares. While she popped them one by one into her mouth, she opened the stainless steel refrigerator. Gasping, she nearly choked on the cereal.

The fridge, too, was fully stocked. Again, all her favorite foods lined the shelves and filled the crispers. She pulled open one of the drawers and found a bushel of lush purple grapes. They were perfect and plump. She grabbed them, a can of cola, kicked the refrigerator closed, and set them on the counter. Looked like she didn't have to grocery shop after all.

Thomas must've phoned someone to come in and stock the kitchen for her. Maybe the people that did the landscaping also had access to the house. Surely, one of them must have done this.

She'd have to phone Thomas later and thank him. It was such a simple thing, but it was one of the most thoughtful things anyone had done for her in a long time. And for him to remember what she liked and didn't like was purely flabbergasting. Especially, since some of her tastes had changed in the past few years. But if anyone knew her, it was Thomas. He had been the only person she had stayed in contact with over the past fifteen years.

Her last link to her past.

Popping the tab open on the soda, she took a sip and wandered to the nook's glass doors. The sun was shining out on the garden, playing over the lush green of the plants and grass. Branlyn opened the door and stepped out onto the porch. She squinted up at the sun, loving how it felt on her face. How many times in the past had she'd done this very thing? Thousands. Sighing, she took another sip of her drink.

Home. She was finally home.

After finishing the grapes and her pop, Branlyn changed into jeans and a t-shirt and set about to clean the house. She started in the living room and made her way through the first floor, including the dining room and family room, then up to the second level.

It was late afternoon when she stood in the doorframe of her father's office. She had fond memories of sitting on the floor playing with her dolls while her father worked at his desk. Every once in while he would stop what he was doing, turn to her, and say *'Hey, Angel Face, whatcha doing?'* Then Branlyn would get up, sit on his lap, and proceed to tell him everything.

Tears fell as she recalled those wonderful moments. She wiped at her face and stepped back out of the doorway. Maybe she'd leave his room until the end. Turning to the left, she wandered into her stepmother's workroom.

Tamora had loved to sew and weave. She had made most of Branlyn's doll clothes. Branlyn had often watched her work the loom. Tamora would chatter away about the day while weaving.

Tamora had never tried to replace Branlyn's mother but was there as a friend—someone for Branlyn to talk to whenever she needed an ear or a shoulder. They had gotten along very well until right before she had died. During the few months leading up to her death, Tamora had changed. No longer the sweet caring woman, she had turned into a bitch. Branlyn couldn't have described her any better than that.

The two of them had fought constantly. Tamora started criticizing her about everything—her hair, her clothes, her schoolwork, her friends, her lack of boyfriend. Then there had been the fights between Tamora and Branlyn's father.

Branlyn could still remember lying in her bed at night, her pillow over her head, while they screamed at each other. Tamora had yelled the vilest things Branlyn had ever heard so far in her young life. She remembered some nights crying herself to sleep.

She had never found out what had caused her parents rift, but it had all ended that one night in the garden.

Branlyn closed her mind off from those thoughts and started pulling the cotton sheets off Tamora's loom and her sewing machine. She didn't know how to do either, so maybe she would sell them. Make the room into something else. Maybe she could take up painting again. Give some meaning back to her life.

Before she could go any further, Branlyn spotted a small square trunk in the open closet. She put her hand in her pocket and fingered the skeleton key on the keychain. Maybe this was what it was for.

Bending down, she eyed the trunk. It didn't even have a lock on it. Branlyn grabbed the lid and opened it. Inside, there were papers and trinkets. It looked like Tamora kept some of her childhood memories in there.

She picked up a small rectangular box. Inside was a silver fork and spoon with Tamora's name engraved on them. Smiling, she set that down and picked up a bundle of what looked like letters tied together with a red bow.

She untied the bow. There were no addresses on the cream-colored envelopes, just one name *"Tamora"*, scrawled in beautiful handwriting with what looked like real ink and not a ballpoint pen. Opening one of the envelopes, Branlyn slid out the letter and began to read.

It was written in the same flowing handwriting, a love letter filled with flowery prose and promises of a world with unending passion. It was simply signed with a capital letter G. Obviously, they weren't from her father, Harrison. Branlyn opened another two envelopes finding the same type of letters, all from the same mystery person.

There were no dates, so Branlyn couldn't tell when the letters had been written. Was this what they had been fighting about? Was Tamora having an affair? Who was this G?

Branlyn ran through a mental list of people that had come in and out of their lives around that time, and she couldn't recall any man with the first initial G. However, it could've been a nickname, so his identity would be harder to decipher.

As thoughts raced through her mind, she ran her fingers over the elegantly scrawled G. The ink was smooth under her touch, and she immediately thought of skin and hot flesh. How soft a man's skin could be. How it could clench and vibrate under her palm.

While her finger began to circle the letter repeatedly, Branlyn felt like she was floating. Then she was sucked into a dark tunnel. At the end of the tunnel was a light, and she floated toward it. When she came out, she was in a candle lit room with no windows.

Instantly, the scent of sex wafted up her nose. There was a massive bed in the room draped with red satin sheets, and there was a couple on it both naked. She could see and hear them as clearly as if she was right there on the bed with them.

The woman was on her hands and knees facing the wall, and Branlyn couldn't see her face. However, she could clearly see her ass, her cheeks spread wide, and the thick plump lips of her glistening sex.

The equally naked and exquisite man on the bed was kneeling behind her, rubbing his hands over her cheeks. He had longish black hair, a lean sinewy frame, and a fabulous tight ass. A long scar marred his back from shoulder blade to hip. It only added to his allure, his sexiness. Branlyn had a craving to run her tongue along that pale scar.

Branlyn watched in heated fascination as he rubbed the woman's flesh up and down and in circles and then he raised his hand and brought it down hard on her right cheek.

The sound of flesh on flesh reverberated through the room. The woman on the bed cried out, but Branlyn knew it wasn't a sound of pain but one of pure pleasure. She knew because she could feel the first stirrings of desire deep in her belly as she watched the man spank the woman again and again. Soon the flesh on her ass was pink from his attentions.

"You like that, don't you?" he growled to the woman.

She mewled in response.

Branlyn nearly gasped aloud as the man moved his hands over and slid them down between the woman's cheeks and into the slick wetness of her sex. He slipped one than two more fingers into her and pumped them in and out vigorously. The woman ground her sex back, encouraging him to push them in further. He didn't disappoint.

Keeping his fingers buried inside her, he leaned down and slid his tongue into her soft folds, nuzzling her clit with the tip. The woman swore and moaned loudly as he lapped at the little bundle of nerve endings.

The sound of the woman's voice unnerved her. It was somehow familiar.

After a few more licks of his tongue, the man sat up and withdrew his fingers. His hand went down to his groin, wrapped around his huge cock, and he guided himself to her opening. Branlyn sucked in a breath as he pushed into the woman. She couldn't imagine stretching around his wide girth. But the woman didn't sound like she was in any pain.

Once sheathed completely inside, he began to rock back and forth, digging his fingers into the flesh of her ass cheeks. "Say you want me to fuck you."

The woman just groaned and mewled in response.

He raised his hand and slapped her flesh. "Say it!" he demanded.

Branlyn shivered in response to his demand. She could feel the wetness of her lust between her legs. She'd never been this turned-on before. And she didn't know if what she was watching was even real.

"Say it!" he demanded again as he spanked her repeatedly in rapid succession.

The woman turned her head to look over her shoulder. "Fuck me, Gregorian. Fuck me!" She growled.

Branlyn cried out. Not because of the words the woman spoke. No, they didn't matter at all. It was because she recognized the woman writhing and whimpering on the bed.

It was her own face staring back at her.

Branlyn dropped the letter and was instantly transported back to her stepmother's room. Shaking her head, she glanced around her surroundings, unsure if she had drifted off to sleep or what exactly had happened. Everything she'd seen, heard, and smelled seemed so real. She could even smell her own desire in the air. If the chaffing of her jeans were any indication, Branlyn was as wet as a sauna between her legs. Her desire was definitely real.

Before she could decipher the meaning of her waking dream, she heard a noise from downstairs. It sounded like breaking glass.

Jumping to her feet, Branlyn raced down the stairs and into the kitchen. She rounded the counter and saw shattered glass on the floor and the bottom end of a vase. On the counter, there was a beautiful bouquet of flowers.

Fear and confusion raced around in her mind. Who had been in the kitchen? Before she could begin to answer, she noticed that the back glass door was open. She rushed to it, threw it open, and ran into the garden. The intruder must've escaped this way. However, what kind of intruder breaks into a house to put flowers in a vase?

As she ran through the garden, she couldn't see anyone around. If the intruder had gone this way, he or she was a lot faster than she was, had already jumped the fence, and was running down the road. Before she reached the fence, Branlyn tripped over one of the cobblestones on the path and fell.

She landed hard on her hands and knees. Pain ripped through her from her leg and the palms of her hands. She likely scraped them both. Before she came to her senses, she glanced up and noticed something odd near the back fence, partially obscured by one of the azalea bushes. Pushing to her feet, Branlyn carefully picked the tiny rocks out of her scraped palms, gently wiped the dirt off on her jeans, and walked toward the strange clump of greenery.

When she neared, she could see what looked like a door in the bushes. An old wooden door cracked and weathered with age, vines, and green framing it. The doorknob looked like ancient brass, and below that was a brass lock.

Branlyn went into her pocket and came away with the skeleton key. Hands shaking, she brought the key toward the lock. She'd never heard of anything being out in the garden. No shed or old war bunker. The land was old enough surely, but she would've remembered if there had been something like this in the garden.

A sense of dread surged over her as she neared the door. Something was ominous about it. Darkly mysterious. But Branlyn wouldn't let fear stop her. The feeling that this was the answer to all her problems flashed in her mind. That opening this door would finally bring her a sense of peace.

"Branlyn?"

Flinching, Branlyn glanced over her shoulder and watched as a heavy-set woman near her age, dressed in shorts and a t-shirt, walked toward her. She turned back to the door, the key still shaking in her hand, but it had disappeared.

Branlyn pulled back, frowning and quickly pushing her hands into the azalea bush. Where was the door? It couldn't be gone. Her search was fruitless. The door was not there. Had it ever been there?

The woman stepped up right behind her. "Branlyn?"

She turned around again, and the woman smiled. Branlyn recognized that lop-sided grin and crooked nose. "Darla?"

The woman nodded, and her grin grew wider. She opened her arms and wrapped Branlyn in a big hug, squeezing her tight. "Damn it, girl, it's been too long."

Twenty minutes later, they were sitting on Branlyn's back porch drinking iced tea. She had learned that Darla wasn't married nor did she have any children. That she, in fact, was living with another woman. Branlyn had suspected as much when they were teens but didn't want to say anything. Being gay just wasn't something a young person talked about. Now, Darla was busy spreading the gossip about all of Branlyn's other past friends.

"Corey Ann got pregnant in twelfth grade and quit school."

"Let me guess. Jake Kipfer?"

Darla nodded. "They got married and moved to Vancouver. Last I heard, they're divorced, and Corey Ann's shacked up with someone else with kid number three on the way."

"What about Trevor?"

Trevor Jones had been her junior high school crush. She had learned he was going to ask her out for a movie that day before the night in the garden. Branlyn remembered how giddy she had felt all that afternoon, hoping the phone would ring and it would be Trevor asking her out.

"He joined the army," Darla answered, breaking Branlyn from her thoughts. "I think he was shipped out to Iraq."

Branlyn just nodded and sipped her iced tea. It seemed like a lifetime ago when she harbored those feelings. A lifetime ago when she had been a child. She had grown up quickly in the days that followed her father and stepmother's deaths.

"I'm so happy you're home, Bran."

Turning, she glanced at her old friend and smiled. But she knew it didn't quite reach her eyes.

"The last time I heard anything, you were in Paris."

"Yeah, I was there for about a year. Before that, Madrid for a year, before that Italy, before that some other place. It's all a blur sometimes."

"Well, you're home now. That's all that matters." Darla drained the last of her drink, set the glass down on the little table, and patted Branlyn on the shoulder. "And I need to take you out and have some fun. We'll go eat. You look way too thin."

Branlyn just nodded. She couldn't tell her old friend that she hadn't had an appetite in fifteen years. Not since she watched her father and stepmother get torn apart.

Darla stood and hitched up her shorts. "Well, I've got to get back to work. Those lawns don't mow themselves."

Branlyn stood and hugged her friend, patting her on the back.

"I'll come by tomorrow?"

"Yeah, sure. Sounds good." She watched as Darla walked down the steps and back into the garden. "Hey, Darla?"

She turned around. "Yeah?"

"You've been keeping the place right? The garden I mean?"

She nodded. "Yeah, Thomas makes sure my landscaping company comes out once a week to keep things up. Why? Something wrong?"

"Did you stock the kitchen, too?"

"No. I haven't been in your house since you left, Bran." She frowned. "Are you okay?"

Shivering, Branlyn wrapped her arms around her body. She nodded. "Yeah, I'm fine. I'll see you tomorrow."

"Are you sure? I can stay if you want."

Branlyn shook her head. "It's fine."

"Right." Darla grinned. "You know the whole town's excited that you're back. We've been waiting a long time to finally have you home, safe and sound." A feeling of dread spread over Branlyn. *We've been waiting*…those words sent shivers rushing over her body. Who was waiting for her?

Before she could respond, Darla turned on her heel and walked back to the rear gate in the garden. Branlyn watched her go and then went back into the house. She no longer wanted to spend time in the garden. There was something wrong there, and she couldn't put her finger on it. Maybe she was hallucinating. Maybe she was losing her mind. But one thing she knew for certain, whatever was causing her anxiety was somewhere in the beauty of her family's home.

Bad dreams came to her that night. Having spent so much time in the garden, Branlyn knew they would come.

She was back in that night. The beautiful moonlit night that she watched in horror as her father and her stepmother were murdered by an unknown assailant.

She walked down the cobblestone path, enjoying the warm night air. Too anxious to stay indoors, Branlyn had opted for a quiet stroll through the garden. As she weaved her way around the meandering paths, loud voices near the back fence caught her attention.

Creeping nearer, she crouched down behind one of the strawberry bushes and watched as her father and stepmother argued. Guilt swarmed around her heart, but she couldn't turn away. They'd been going on long enough. She'd spent too many nights listening to their screaming matches. She wanted to know the cause of their fights.

Harrison grabbed Tamora's arm. "You must stop seeing him."

She tried to pull away, but obviously, his grip was too tight. "I can't," she spat at him.

"You have the will to break his spell, if you wanted to."

"Well, I don't want to. He's a delicious lover." She pulled her arm away. "It's your fault anyway, Harrison. You brought him here. Reap what you sow, darling."

Branlyn sucked in a breath as he raised his hand to slap Tamora. She'd never known him to lift a hand to anyone. Even when she had been bad, he never spanked her. He didn't believe in that kind of punishment.

Harrison lowered his hand and took a distancing step back. "For years I've tried to keep him at bay, but he's too strong to deny."

"No, it's your greed that keeps him here. You had to have the big house, the fancy cars, and the unlimited spending money. You wanted me, and he made that happen. It's your own lust for riches that *you* can't deny."

Branlyn was startled at the things she was hearing. Whom were they talking about? What had her father done? She didn't remember this conversation from before. Her father, a greedy man, never. He was gentle and loving and always had a kind word for everyone. He gave much of his money to charity every year.

Before she could question it any further, a dark shape appeared as if from nowhere. As if materializing from the shadows itself.

"Tamora is right, Harrison. You are much too greedy," the black form said.

When he stepped into a beam of moonlight, Branlyn gasped. He was ethereally beautiful. Hair as dark as midnight, and skin so pale he seemed to glow, competing with the moon.

She thought he looked like a dark angel. She'd never seen anyone as enchanting before, yet he seemed very familiar. As if she'd been seeing him her whole life.

"What are you doing here, Gregorian?" Harrison asked, a quiver in his usually commanding voice.

"To negotiate my payment, naturally." The dark haired man trailed his finger over Tamora's shoulder as he stepped around her.

Her father clenched his fists at his sides. "I have already paid you more than enough."

"Yes, well, that was for the last two years of keeping you in the lifestyle you're accustomed to." The man named Gregorian ran his hand up and down Tamora's back and then patted her backside. "While still lovely, your payment bores me. I grow tired of her attentions."

Tamora flinched then started to cry.

Gregorian leaned toward her and licked away the tears running down her cheek.

Branlyn wanted to run away, but she was frozen in place. Her legs were like rubber, and she knew they would not support her if she stood. She didn't quite understand everything she was hearing and seeing, but she knew that her father had done something unspeakable. And if her figuring was correct, he had sold Tamora's affections for it.

"What do you want?" Harrison asked again, teeth clenched in anger.

"I want something more succulent. Younger. Fresher. Tastier." Gregorian gnashed his teeth at Harrison. "Your daughter's almost of age, isn't she?"

"You bastard!" Her father rushed at Gregorian.

Before he could reach him, the other man had Harrison by the throat and was lifting him off the ground.

Branlyn covered her mouth with her hand, stopping the scream that threatened to escape. Quivers of fear erupted over her whole body.

Harrison kicked at the other man, but Gregorian held on as if Harrison's efforts were inconsequential. "You knew it would come to this, Harrison. Try to deny it, but deep down in your heart you knew when you begged me to make you rich, to make you desirable, that your dear darling daughter would be your final payment to me. Everything comes full circle eventually."

Tamora launched herself at Gregorian's back. Before she could even touch him, he swung his arm around and struck her across the face, sending her flying backwards. She landed a few feet away in a heap and didn't move.

"I'm going to let you down, and we will talk like the reasonable men we are."

Gregorian set her father down on the ground and released his hold on Harrison's neck.

Bending over to take in air, Harrison rubbed at his neck. "I'll expose you," Harrison grunted. "People will come to hunt you down."

Gregorian clucked his tongue. "It's talk like that, that gets people hurt." He turned his back to Harrison and glanced at Tamora still slumped on the ground. "Tend to your wife, Harrison."

But her father didn't move. Branlyn watched in horror as he raised his hand, a long blade of a knife glinting in the moonlight and rushed at Gregorian. He swiped down across the dark man's back.

Growling low in his throat, Gregorian swiveled around, knocked the knife from Harrison's hand and grabbed him around the throat again, squeezing tight.

"It didn't have to come to this, Harrison. We've always been able to work out our issues, haven't we?" He pulled her father close to him and spoke low, but Branlyn could hear every word as if it has been directly spoken to her. "What do you want from me?"

"I want you to die," Harrison croaked.

"You first, my friend, you first."

With that, Gregorian opened his mouth wide and clamped down on Harrison's neck.

Branlyn screamed.

She was on her feet and running toward her struggling father before she could even consider the ramifications of her actions.

Gregorian turned toward, blood dripping down his chin. He released his grip on her father's throat, and Harrison slumped to the ground like a rag doll.

"Ah, there she is. I knew you would come out of hiding sooner or later." He licked the blood from his lips, her father's blood. "I'm sorry it had to come to this, Branlyn, but he just wouldn't listen to reason."

A rage she never knew could exist surged through her as she sprinted toward him. Although she could see his mouth moving, all she could hear was her blood roaring in her ears.

However, before she could near him, bright light flashed all around her. Stopping in her tracks, she had to shield her eyes from the intense glare. Where she had felt cold, sudden warmth spread over her form.

Glancing toward Gregorian, she saw that he knelt in the dirt, his head turned from the light. And he was screaming. A name echoed in her head over and over again.

Thane! Thane! Thane!

Branlyn sat up in her bed, gasping for air. Sweat dripped from her skin, soaking the sheets beneath her. Shivering, she took in some ragged deep breaths.

Calming, she lay back down and wrapped the bed covers tight around her body. Tears leaked from the side of her eyes. For the first time since that horrible night, she could recall every word, every action. Everything had been a bloody blur before, but now, now, she had clarity. And she had a name.

Two names actually. The name of her father's murderer and the name of her rescuer. The man that had saved her life. Her dream lover.

Quietly, she spoke his name, whispering it into the dark. "Thane. Where are you? I need you now more than ever."

"I'm here. Right where you left me."

Jolting up, Branlyn clutched the covers to her breast and gasped.

A beautiful man with golden hair and pale glowing eyes stood in her bedroom doorway, the first signs of dawn illuminating his radiance.

Chapter Three

"Am I still dreaming?" Branlyn couldn't control the quiver in her voice or the vibrations rushing over her skin.

When Thane took a step into the room, it was as if the room shrank. He was a formidable presence. One that couldn't be denied. And she had no plans to deny him.

"No." He took another few steps, closing the distance between him and the bed. "I'm as real as you are, Branlyn."

The lilt of his voice sent shivers over her, and the hairs at the back of her neck and arms stood to attention.

Another couple of steps and he was beside her, gazing down at her with his pale moonlight eyes. Shaking, she reached for him and grasped his arm. He was solid, like silk-covered steel in her hands. The blond hair on his arm tickled her palm. He was very real.

"How can you be here? It's impossible."

Smiling, he ran his hand down over her hair and cupped her cheek. "You called me, and I came." Tilting her head up, he lowered his face and covered her mouth with his.

The kiss was electric and sent ripples of pleasure surging over her. He tasted like sunshine — spicy, smoldering, and rejuvenating. She felt like she was fully awake for the first time in her life. Awake and completely aware of everything around her, especially the flare of desire igniting her body.

After nibbling on her lower lip, he broke the kiss and pulled back to stare into her eyes. "I've been waiting a long time to be able to do that for real."

Branlyn pulled him down to the bed. He sat on the edge next to her leg. Touching his face, she ran her thumb over his soft succulent lips. "You rescued me that night in the garden." She leaned forward so that she was only a mere whisper away from his mouth. "And have been rescuing me in my dreams ever since."

"Yes." His breath hitched in his throat.

"Why?"

"Because I'm in love with you."

Branlyn lost her breath and stared at him. "But how can this be? You're a figment of my imagination, aren't you? I created you."

He shook his head and ran his hands up her legs to rest at her hips. "I have always been here, Branlyn, watching, waiting. I've watched you grow up and blossom into a beautiful vibrant woman. And I've been waiting here for you to return to reclaim Carmichael Manor."

Dropping her hand, she pulled back from him. Confusion and fear of the unknown swirled inside her, battling the desire she felt just being so close to him. "I don't understand. Who are you? Who is the man that murdered my family?"

"His name is Gregorian. He's a very powerful spirit that has cursed your family."

"Spirit? You mean he's a ghost?"

"No, not a ghost, but an entity that surrounds this place." He slid his hands over top of hers and grasped them tightly. "And he's fixated on you."

Flinching, she tried to pull back, but he held her firmly in his grip. "Why?"

"Because you're the only one that can send him back to the hell he came from, and he wants to seduce you, to possess you so you can't send him away."

Images of her on her hands and knees in that bed flashed in her head. Sounds of her pleasurable whimpers echoed in her ears. Clamping her eyes shut, she tried to push the erotic thoughts from her mind. She wouldn't succumb to his seduction, however much passion flared inside her body as she thought of her complete surrender.

Opening her eyes, she concentrated on Thane. He was her salvation. "And you? Why is it that you are here?"

"I'm here to protect you, Branlyn. *You* are the only reason I exist."

As declarations went, that was the most powerful one she'd ever heard. With tears brimming in her eyes, Branlyn turned her hands and intertwined her fingers with his. The heat from his body surrounded her and chased away the shivers of fear. Still she felt afraid. Scared of the intense feelings that blossomed in her heart, in her body for this man. A man that had been with her most of her life, but she didn't know at all. Was it insane to feel this way about him? When she had no idea, who or what he truly was.

"I'm afraid, Thane."

He pulled her to him and wrapped his arms around her, stroking her hair with his hand. "I won't let anything happen to you, my love." He pressed a kiss to the top of her head and lingered there, breathing in her scent.

Sighing, Branlyn nuzzled into his comforting embrace. She could hear the frantic beat of his heart in her chest. Was he as excited to be near her as she was to him?

Moving her head, she pressed her mouth to the side of his neck and kissed him there, inhaling his earthy male odor. He groaned in response. A sound that encouraged her to continue her exploration.

She pressed kisses to his neck, working upwards to his ear, and over to his cheek, and then his mouth. He opened for her, and she swept her tongue over his, sampling his exotic flavor. He tasted of hot summer days by the ocean. He tasted of her past and her future.

Moaning, he buried his hands in her hair and deepened the kiss. He nipped and toyed with her bottom lip, coaxing little gasps from her mouth. His kiss alone was enough to illicit pleasant vibrations between her legs. Oh, how she wanted him to touch her there, to take her as he had in her dreams.

Breaking the kiss, she moved over his cheek to his ear and whispered, "I don't want to think anymore. I just want to feel you inside me."

Sitting back, Thane pulled back her covers and gripped the hem of her nightshirt. Branlyn raised her arms and let him slowly peel off her nightgown. She shivered in the cool morning air. Her nipples tightened into hard peaks. She figured that was more due to the way he stared at her with heat in his eyes than the cool breeze.

Standing, he stripped off his shirt, revealing the pale rippled flesh of his chest and abs that she remembered from her dreams. He was even more breathtaking, standing before her, in the pale pink light of dawn.

When he unbuttoned his pants and let them fall, Branlyn nearly gasped at the sight of him fully erect and quivering for her. She drank him in from head to toe, reeling in the exquisiteness of his form. He was perfect in every way.

Flipping the covers back, she scooted over on the bed, making room for him to join her. Nervous energy surged through her. She felt like a virgin again. Excited but afraid. Although she knew she had nothing to fear from Thane. In her dreams, he had been a generous attentive lover, and she didn't expect anything less in reality.

He slid in beside her but didn't touch her. Maybe he sensed her apprehension. Instead, he smiled and brought a hand up to her face and lightly traced a finger over her lips.

"I will go slowly if you want me to."

Grabbing him, Branlyn stilled his movements and pulled his hand down to her breast. She put her hand on top of his and squeezed, thrilling at the sensation of his touch. Her nipple grew harder under his palm.

That was all the encouragement he needed.

Molding her breast in one hand, Thane nuzzled in closer to her and took her mouth in a long heated kiss. Sighing, she opened for him, letting his tongue dart in and out, tasting her with each sweep. Her inner thighs tightened and pulsed, anticipating him in between them. Oh, how she ached for him. She'd never been this wanton with anyone before. Only him.

As they kissed, Branlyn drew her leg up and wrapped it around his. Thane ran his hand down her torso and over her hip to brush against the cheek of her ass. He gripped her there and pulled her closer to him. She could feel the hard length of his cock nuzzling against her sex. She was already slick and hot, eagerly waiting for him to push inside, to fill her completely, wholly.

Groaning into his mouth, she trailed her hands over him, feeling every hot hard inch of his body. His skin was soft like satin and underneath, his muscles were as solid as granite. Sweeping her fingers over his back, she felt a ridge on his skin. Was it a scar?

Searching further, she found a long puckered line from his shoulder blade down to his hip. Somehow touching it reminded her of something. Something she wasn't sure if she wanted to remember. Pushing the conflicted thoughts away, she ran her hands over his firm ass and around his hip to grip his erect cock.

He bit down on her bottom lip and moaned as she stroked him, urging him to thrust into her. He didn't disappoint. Within seconds, he rolled her over onto her back, spread her legs with his knee, and filled her in one fluid stroke.

Wrapping her arms around him, she hung on as he took them up. Gasping with each thrust, Branlyn could already feel an orgasm building deep within her sex. His cock stretched and filled her, giving her a feeling of being complete. As if the last piece of her complicated puzzle had finally settled into place.

Wrapping his hands in her hair and nuzzling into her neck, Thane found a steady rhythm as he drove into her. With each thrust, Branlyn met him stroke for stroke. When he plunged forward, she pushed up with her pelvis, meeting him and burying his cock so deep into her sex, she could feel him touching the top of her womb.

Gasping, panting, she dug her nails into his back as he drove them to the edge. A smoldering ball of heat burned at her center, threatening to gush like molten lava from her body. She was so very near climax, she could barely breathe. One flick on her aching clit would send her spiraling off into rapture.

Thane pushed up onto his elbows and trailed kisses from her neck down to her breasts. Sliding his tongue over a nipple, he gently sucked it into his mouth.

A sizzling whip of pleasure cracked over her as he suckled on her throbbing peak. She pushed up, urging him to take more of her into his talented mouth.

Groaning, he licked and sucked on one nipple then gave the same glorious attention to the other. While his mouth was busy, he slid one hand down her torso to her navel, circling it seductively, and then dipped lower to her sex. He slid this thumb into her soft wet folds and found her hard swollen nub. As he thrust hard, burying his cock as deep as it could go, Thane pressed down on her clit and rubbed it back and forth.

Clamping her eyes shut, she arched her back as she came in a blazing thunder. White light flashed behind her eyelids, and she could hear nothing but the roaring of her blood through her veins.

Crying out her name, Thane followed her down into bliss. Collapsing on top of her, and biting down on her neck, he emptied himself with a violent surge. A sharp pinch of pain radiated from her throat, but it soon faded into mind-numbing pleasure.

Together they came, spiraling down into a state of total ecstasy. Branlyn had never felt so in tune, so in synch with anyone before. It felt like they had melded into one body, one entity. She swore she could hear his thoughts.

He whispered her name over and over again as if swearing allegiance to her.

Maybe he was.

After her breathing regulated and her heart stopped feeling like it was going to burst from her chest, Branlyn opened her eyes and stared at Thane. His eyes were closed, and he had a small smile of satisfaction on his face. He looked completely at peace.

Smiling, she closed her eyes again, and let the grogginess of great sex pull her under into sleep.

* * *

Branlyn startled awake to the soft sounds of Thane's rhythmic breathing.

Turning her head, she watched him as he slept. Face down with his arm hanging over the edge of the bed, he looked like any satisfied man after a heavy bout of amazing sex. Except he wasn't an ordinary man.

Sitting up, careful not to disturb his sleep, she stared down at him, memorizing his magnificent features. But what she saw on his back froze her blood in her veins.

A scar dissected him from top to bottom. She had felt it earlier with her fingers as she streaked up and down his back. A similar one marred Gregorian's flesh. Could it be coincidence? Or something more? Something beyond her reasoning.

She touched her neck where an ache still pulsed. She could feel nothing there—no holes, no scabs—but swore he had bitten into her skin when he had climaxed. Had she imagined it? Remnants of her bad dream still clung to her like a spider's cobweb.

Ever since she'd seen Gregorian in her vision, she felt like something was off. That there was some piece of the puzzle she was completely missing. The most important part.

Thane had said that Gregorian was some sort of entity tied to this place, to her. Maybe she could find the answers in the past. Not her past, but somewhere deeper, farther back.

The land her house sat on was old. Settled on over a hundred years ago. Her house had only been built a few years before she had been born. What had been here before? Who had been here before?

Shifting, Branlyn crept over Thane's legs and off the bed. She watched his face to make sure she didn't wake him. She needed to do this by herself, to find the answers on her own. Face them dead on. She wanted to prove that she wasn't a coward any longer. She was ready to battle her demons, however horrific they turned out to be.

Stepping quietly from her room, she padded down the hallway and into her father's office where she had set up her laptop. She sat down in the old leather chair. It creaked when she moved it up to the desk, but she didn't think it was loud enough to wake Thane.

Using her mouse, she plugged into the internet and found a search engine. She typed in Gregorian and Vancouver Island. Several links popped up referring to Gregorian chants, and the Gregorian calendar, but nothing so far on anyone named Gregorian. Determined, Branlyn kept scrolling through link after link until finally she spotted something worthwhile. She skimmed through the contents of a couple old newspaper clippings now archived.

April 2, 1904. Rich Industrialist's Wife Found Dead.

Delilah Elizabeth Thane, age 29, wife of Gregorian Alan Thane, wealthy land owner, was found dead this morning at the bottom of Thane Cliffs. Thane suspected of foul play.

Her death found to be a suicide.

Gregorian Alan Thane jumps from the same cliffs.

Body disappears from the grave.

Gregorian Alan Thane.

Branlyn read the name over repeatedly, making sure she was reading it correctly. Thane. Were they related? She didn't believe in coincidences. But else could it be?

"What are you doing?"

Branlyn jumped, nearly knocking her laptop off the desk. "You scared me." Recovering, she tapped her mouse to close the application and smiled at Thane as he stood leaning against the doorframe clad only in unbuttoned pants. "Did I wake you?"

He shook his head and stepped into the room. "What were you doing?"

Standing, she took his hand and nuzzled into him, keeping him from the computer. "Just checking my emails. Thomas likes to check in with me now and then."

He stroked his hand over her hair and kissed the top of her head. "How about some lunch?"

She nodded. "Sure. I'm starving."

"Is there something wrong?"

She could hear the suspicion in his voice. She pressed a kiss to his chest. "Everything's great. Let's go eat. We earned it from that workout." She glanced up at him.

He smiled, and his face softened. "We sure did." He leaned down and covered her mouth with his.

The kiss was gentle but potent. Branlyn's knees wobbled again, threatening to melt into his arms. But before she gave into the lust beginning to build again inside, she needed some answers.

If she was going to fall in love with this man, she wanted to make damn sure what he was.

Chapter Four

After a long relaxing lunch of salad and turkey sandwiches, both of which Thane had prepared, they made love again. It was slow and lazy like the afternoon, but he managed to bring her to orgasm twice. He was an amazing lover, and she could easily become accustomed to him being there with her. In her house, in her bed.

She felt strange for accepting him into her life so quickly. She had no idea who or even what he was. He was a man certainly, but someone definitely not of this world. However, he had been a part of her for a long time. Although not physically, he had occupied a huge part of her life. It was in her dreams, with him, where she felt the safest, the sanest, as if nothing could harm her again. A place where everything made sense.

But out here in the real world, it was all a bit more complicated. She couldn't just bury her head in the sand and pretend that everything was all right, that everything was normal. Because it certainly was not.

As dusk drew near, Thane began to fidget and pace. Branlyn could see the difference in him, a change. Something about the approaching night unnerved him to no end. While she drank a glass of red wine, she watched him move back and forth in front of the patio doors facing the garden.

"I have to leave when night comes, Branlyn. You know that right?"

"I figured. You came to me at dawn, but the rest of the time it has been in dreams." She eyed him, an unpleasant thought forming in her mind. "You can't take physical form during the night?"

He shook his head. "No."

"Why?"

"I don't know. It has always been this way."

She sat forward in her chair, wanting to touch him. To soothe his obvious apprehension. But she needed answers. If she didn't get any soon, she knew she'd finally succumb to madness, because surely this couldn't be anything but.

"Why won't you answer my questions, Thane? You must have some idea why this is happening. Why Gregorian has forsaken this place and my family."

He turned to her, his eyes flashing like twin moons. "Do not try and find the answers yourself, Branlyn. It is too dangerous. You have to promise me you won't go into the garden tonight."

She flinched, fear cascading over her. "I won't."

"Even if he calls to you." He knelt down in front of her and took her hands in his. "You must fight him. He will stop at nothing to have you. I can feel his obsession for you."

Branlyn shivered. "Is there something you're not telling me? I know there is more going on than you're saying."

Sighing, he closed his eyes and bent his head. When he looked up again, he looked weary and sad. "Gregorian is my brother."

"What?" She squeezed his hands. "Why didn't you tell me before?"

"Because I didn't want you to look at me the way you're looking at me right now. As if I was Gregorian himself."

Swallowing the lump in her throat, Branlyn tried to look at him without judgment. But it proved difficult. She had a feeling there was more to it than just being brothers. "I'm sorry. It just comes as a shock."

"Yes, I imagine it does." He let go off her hands and stood to stare out at the garden. The sun was starting to set.

"Why does he call you Thane? Isn't that your last name?"

"Why does it matter what he calls me?" He turned, and she could see anger in his face. Something she never thought to see in her dream lover's eyes.

"What are you afraid of telling me? What are you hiding?"

His hands clenched into tight fists. "Have you not been listening to me, woman? Do not go into the garden for any reason. He will take you without regard."

"But why? Why does he want me so much? Surely, you must know."

He stared at her, and she could see confusion start to cloud his face. A twitch started on his brow between his eyes. He reached up and tried to rub it away.

"I don't...I don't know why."

"Thane, it's all right to tell me. You can trust me."

Without a word, he opened the patio door and glanced back at her. "I'll be back in the morning. I will tell you everything then."

"All right." Resigned to have more questions then answers, she stood to touch him, but he had turned and walked out the door before she could. She watched him as he wandered down the stone path toward the back fence. Standing in the doorframe, she watched until he had disappeared, as if he had just vanished into thin air.

With dread forming in her gut like a hard ball of steel, Branlyn stepped out onto the veranda. She wasn't sure if what she was going to do was the smartest thing, but she couldn't wait in the house for Gregorian to come to her. She needed her answers now.

Keeping an eye toward the back fence, she wandered along the path to where she'd last seen the mysterious door. The azalea bush looked no different. It was still thick and green, with no aging wood inside it. Fingering the skeleton key in her pocket, she leaned forward, scrutinizing the foliage. It had to be there somewhere.

She turned her head slightly to the right and out of the corner of her eye, she saw something beginning to form.

The door materialized inside the bush as if by magic. And magic it had to be. She couldn't explain it anyway else.

Pulling her hand out of her pocket, she brought the key toward the lock on the door. She inched closer and closer to it, her heart hammering in her throat. Right as the tip of the key touched the metal, the door vanished, leaving just a dark hole leading into the bushes. Branlyn leaned forward and stared into the absolute black.

That was the last thing she remembered…

* * *

Branlyn wasn't expecting the smell of lavender when she woke up, the red filmy gown she wore, or the red satin sheets beneath her. She definitely hadn't anticipated the silk ropes securing her wrists to the headboard of the massive bed she seemed to be lying on.

Pulling on her arms, she tried to sit up, but to no avail. She was securely fastened to the bed, her arms splayed out in a V. She flailed her legs, thankful that they too weren't tied to the bedposts. Glancing around the room, she tried to figure out where she was. The last thing she could recall clearly was going into the garden.

When a door opened, and a dark form filled the doorway, the answer became very clear.

Gregorian glided into the room, clad only in a pair of loose fitting black pants. They shimmered in the flickering candlelight as he moved toward the bed. Once aside the mattress, he looked down at her and smiled, sharp incisors glistening in the low light.

Fear rippled over her like waves threatening to drown her in its power.

Here was her worst nightmare, the man that ripped her family apart, staring down at her with her dream lover's eyes. She suspected the truth, but actually seeing it before her nearly sent her spiraling into madness.

"Hello, my love."

"Please," she begged, turning her head from his intense gaze. "Please don't call me that."

Chuckling, he sat down on the bed next to her hip. She tried to pull away from him but found she had nowhere to go, her bound hands keeping her immobile.

"Resist me all you want, Branlyn, but you know as well as I, that our meeting is fated." He splayed his hand over her stomach. "And that is something neither one of us can run from."

Shivers radiated over her body from his unexpected gentle touch. However, it was the sensations between her legs that caused her anxiety. His touch sent delicious tremors over her thighs and in between. Already she could feel the insides of her thighs moisten from her desire. She squeezed her eyes shut from the treacherous feelings blossoming inside her body.

He moved his hand up her form, slowly circling a finger around her breasts. "Don't fight it, my darling. I can awaken your body to more pleasure than you've ever thought possible."

She shuddered as swells of pleasure rippled over her. "Please, don't hurt me."

"Hurt you?" He clucked his tongue. "I wouldn't dream of hurting you, my darling. I've been waiting so long for you to come home." With both his hands, he cupped her breasts, running his thumbs back and forth over her nipples. "And now that I have you, I'll never let you go."

Again, ripples of pleasure washed over her. She couldn't stop the sensations bombarding her body. Arching her back, she pushed her breasts into his talented hands, eager for more of his attentions.

She swore to herself for giving over to him, but she couldn't stop it. It was as if her body recognized his touch, craved it, hungered for it. It was inexplicable, but her body didn't reason that way.

Gregorian moved his hands up to the neckline of the transparent gown she was dressed in. He stared deeply into her eyes. His gaze was penetrating. "I won't take you against your will, Branlyn." He ran a finger over the exposed skin just above the fabric. "Just say the word, and I will stop. Do you want me to stop touching you?"

Gritting her teeth, she shook her head. "No. God help me, no, I don't want you to stop."

With a smile, he hooked his fingers under the neckline of her gown and pulled down. In one violent tug, he rendered the top half of the garment into two pieces.

She gasped at the violence of it but reveled in the cool breeze that blew over her rigid nipples, making them tighter, harder—throbbing with intense need.

Leaning down, Gregorian laved his tongue over one nipple then the other. She nearly jumped out of her skin as sizzling sensations bombarded her. Urged on by her writhing, he nestled at one breast, licking and sucking on her taut peak.

She writhed and squirmed while he feasted on her flesh. After teasing the one nipple into a throbbing mass, he moved on to the other to inflict the same delicious torture.

"Oh, you are so lovely. So delectable, like ripe peaches," he growled as he moved off her breast and pressed kisses to her skin, slowly making his way down her form.

As he moved closer to her sex, she thought she'd go mad with lust. Already she was wet, eager for him to touch and taste her. Groaning, she bit on her bottom lip as he trailed his tongue over her navel and then even lower.

He put his nose to just above her pubic mound and inhaled deeply as if smelling a flower. "Your scent drives me mad with desire. I want you like no other."

Heart hammering in her chest, she watched as he slid down lower pushing her legs apart and nestled in between them. Grapping her thighs, he pushed her legs wide open. She could feel the light cool breeze brush against her slick inner folds.

He eyed her sex, as if drinking in his fill of her. "So beautiful. So inviting." Leaning forward, he slid his tongue into her cleft.

She jolted off the bed. A hot flow of intense pleasure washed over her. An orgasm was near. She could feel it building like a ticking time bomb deep within her sex.

He licked and sucked on her intimate flesh. She'd never been so thoroughly feasted on before. Flicking his tongue over her clit, he slid a finger into her, then another, then another. Jolts of pleasure seared her as he devoured her.

She pulled at her restraints as swell after swell of intense pleasure surged over her. She wanted nothing more than to dig her hands into his silky black hair and hang on as he sent her spiraling into bliss. Her body jerking, she was so close to climax she could feel it like a sneeze in her belly.

Moving his tongue around in circles, he settled at her clit sucking the swollen pearl into his mouth. While he rolled it between his lips, he buried his fingers deep into her and swirled them around, feeling every inch of her sex.

With a blinding punch of pleasure, Branlyn came, yanking at her bindings and ripping the silk. She tried to close her legs, but he held her open, still torturing her clit.

"Thane!" she cried. "Thane!"

Lifting his head, he glared at her. "Why do you call his name? He is not here. He didn't give you this pleasure."

"Yes, he is," she panted, still quivering from the violent orgasm she sustained. "You are Gregorian Alan Thane. And so is he."

Wiping his mouth, Gregorian sat up and pushed her leg out of his way so he could stand. His eyes were a solid black, and they seemed to burrow into her soul. "You are insane if you think this. I am Gregorian. He is Thane, my enemy. It has always been this way, for a lot longer than you can even imagine, little girl."

"Gregorian —,"

"You can lay here in this room until that notion leaves your mind." He leered down at her. "Then I will be back to show you how much you are so totally wrong, my darling." He smiled, and she could plainly see the fangs poking from his gum line.

Swallowing down the bile in her throat, she watched as he floated out of the room as if on air. She sunk back into the mattress and began to think. She was right about her assessment. The moment Gregorian had come into the room she could feel Thane's presence. She knew that feeling like her own body. She'd been feeling him for fifteen years. Long enough to memorize his aura, his spirit.

She believed that over a hundred years ago, Gregorian Alan Thane had somehow split his psyche after the death of his wife. Maybe guilt had consumed him so completely he manifested a dark and light side of himself to deal with it. Was it a logical assumption? Hell no! But it's all she had to go on. Everything that had happened since returning home had bordered on the unbelievable.

However, for now, she had to get out of here. Gregorian had not been pleased when she confronted him with her assumptions. His anger wafted off him like a tangy cologne, bitter and tart. She didn't want to be here when he returned.

She pulled at her silk ropes. She had felt it give earlier when she had been in the throes of her pleasure. Maybe with a little more power she could rip one hand free. Yanking and twisting, she could feel the fabric cutting into her skin. But she continued. She had a feeling she'd be in a lot more pain if she remained when Gregorian returned.

With one final tug, the silk tore, and her right hand was freed. Twisting, she quickly untied the over hand and slid off the bed. Glancing around the room, she searched for her clothes. She couldn't run around in the torn gown.

She couldn't find them but spied a white tunic in the corner. One of Gregorian's flowing shirts she assumed.

Discarding the ripped dress, she pulled the loose tunic over her head. The hem came to her thighs. It would have to do. She went to the door, opened it slowly, and peered out into the long deserted hallway.

She waited and listened but didn't hear a sound. No movement, no voices, no anything.

She stepped out into the hall and looked both ways. She had no clue how to get out or where exactly she was. She supposed she would just start running and deal with the consequences later. Without any more delay, Branlyn turned to the right and started to run.

Within minutes, she realized that she wasn't getting anywhere. As she ran, it soon became clear that she was going in a circle. She nearly cried when after fifteen minutes of non-ending hallway, she ended up back at the open door.

Bending over and breathing hard from the exertion, Branlyn looked the way she came and decided to walk that way. Maybe she missed an exit in her haste. But as she walked, she noticed nothing but smooth rounded walls. No doors, no windows, no anything but ornately decorated wood. Then she saw a painting on the wall that stole her breath.

The picture was old, of a woman dressed in wealthy finery, her hair up in an elegant bun. However, Branlyn's face stared back at her. There was no mistaking the cut of her cheeks, line of her jaw, and the same startling green eyes.

Was this Delilah? Gregorian's dead wife? Was this why he was so obsessed with her? He thought her to be his dead wife.

Tears started to well. She didn't want to believe this. It was too far-fetched. Too outside the realm of possibility. Wasn't it?

When she ended up back at the opened door, the tears started to fall. Maybe it was all an illusion. Maybe if she tried hard enough she could wish it all away like Alice in Wonderland. She clamped her eyes shut and envisioned being back in the garden. But when she opened her eyes again, she was still in her nightmarish maze. Sighing, she put her hands on her hips and looked up.

Wait. What was that?

Squinting, she scrutinized the ceiling, or what seemed to be the ceiling. But what she was looking at was dirt. Hard pressed rich black soil.

She was underground, beneath her family's garden.

Branlyn stepped back into the bedroom and looked up. The ceiling in the room was solid, ornately decorated just like the walls. Glancing around the room, she spied a chair set by an elegant desk. She grabbed it and carried it out into the hallway.

She stood on it and reached up to the ceiling, thankful that it wasn't lofty. It was hard, but she managed to dig into it. Soon, dirt fell over her and to the ground. Did she really think she could dig herself out? She didn't know, but she had to try. For her sake and for Thane's. Maybe there was some way she could help him stitch his soul back together.

After ten minutes of digging, Branlyn reached high, dug her hands into the hard soil, and pulled herself up. She braced her feet against the wall and her back into the little hole she had burrowed out. Her arms began to shake from the strain of keeping her body suspended, but she continued to dig upwards, determined to escape.

After a few more feet of digging, the soil began to fall more freely, giving way to her. She must be nearing the top where the dirt was rich and flaky. Desperate, she started to dig faster, her fingers throbbing, her wrists aching with the exertion.

Another five minutes passed until she saw plant roots in the dirt. Laughing hysterically, Branlyn pushed up with her hands clawing frantically at the soil and greenery. Soon, her hand pushed through the top soil and she could feel air on her fingers.

Then she felt someone grab her hand and start to pull her up.

She struggled against the force of the drag but to no avail. Whoever was yanking her out of the ground was a lot stronger than she.

"No!" she screamed.

Covered in dirt from head to toe, she was wrenched from the earth and into strong masculine arms. A familiar scent enveloped her.

She looked up into her dream lover's beautiful pale face.

"I have you, my love. You're safe now," he cooed.

Looking up, she noticed the sky turning pink. It was a new day dawning. She had spent the entire night underground.

"Gregorian, he —,"

Cutting her off, he pressed his lips to her brow. "He can't hurt you now."

She pulled away, determined to tell him what she'd learned. To make him see that the two men were actually one. "Listen to me. You and Gregorian —"

Something grabbed her ankle and pulled her down into the hole.

She screamed as Gregorian yanked on her foot, trying to force her back into the dirt tunnel she'd just escaped from.

Thane grabbed her around the waist and pulled her back. Gregorian momentarily lost his grip on her. She managed to yank her foot out of the soil, but it didn't last long as his hand snaked out of the hole and grasped her tightly once more, his nails digging into her flesh. Soon, a game of tug-o-war ensued.

If she hadn't been so frightened, she would've laughed at the absurdity of it. Two men literally fighting over her. But she knew it was more than that. The struggle was for much much more. She believed it was for their soul.

After pulling and yanking back and forth, her body began to scream in pain. Her leg felt like it was being ripped off. If Gregorian pulled any harder, she'd be surprised if it didn't.

Thane must have heard her grunts of agony. He lessened his grip on her waist and lowered himself into the dirt. He reached forward and grabbed Gregorian's hand, intent on prying it loose. What happened next was anything less than mesmerizing.

Both men cried out in pain as their skin touched.

Branlyn fell backwards in the dirt, landing hard on her butt, and watched in horrified awe as a white glow emanated from their joined hands on her ankle. Thankfully, she didn't experience any of the pain that they both seemed to be enduring.

Grimacing, Thane secured his feet into the hard packed earth and wrenched back with all his strength. Finally, Gregorian's hold slipped off her foot, and he was yanked out of the dirt tunnel with the force of Thane's pull.

Hands connected, the two men stood staring at each other, as if truly seeing for the first time.

Branlyn scrambled back, transfixed on the two men. Looking at them together, face to face, there was no doubt in her mind that they were two forces of the same person. They were identical in every way. Except Thane was light, blond hair, pale ethereal eyes, and Gregorian dark, with black hair, and dark eyes. However, everything else was the same. Their faces, their bodies, their stances. Identical.

"What magic is this?" Gregorian demanded, his voice not as commanding as before. "What have you done to my hand, Thane?"

"Can't you see?" Branlyn pushed to her feet. "You are the same man. You are both Gregorian Alan Thane."

Thane turned his gaze toward her. She could see the horror in his eyes, but she could also see the beginnings of acceptance. He knew. Somehow, he had always known.

It was Gregorian that needed to be convinced.

"Lies!" he growled, still trying to wrench his hand free from Thane's. The glow intensified from where they were joined, their flesh seemingly being fused together.

Branlyn took a step forward toward the two men. Finally, she knew what she had to do. Seeing her face on the old painting in Gregorian's lair had confirmed it. She was the key and always had been.

"Look at me, Gregorian." She took another step closer. "See my face."

At first, he averted his gaze, but something made him lift his eyes and study her. Then she could see a dawning in his face. Recognition flickered in his eyes.

With her next step, Branlyn was within touching distance of him. She reached out and placed her hand on his cheek. "You did not kill your wife, Gregorian. You are not at fault. She jumped."

He gnashed his teeth and tried to pull away from her. But she held firm, staring him in the face. "I forgive you for all that you have done."

He raised his other hand and smacked her across the face. The blow sent her spiraling to the ground.

"No!" Thane yelled as he launched forward, wrapping his free hand around Gregorian's neck. The momentum of his movements sent them both tumbling to the dirt.

Branlyn watched in horror as the two men rolled around on the ground, the glow from their joined flesh growing brighter still. Soon, their bodies were basked in light, and she could no longer distinguish between them.

Eventually the glow became so bright she had to avert her gaze and shield her eyes.

It became a glaring ball of white light in her garden. So intense she thought she'd go blind from it.

Then it vanished into itself, and she was back in the soft glow of dawn creeping across the sky.

With her heart pounding, she stood on shaky legs and walked toward the form laying face first in the dirt. His golden hair glinting in the blossoming light of day. Bending down, she touched his shoulder.

Groaning, he opened his eyes and rolled over onto his back. He stared up at her, a look of complete astonishment on his perfectly sculpted face.

"Am I awake?" he asked.

With a wane smile, she wiped away a streak of dirt on his brow. "Yes, Thane, you're awake."

He grabbed her hand and held it tight. She could see the horror in his eyes as he finally accepted who he was and that, a hundred years ago, he had literally ripped himself apart into two men. The dark and the light. The evil and the good.

Tears swam in his eyes. "I'm sorry, Branlyn. I have done you so much wrong."

Shaking her head, she touched one of his tears and wiped it away. "No. Gregorian did me wrong. You are not that same man."

"But he is a part of me."

"*You* are a good man, Thane. I believe that in my heart and in my soul."

He brought her hand to his lips and pressed a kiss to the palm. "Can you ever forgive me?"

With tears streaming down her face, she nodded. "I already have."

Thane sat up and wrapped his arms around her, hugging her tight. He cried into her shoulder, purging himself. She could feel one hundred years of grief and anger flowing from him. It dripped down his face and into the black soil beneath them.

Warmth spread over her as she hugged him close. A light began to build between their bodies. She could see it when she glanced down. Pulling back, Branlyn watched it intensify until the white glow completely encompassed them. She looked up into Thane's face and saw that he was smiling.

He reached for her face, cradling her cheek in his palm. "Thank you."

Lifting her hand, she covered his. "Now, you can have the peace you deserve."

"As can you."

He leaned forward and pressed his lips to hers. When she opened for him, the white glow poured into her mouth like liquid honey, filling her with warmth and tranquility. Burying her hands in the golden silk of his hair, she hung on as he seared her with his passion, with his love.

When he broke the kiss and pulled back, she felt complete. For the first time since her life was turned upside down fifteen years ago, she was no longer afraid and confused. Understanding and acceptance filled her heart. She knew that she could finally move on with her life and find happiness.

With his healing came her own.

"Will I see you again?" she asked, not wanting to let him go but knowing she had to.

"In our dreams. For as long as you want me, I'll be there." He kissed her on her brow one last time then stood.

Branlyn remained on her knees and watched as he slowly stepped backward into the light. She stayed until he vanished along with the bright glow. All that remained was a beam of sunshine piercing the gray morning sky.

Wiping the last of her tears away, she stood, brushed the dirt from her pants, and took in a deep breath of the crisp ocean breeze. She felt cleansed and renewed.

Ready to start again…

Night Whispers

Night Whispers
Volume 2
Coming August 2007

Sleight of Hand by Lauren Dane
Hot Gossip by Tawny Stokes
Public Domain by Bridget Midway
One Naughty Night by Devyn Quinn

For more information, please visit our website at <u>www.whispershome.com</u> or contact us at <u>customerservice@whispershome.com</u>.

Night Whispers

Printed in the United States
75082LV00001B/16-18

9 780978 536886